a mother's
lie

LEAH MERCER

a mother's lie

bookouture

Published by Bookouture in 2021

An imprint of Storyfire Ltd.
Carmelite House
50 Victoria Embankment
London EC4Y 0DZ

www.bookouture.com

ISBN: 978-1-80019-668-1
eBook ISBN: 978-1-80019-667-4

This book is a work of fiction. Names, characters, businesses,
organizations, places and events other than those clearly in the
public domain, are either the product of the author's imagination
or are used fictitiously. Any resemblance to actual persons, living or
dead, events or locales is entirely coincidental.

CHAPTER ONE

Violet

May 2018

Shouts pull me from my sleep – at least I think I was asleep. The older I get, the less certain I am of the difference between dream and reality. I sit up slowly, the bones in my back grudgingly creaking into gear, and listen. Yes, there it is again: a cry ringing through the night air. What on earth is happening?

I throw aside the duvet and slip into my robe, shivering as I pull it tightly around me. It might be spring, but here on the coast the air is damp and cool. I slide open the back door of my cottage and stand on the worn decking, staring out into the night. The house next door is dark. The string of summer homes and empty cottages clinging to the top of the land lie silent and dormant, as if in hibernation.

The moon is high in the sky, clouds scudding across like they're in a hurry to head home to sleep. I'm lost in watching them when another shout pulls me back, and I cross the lawn to the edge of the cliff, where the land drops away to the beach below… a beach I haven't set foot on for years. I walk towards the edge gingerly – after the last big landslip, I can never be sure when more might give way – and squint at two shapes undulating in the water.

For a second, I'm not sure what I'm seeing. The moonlight on the waves and the wind roaring in my ears make me feel like I'm in some strange hinterland, a place not tied to past or present. As I keep staring, the two shapes turn into people, one bigger than the other, ducking and diving under the surface. They pull at each other, then move away, as if performing an elaborate dance they've choreographed over time. Their shouts spin around them in perfect pirouettes before the wind whips them off.

I watch their performance, unable to look away; unsure whether to be horrified or entranced at the way they're grabbing at each other… unsure whether one's trying to drag the other down or pull them up again. Are they all right? Do they need help? And what are they doing in the water, anyway? The beach is popular in the summer, but it's only May and hardly a soul visits this time of year. Not to mention it's the middle of the night and the water is freezing.

Are they real? Or are they something from my memory – a scene unravelling, projected from my mind's eye as if I'm at the cinema? As the years pass, the memories clamour louder and louder inside of me, like they're afraid of being forgotten.

You don't need to worry, I want to shriek when they press in on me so hard I can barely breathe. *I will never forget. I couldn't, even if I wanted to.*

As I watch, one swimmer starts moving out to sea, struggling to swim even faster or break free from a current… it's impossible to tell. The other comes into the shallows and stands on the sand, stock-still. I can only just make out the swell of her very pregnant stomach, and I shake my head. That cold water can't be good for her or the baby. What are they doing?

The cries have stopped now, and all seems fine as the lone swimmer moves towards shore, then staggers through the waves to the sand where the other is waiting. They face each other, as if frozen, before finally turning to make their way back up the cliff.

I catch my breath as they near me: it's the young couple from next door. I had no idea she was pregnant… not that we're close. I see her swimming almost every day from my perch up here, but I escape into my cottage before she gets out of the water. I'm not one for small talk.

I go back inside before they see me, uneasiness lingering as my brain tries to make sense of what I saw. I lie on the bed and draw the duvet over me, reminding myself that when it comes to life, making sense of anything is impossible. Whatever that couple gets up to, it's none of my business, anyway.

I came here to be alone, and that's how I'll stay.

CHAPTER TWO

Ali

Thirteen months later

'I'm sorry, Ali. I *can't*.'

Ali Lawton stared into her husband's eyes, pain circling through her. His face was every bit as familiar as her own, and yet now he seemed a stranger. It was difficult to believe that just yesterday, they'd sat in the waiting room of the antenatal ward, full of anticipation and expectation. She'd squeezed Jon's hand, love gushing through her for him, for their child and for their future. Everything was perfect. Soon, she'd have the family she'd always longed for. The family *they'd* always longed for, because Jon had spent years saying he couldn't wait to be a father. And then...

Then everything had changed.

Ali cradled her belly, as if she could shield the child inside from what had happened – what was happening still. Ugly words, unbearable words. Words that even in her worst nightmare, she never thought she'd hear. Words she couldn't grasp.

Words she'd never have imagined her husband could speak aloud.

I don't want this baby.

She hadn't believed Jon the first time he'd said them. It was only a knee-jerk reaction after seeing the ultrasound. He'd been so quiet since they'd viewed their baby on the screen, turning inwards away from her. Everything was real now; he was overwhelmed. She could understand that. She'd held him close, anchoring her body to him as if she could make the three of them one solid mass. 'We'll be okay,' she'd told him over and over.

But the night went by, and then the day, and his words remained the same. Endless hours passed, where Ali felt as if she was drifting in dark water, suspended in an ocean of uncertainty and horror. Jon had always been the one to lift her up, but now... now, he was a heavy weight threatening to drag her down.

I can't be the father you need me to be. I can't be the father this baby deserves.

She struggled against him, trying to remind him of everything he'd said to her – all the promises he'd made; how he'd never let her down. But Jon would only shake his head, and she'd sink further into the black brine. Panic gripped her throat so strongly she could barely take in air – barely *move*. She was tired, so tired. How much more could she take?

She had to go, she realised suddenly. She had to get away from him – away from his words – before the water sucked her under and she could never escape. She had to leave *now*, before it was too late. Without even thinking, Ali knew where she'd stay: the run-down cottage she'd inherited from her grandmother Violet after her death last year.

'Jon...' She held his gaze, still unable to believe that any of this was happening. 'I'm going to my grandmother's. To give us space.' Space for her to breathe. Space to absorb everything; space for him to come around because she was sure he didn't mean what he'd said. 'Just... just take some time to think, okay?' *Think about our child. Think about me. Think about* love *because surely that trumped everything.* 'I'll be fine, don't worry. Just call… call me when you're ready.' Ready for the baby and their life ahead.

She rushed into the bedroom before he could respond. Tears blurred her vision as she pulled her holdall from under the bed. With every item she threw into the bag, she prayed that Jon would tell her to stop. That he'd say he didn't need space or time. That he'd wrap his arms around her and tell her of course he'd be there, this was their *child*, and he loved them both no matter what. But all he did was watch as she zipped the bag closed and picked up her keys.

Ali turned to face him one final time, stunned by the pain and exhaustion on his face. They stared at each other, each waiting for the other to speak. But finally, after hours of talking, there was nothing left to say.

Nothing but the horrific words clogging the air like poison, slowly suffocating her and the child inside.

She had to get out of here.

She grabbed her bag and closed the door behind her, then got into the car. Her heart pounded and her hands shook as she started the engine, but a tiny bit of calm descended as she drove away, as if her toes had touched the sand after struggling in choppy waters. As she headed towards the motorway, an image of her very first trip to Seashine Cottage came to mind. She must have been… ten, maybe, right after her parents' divorce? She'd sat silently in the car with her father, full of hurt and anger that instead of spending the promised holiday with her, he was dumping her with an old lady she barely knew – an old lady who, judging by the hurried conversation at the front door – had no idea Ali was coming and wasn't best pleased. One glance inside the dilapidated cottage and Ali had wanted to take off, but after her father had driven away, Gran had sat her down with a cup of camomile tea.

'I have a feeling this place may not have been your first choice,' she'd said with a gentle smile. 'But sometimes in life, things don't go as we planned.' Her face had twisted, and Ali had wondered what she was thinking. 'But you're here now, so let's get through this, all right?'

Ali had nodded, staring up into her grandmother's grey eyes. Despite the years between them, she'd felt a connection... a feeling that somehow, her grandmother understood. And although Ali had been far from keen at first, that summer had been one of the best in her life. After listening to her mother's endless stream of bitter and angry words, the quiet of the cottage wrapped comfortingly around her. Staring out to sea, she'd felt all the whirling emotions and confusion still; the fog inside her clearing. Gran had just let her be, and that was exactly what she'd needed.

Ali had spent the next few summers there, too, the sound of the sea the backing track of her memories. She'd loved racing across the grass in her bare feet, making her way down the cliff path at the back of the garden, then streaking across the sandy beach below. The sense of freedom after hemmed-in London was exhilarating, even if Gran did have a fast and firm rule about never being on the beach without her watching. The cottage – and Gran – had been a refuge during the turmoil of those years after the divorce. When her dad had told her the place was hers, she'd been shocked but thrilled. It had been so special to her, and even though she'd never said anything, it seemed Gran had known that too.

A couple of hours later, Ali pulled into the cottage's grassy drive and turned off the engine. She yanked open the car door and inhaled the salty air, feeling her lungs expand for the first time in days. The sound of the crashing waves washed over her, drowning out everything else. She closed her eyes and let herself float on the gentle swell, her emotions quieting the way they had when she was young. This place was exactly what she needed now too. In a way, it felt as if Gran had led her here.

Lifting her bag from the boot, Ali crossed the dewy grass, shivering in the cool air. Although it was June, the wind whipping in off the water made it feel more like October. She tipped up the flowerpot and slid out the spare key her grandmother had always kept underneath, ignoring her family's protests that was the first spot burglars would look.

'There's nothing valuable inside, anyway.' Gran would shrug, brushing aside objections that it was *her* they were worried about. The population of Fairview was mainly geriatrics and holidaymakers, and Ali could hardly envisage a thief targeting the dingy, cramped cottage, but she knew Gran could take care of herself. She'd lived here for years on her own, and although the place may not have monetary value – it was impossible to sell, thanks to the looming threat of subsidence – her gran had treasured its silence and isolation.

She unlocked the door and snapped on a light, shaking her head at the damp-stained walls. The cottage had been practically falling down when Ali was young, only getting worse with each passing year. During one of Ali's rare visits – maybe ten years ago now? – she'd offered to help her grandmother paint the tiny open area to freshen things up a bit. But Gran had simply shaken her head and said these scarred walls were beyond brightening and anyway, she preferred them this way.

Ali dropped her bag on the sagging double bed squeezed into the small bedroom off the kitchen, then filled the kettle and flicked it on, desperate for a warming cup of tea. Waiting for the water to boil, she threw open the back door and crossed the faded decking into the garden. From here, she could see the black hulks of cottages and houses strung out along the clifftop. Most, including the huge house next door, were dark and silent; cottage season had yet to begin in earnest.

Stars garlanded the black sky with pinpricks of light, moonlight shimmered on the water, and Ali slowly exhaled. As she stared out to sea, the wind carried the sound of a baby crying towards her. For a second, it felt like her own baby was reaching out to her, and a fierce rush of love swept over her. She cocked her head and tried to listen, wondering where the noise was coming from. But before she could trace it, the cry faded into the dark night, merging with the crash of the waves.

Whether it had come from inside her or not, it didn't matter. She and her baby were safe here, miles from any torment or pain.

Miles from anything or anyone who would threaten them.

CHAPTER THREE

Ali

Sunlight blazed through the window so strongly that Ali could see the red glow through her closed eyelids. For a second, she thought she was back home in North London and Jon had done that annoying thing she'd thought she'd trained him out of: yanking up the blind first thing every morning when he got up for his job as music teacher at the local secondary school. He was *such* a morning person, greeting the day with a little tune and a jig down the corridor to the loo, while she preferred to laze about in bed and wake up slowly, letting consciousness roll over her.

'You won't be able to sleep in when the baby comes,' Jon had liked to remind her. 'We'll be on call, 24/7.' He'd rubbed his hands together gleefully, as if he couldn't wait to experience sleep deprivation. In fact, he couldn't wait for anything to do with this baby, that's how excited he'd been. The strength of his anticipation had taken Ali by surprise – as a dedicated bachelor until they'd married, she'd assumed at first that there might be a little persuasion involved when it came to having a child. But Jon had told her soon after they'd met that he wanted not just one child but several, eager to recreate his idyllic but crazily chaotic childhood.

'The more kids, the more love,' he'd said, smiling that wide grin of his. And although their upbringings couldn't have been more different, Ali loved that they shared the same vision for the future. Jon's eagerness couldn't be further from her own absent father, and the thought of a house bursting with kids clambering over him as they vied for attention filled her with warmth. Every child would be loved no matter what – every child would know they were loved, beyond a doubt. Jon had promised nothing would change that.

Her insides twisted, and she let out a cry. How could he say that he *wouldn't* love each of their children, no matter what? How could he stand there, in the middle of the life they had been making together, and tell her that?

How could he let her leave?

Her mind raced back to the moment she'd found out she was pregnant, as if by remembering his excitement, she could negate the awful words still ringing in her ears. Not wanting to disappoint Jon if the test was negative, she'd waited until he was asleep. She'd crouched over the sink in the bathroom, heart pounding as she tried to make out the result with only the light on her phone.

When she'd seen it was positive, a mix of love and determination had filled her, so strong she'd started shaking. She'd wrapped her fingers around the stick as if she was cradling her child and whispered a vow that she would never let it down, not like her parents had with her. She'd give it all the love, the time and the dedication it deserved. She'd give it everything… and more. They both would – she and Jon. She'd never been surer of anything in her life.

Then she'd burst back into the bedroom and screamed that they were having a baby, too full of emotion to even think of waiting until morning. Jon had hugged her hard, and they'd talked all night, making grand plans of how they'd decorate the nursery, dreaming of the future ahead. Jon had even grabbed his phone and ordered a mini-guitar and *Rock Hits for Babies* album. Ali hadn't even known such a thing existed, but it was amazing how peaceful Guns N' Roses could be on acoustic guitar.

Her mobile alarm started ringing, and she sat up slowly. Right now on a normal day, Ali would be getting ready for her job as a data analyst. But today was hardly normal, was it? She bit her lip, thinking she needed to call her boss Sarah and tell her she wouldn't be in again today or for…

How long? How much time would Jon need? Unless… unless maybe he had already called? Hope darted through her, and she picked up the mobile, her heart dropping at the empty notification screen. She breathed through the pain as she typed a message to Sarah saying that she had an emergency and wouldn't be at work for a few days. Surely, Jon wouldn't need longer than that?

Ali put down the phone and wandered into the lounge, desperate for something to help keep the pain at bay; something to fill the hours ahead. Gran's voice floated into her mind, bearing words from those long idle summer weeks: 'There's always work in the garden that needs doing. The outdoors never rests.'

God, how she wished her grandmother was still here. Sadness flowed through Ali as she realised that she hadn't actually spoken to her grandmother for months before she'd died. Gran had never been one to reach out, and Ali, well… she'd never been great at keeping in touch either. Ali's mum filled her ears with a litany of complaints and demands on the off-time Ali did call, but Gran was different. She always listened, but she never expected anything in return, and there was something so restful about that. She barely even spoke about herself unless prodded.

Ali nodded, as if Gran *was* here now. Work outdoors was exactly what she needed – something to keep her mind focused and body busy – and God knows the gardens could use some TLC. The rose bushes by the front door had grown so much that they were almost level with the small lounge window, their prickly tentacles reaching out to snag anyone who dared stray from the steps.

She padded back into the bedroom and tugged on jogging bottoms and a shapeless T-shirt, then grabbed the pair of rusty garden shears Gran kept hanging by the front door and went outside. After an hour or so, her arms were aching, and her lower back was on fire. When was the last time she'd actually done something physical? She and Jon were less of the exercise kind and more of the gluttony kind.

'Hello!' A cheerful voice cut into Ali's thoughts, and she turned from where she was crouched under a troublesome thorny branch. A man and a woman were smiling down at her, the sun creating halos around their heads as if they were glowing.

Ali groaned to herself. She dreaded small talk at the best of times, and right now, all she wanted was to be left alone. She stood and ran a hand through her hair, conscious that she must look an absolute mess – and even more so, compared to this woman. Copper-coloured hair fell in perfect waves down her back, and she was dressed in a crisply pressed yellow summer dress. The man beside her was wearing shorts and a T-shirt, but somehow, he managed to make the casual clothes look stylish and cool. And beside them was a Silver Cross pram, which Ali knew from her copious online research cost an absolute fortune.

Although Ali couldn't see the baby, she had no doubt it was beautifully clad in something pristine too. They looked like they'd stepped from the pages of a Boden catalogue... and Ali should know, given the amount of time she'd pored over one recently. An image of the family she'd envisaged swept through her mind – she and Jon and their baby swaddled in their cosy nest of a flat – and longing poured into her.

'Hi,' she said curtly, hoping they'd get the hint and leave.

'Are you here on holiday?' The woman gestured towards the cottage. 'I didn't realise the place was being let out now. It's been empty for a while.'

'Holiday, yes, I guess you could call it that.' It was so far from reality Ali could barely drag the words from her mouth. 'I'm not renting it, though – I own it. My grandmother passed it down to me.'

'Oh! Your grandmother!' The woman darted a glance at the man beside her. 'I'm so very sorry for your loss.'

'Thank you.' Despite herself, Ali couldn't help wondering if this couple had known her gran. Given how Gran had kept to herself, it wasn't likely. But something in this woman's tone made her think the condolence was genuine, not simply an automatic response. 'Did you know her well?'

'We were her neighbours, actually, right next door here.' The man pointed at the huge house, and Ali's heart sank. She'd thought the house was empty last night. The last thing she needed was nosy neighbours invading the quiet cocoon she desperately craved.

The man met Ali's gaze. 'That afternoon your grandmother died... I want you to know we tried everything we could to resuscitate her.'

Ali's eyes widened. 'You found her?'

He nodded. 'We'd come out that afternoon to go to the shops, and your grandmother was lying on the grass.' He pointed to a spot between the two houses. 'I called 999, but...' He sighed. 'I'm really sorry we couldn't do more. Maybe if we'd got there sooner... I don't know.'

Ali shook her head. 'I'm only happy she wasn't alone for too long. Thank you.' Those words weren't enough, but she couldn't think what else to say. She'd hated the image of her grandmother lying on the hard ground, by herself and in pain. Knowing someone had been with her was a huge relief.

'Oh, we haven't introduced ourselves!' The woman's lively tone lightened the mood. 'I'm Meg Walker, and this is my husband Michael.' If Ali hadn't been so thankful about how they'd tried to help her gran, she would have rolled her eyes. *Meg and Michael* – even their names sounded good together. She took Meg's outstretched hand, conscious of the dirt under her nails.

'Welcome to Fairview,' Michael said in a warm, deep voice, stepping forward to shake her hand once Meg had released it.

'Hope Jem didn't wake you up last night. She can be *quite* the noisy one.' He grinned as if he was proud of his daughter's lung capacity.

'Jem?' So the crying last night *had* come from next door. Ali couldn't resist peeking into the buggy, where a pink-faced baby was sleeping. Sorrow hit like a physical blow, and she jerked her gaze away. She'd been so excited for her and Jon to meet their own child, and now... She took a step back, pushing Jon's tortured face from her mind.

'Jemima, but we call her Jem. She just turned one,' Meg said. 'Hard to believe! We love her, but she does keep us on our toes. If only she'd sleep!' She gently tweaked her daughter's nose before running a hand over her face. 'That's okay, though. Being tired and a little haggard is more than worth it.'

Ali forced a smile, thinking that despite Meg's words, she looked anything but tired and haggard.

Michael glanced at his watch. 'Right, we'd better get inside. It's almost time for Jem's lunch.' He paused. 'Listen, why don't you come over for dinner tonight? If you're going to be right next door, it'd be great to get to know you better.'

'Ooh, yes! Good idea.' Meg put a hand on Ali's arm. 'Please come. Fairview is perfect if you're a kid on holiday or a pensioner looking to relax, but there's hardly a soul my age. It'd be so nice to chat to someone who doesn't need nappies.' She grinned up at Michael. 'Someone besides my husband, anyway.'

Ali met Meg's eyes, her mind spinning. Tonight, she'd planned to climb in bed early, pull the covers over her, and listen to the sound of the waves as she drifted off – not sit and exchange pleasantries with a perfect couple who, with every loving glance and joking gesture, would only remind her of everything she'd left behind.

But then... these were the people who had helped her grandmother. These were the faces Gran had seen before she'd died. In a way, it felt like they were all connected through her grandmother, and as much as Ali loathed the thought of dinner with them, she couldn't bring herself to say no. Gran might have wanted to live her life in isolation, but thanks to this couple, at least she hadn't died alone.

'Okay,' Ali said finally, nodding. 'Thank you – that's really kind.'

'Great!' Meg beamed. 'Seven okay? We'll get Jem down, and then we can have the whole night to ourselves. See you soon!' She gave a cheery wave, and then she and Michael continued down the path.

Ali watched until they disappeared, then picked up the shears again. She chopped at the prickly branches, trying to dislodge the pain that had ballooned inside after seeing this perfect family. Just one evening, she told herself. Just one night, and then she could retreat to her refuge once more.

CHAPTER FOUR

Ali

Ali shoved her flyaway brown hair behind her ears as she crossed the narrow patch of grass to the house next door. The glorious sunshine of the morning had given way to heavy clouds, and even though she'd only wielded the shears for an hour or so, she'd collapsed on the sofa and fallen into a deep sleep. She'd awoken in a sweat after dreaming she was sinking in deep water, screaming out to Jon for help as he walked away. She'd sat up in bed and grabbed her mobile as if it was a lifeline, but the screen was still empty. No texts, no calls… nothing.

To say she was dreading this meal tonight was putting it mildly.

Ali climbed the steps to the front door, then gazed up at the house, taking in its haphazard design. It looked like it'd started out the same size as her own tiny cottage, but over the years bits and pieces had been added here and there, making it about double the footprint now. She smoothed down her T-shirt in a futile attempt to make it look less wrinkled. She'd only packed shapeless tops and baggy jeans, selected solely for their ability to accommodate her swelling stomach. From her reflection in the glass door, she could see that despite her efforts, she was barely presentable. Her dark hair hung limply around her shoulders and her cheeks were pale, making the freckles stand out like pox.

A memory popped into her mind of Jon, tweaking her nose affectionately and playing a game he called 'freckle watch' as more and more freckles appeared on her fair skin. He'd loved her spots ever since their first date. They'd picnicked on Hampstead Heath, then lay down on the springy grass. Jon had rolled to face her, tenderly touching every freckle he could and counting in a soft voice. She'd sat there, savouring the gentle sweep of his fingers on her skin, half wanting to discover they were wholly incompatible so she wouldn't have to risk letting him into her life – risk someone else she loved letting her down. Instead, they simply fit... as much in harmony as Meg and Michael seemed to be.

Panic and fear swept over her, and she drew in a breath. Jon *would* call. He had to.

'Hello, neighbour!' Meg appeared, wearing a different dress from this morning. This one was black with little red flowers, the same colour as her hair. Her blue eyes leapt out from her milky skin, and Ali self-consciously plucked at the faded material of her T-shirt. 'Good timing – Michael just got Jem down. Come on in.'

She swung open the door, and Ali's eyes widened. The higgledy-piggledy design from the outside was deceptive: inside, the space was airy and light. A modern kitchen opened out onto a lounge with huge glass panels creating one whole wall, looking out onto the ocean... miles and miles of water the same colour as the sky, so you couldn't tell where one stopped and the other began. The effect was disconcerting and, for a second, Ali felt like she was falling. She blinked and forced herself to look away, taking in the solid wood furniture scattered around the lounge.

'This is lovely,' Ali said, reaching out to touch a large coffee table. A solid plank rested atop three rough-hewn legs. It would have looked right at home in an art gallery.

'Michael made it,' Meg said, tucking her legs underneath her on the sofa. Ali had always wondered how anyone could sit comfortably like that, but Meg didn't appear to be in pain. Flexible as well as beautiful, Ali thought wryly. God, some people really did have it all.

'He crafted all of the pieces here, actually. He designs and makes furniture for a living. Remind me to take you to his studio out back some time to show you more of his work. I'd take you now, but he's working on a huge commission and the studio's rammed.'

'Wow.' Ali raised her eyebrows, impressed. She could barely assemble IKEA furniture, and Jon was even worse. She closed her eyes, picturing the day they'd rented out their own place together. After years of living in furnished accommodation, neither one of them had any furniture. One quick trip to IKEA later, and they'd come home with box after box of flatpack furniture... all of which Ali had assembled while Jon watched from the sidelines, providing her with the drinks. He claimed he was allergic to Allen keys, and Ali could only laugh and roll her eyes. With all the gins he'd given her, everything seemed funny.

'Speak of the devil.' Meg unfurled from the sofa as Michael entered the room. Dressed in jeans and a stripy shirt, he should have looked casual but, framed against the backdrop of the ocean, he could have come right off a fashion show runway. If Jon had been wearing that, the jeans would have been faded and torn; the shirt wrinkled and scruffy. But that was what had attracted Ali to her husband: what you saw was what you got. He was unabashedly himself, unable to live with pretence or illusion.

'Can I get you a drink?' Michael asked. 'Sparkling water, lemonade, elderflower pressé? I'm sorry we can't offer you wine or anything harder. We didn't have time to pop to the shops, and I stopped drinking ages ago in solidarity with Meg. She's still breastfeeding.'

Ali raised her eyebrows, impressed. She'd read somewhere that you should breastfeed for a year, but that most women stopped after a few months – if they even made it that far. Not that she was surprised Meg was still going. This family seemed to have it all together, and Michael was obviously supportive. He'd stopped drinking alcohol for over a year! Jon had stopped mixing G and Ts once she'd asked him to, but he'd still kept the fridge stocked full of beer.

'That's more than fine, actually, because I'm not drinking either.' The words were out before she could stop them, and for a second, Ali wondered if she should fabricate an illness; to say anything other than the real reason. Telling this couple she was pregnant meant opening up, and the last thing she wanted was to get personal with them – or to think about all that was at stake right now.

But it was too late because Meg's eyes had already lit up as she examined the swell of Ali's belly beneath the T-shirt. 'Ahhh! You're pregnant!' She paused. 'Please say you're pregnant. Or I've been really rude.'

Ali couldn't help laughing even as her heart sank. 'Yes, I am.'

'Oh, that's wonderful!' Meg clapped her hands. 'I can't believe I didn't notice when we first met you.'

'Congratulations.' Michael smiled warmly.

'Do you know what you're having? How far along are you? Do you have any names picked out?'

Michael laughed, putting an arm around Meg. 'Please excuse my wife. You don't have to answer any of those if you don't want to.'

'I'm sorry.' Meg grinned. 'But pregnancy is so special! It might feel like it's dragging now, but when you look back on it, it'll seem like it was over in a flash. Make sure you enjoy it.'

Ali nodded, meeting Meg's eyes. Pregnancy *was* a special time – a time that would pass too quickly. It hadn't felt like it was dragging at all. She loved it: loved her belly growing bigger, the thought that she was creating something inside of her. She'd been enjoying everything about it, until…

'I'm a little over twenty weeks now,' she said, resting a hand on her stomach. 'And I'm having a girl.' Her heart pinched as she remembered the sonographer telling them that.

'You look amazing!' Meg said.

'Thank you.' Ali knew she looked anything but, but she appreciated Meg's kindness. She said it with such enthusiasm that Ali could almost believe she actually did think Ali looked amazing.

'I have loads of things you can have, some sleepsuits that Jem has outgrown and lots of other stuff we're not using any more. And—' She stopped as Michael put a hand on her arm. 'Sorry, sorry. I'm sure you've got all that back at home. It's just that it's such an exciting time. I'm thrilled for you and your husband.' She paused, as if realising she might have said something wrong. 'Or… your wife?'

'Husband.' Ali swallowed back the emotions, trying hard to keep her face neutral. 'He's, er… he's working back in London,' she mumbled, hoping Meg didn't ask more.

'I loved being pregnant.' Meg smiled, her eyes meeting Michael's. 'The anticipation, the waiting… like getting ready for Christmas with the best present ever. We'd have ten more if we could. Right, Michael?'

'Well, maybe more like five.' Michael squeezed her arm. Meg reached up to kiss him, and Ali felt the pain rising again. She and Jon had wanted that big family too. *The more kids, the more love.* Tears filled her eyes, and she blinked them away, trying not to stare at Michael and Meg as they embraced. God, it was as if the two of them were on honeymoon or something! Even when she and Jon had been on their actual honeymoon, Ali didn't think they'd been like that. Granted, they'd decided to go camping in the Lake District in October and spent the whole time in a leaky tent, both coming down with killer colds within two days of arriving. They'd huddled together to stay warm, but romance right then had been the last thing on their minds.

It wasn't exactly the stereotypical notion of a honeymoon, but somehow it had confirmed to Ali that she was with the right man – not that she'd needed extra confirmation, of course. It was just… if you could get through that without killing each other, she'd thought you could get through anything. Couldn't they? She shifted in the chair, drawing in a breath to try to stay calm.

A buzzer sounded, and Meg leapt to her feet, then called them all through to the table for dinner: a beautifully golden fish pie with sparkling water for them all. The table was picture-perfect with fresh flowers and white linen, and Ali almost didn't want to sit down for fear of sullying the setting. They all tucked into the food, with Michael and Meg keeping up a steady stream of conversation, and before Ali knew it, the sky had darkened, and her dessert plate was empty.

'Were you and your grandmother close?' Michael's voice cut into her reverie.

Ali tilted her head, wondering how to answer. Were they close? Probably not in the way Michael meant: as relatives who kept in touch and saw each other regularly. But despite the distance between them, Ali *had* felt close to her grandmother… closer than she did to her mother and father, anyway. She and Gran hadn't needed constant physical contact to have that connection.

On the rare occasion Ali needed to, Gran would let her talk and talk – Ali never chatted to anyone like she did to Gran. Gran seldomly offered advice, but when she did, it always made *sense*… as if she could see everything clearly. That first summer, Gran would make her endless cups of camomile tea as Ali choked out through tears how she'd pack her bag each Friday night and wait upstairs in her bedroom, praying she'd hear a knock on the door… praying her dad would fulfil his promise of spending weekends with her after the divorce. How she'd done it for weeks. Months, even, and of course the knock never came.

And how finally, she'd stopped packing her bag. She'd lain on her bed, full of anger and hurt, vowing she'd never, not in a million years, treat her children that way. She'd never break a promise to them, no matter what. She'd never let them down.

Gran had never said anything; never interrupted. She'd let Ali cry, then tuck her up into the tiny bed in the back room. She'd sit there until Ali became drowsy and started drifting off. Ali could have sworn that one night, she'd spotted tears on Gran's cheeks as she stared out the window at the sea. But then Ali had fallen asleep, and Gran had been her usual bustling, no-nonsense self the next morning.

'I used to come here every summer to spend a few weeks with her, but as I got older, I preferred staying in London. Typical teen, I guess.' She smiled at Michael as an image flashed into her mind. She must have been fourteen, maybe, standing in front of her father, begging him to go to Gran's like she used to. But he'd said no, she couldn't, not any more, and then dragged her off to computer camp. She'd enjoyed it, but she'd loved Gran's more. She'd bugged her father the next summer, too, then given up.

God, she'd forgotten all that until now. Why hadn't her father wanted her to go to Gran's again? Or was it Gran who hadn't wanted her?

'Did you two see her much?' Ali asked. Gran might have favoured solitude, but hopefully someone had been watching out for her.

'Not really,' Michael said, pouring more sparkling water into Ali's glass. 'We kept an eye on her as much as we could, but she kept to herself. We'd see her sometimes around the garden or out back, staring at the ocean. She used to sit there for hours.' Ali nodded. Gran used to sit watching the water even when Ali was young too. Once Ali had asked her what she was staring at, but Gran had shaken her head and said nothing.

'Meg loves to swim, and your grandmother would always be watching,' Michael continued. 'Our own self-appointed lifeguard. Which is great since I'm not the world's strongest swimmer. It's the only place this one can get away from me.' He grinned and touched Meg's hand, and she smiled back. 'Not that she needs to, of course.'

'Gran was always worried about the water,' Ali said, twisting the wedding ring on her finger and glancing away. She liked this couple, but watching their constant love and affection was like scraping shards across her skin. She needed to get back to the cottage before it was too much to bear. 'She said the currents were too strong for children to swim.' Ali remembered pleading to go in, but Gran would always shake her head no. On hot days, it was pure torture.

Ali pushed back her chair. 'Well, I guess I should be going. Thank you so much for dinner.'

'Hang on!' Meg dashed from the kitchen and up the stairs, returning a minute or two later with a carrier bag. 'Here,' she said, shoving the bag towards Ali. 'Just a few onesies and muslins. You can never have too many, right? Some days Jem goes through five outfit changes. I never realised how explosive babies can be.' She laughed and poked Michael. 'Luckily, I have this guy to help out. Expert nappy-changer right here.' Michael grinned proudly. 'Anyway, I'm sure your husband will be fantastic too.'

Ali somehow managed to nod. 'But what about the next ten?' she asked. 'Won't you need these?' They might have been joking about the number, but they'd seemed certain enough about wanting more.

Meg waved a hand. 'You can give them back to me, if you want. Anyway, these are only a few bits and bobs.'

Ali reached into the bag and drew out a tiny onesie in a soft, buttery yellow. Her heart shifted, and she met Meg's eyes. Meg was watching her with a smile. 'I know,' she said quietly. 'It's hard to believe, isn't it? That the baby inside of you now will one day – soon! – be in your arms.' She reached out to touch Ali's arm. 'You'll be her mother, her whole world. You'll do anything for her.' She smiled. 'It's wonderful, really.'

Ali nodded again, a current of understanding swirling around them. Meg was right. Ali would do anything to keep her baby safe, away from anyone who might harm her. Wasn't that the very reason she'd come here? In the midst of this turmoil, her daughter was the most important thing. This pregnancy was special, and no one should ruin that – *nothing* should ruin that. If Ali focused solely on her baby, she didn't have to let even one day be darkened by fear and uncertainty.

'Thank you,' she said, then turned and went into the night, clutching the yellow onesie like a guiding light.

CHAPTER FIVE

Violet

June 2018

I yank up a dandelion, one of many that persist in growing in my carefully weeded front garden, even when I constantly rip their roots out. It's as if they're *commanding* me to be happy with their cheerful yellow bobbing heads… reminding me that even in the most challenging of places, they can thrive.

I don't want that reminder. I don't need that reminder. I may still be alive, but I'm barely surviving. I'm hunkered down, lost in the voices that seep into me, bobbing somewhere in a sea of memories. An image floats by like jetsam: a tiny hand outstretched as he wobbles towards me on unsteady legs, yellow dandelion heads falling from his fist. I try to grasp onto it; try to see his face, but it drifts off before I can grab it, replaced by the old familiar pain. I give another dandelion a furious tug, throwing it to one side. Then I remove another and another, working methodically as my back aches and my knees sting.

A door slams, and I raise my head to see the couple next door coming outside. I haven't spotted them since that strange night in the ocean a few weeks ago – I haven't seen the woman doing her usual swims either. Everything has been as silent as a tomb… exactly how I like it. Angry doesn't come close to describing how

I felt when the owners decided years ago to extend their cottage into a proper, full-time residence. I shut myself away and seethed as the sound of hammers rang out and the edge of the property inched closer and closer to mine. I tolerated months of noise before the project was completed, and when it was, the owners only lived there for a couple of years before heading off to a country with guaranteed sunshine.

The house was empty for ages before this young couple moved in... maybe five years ago now? When they first came over to introduce themselves, irritation swirled inside. They were young and beautiful (I saw them through the window; never opened the door), and I knew that they'd want to have BBQs, parties, *children*... all the trappings of a full life with friends and family, everything I put behind me. Thankfully, they're as quiet as I am. After that one attempt to introduce themselves, they've let me be.

Fifty years I've been here. Fifty years, all on my own in this ramshackle cottage that's falling down around me – a cottage my husband and I built for family summer getaways. Life back then seemed shiny and bright, just like the young couple next door.

Little did we realise it would change in a blink of an eye.

I should have known how quickly it could fall apart. Before I came to live here, I worked as a part-time GP in a busy practice in North London. I'd seen people come in for a regular check-up, and I'd known in an instant that their lives would never be the same. But that was *them*. I was fine. I was perfect, with my job that still let me be a mother, a husband who loved me as much as he had when we married, and two adorable children who would drive me to the brink and back again, but who I could never imagine life without.

I watch as the woman clutches her stomach and groans, in the throes of a contraction. I should go and see if she's all right. I am a doctor, after all, and even if I'm not in obstetrics, I have delivered the odd baby here and there. But it's been years – decades, even – since I practised… since I left behind the job I loved; left behind the children I cared for. I'm on my own now, and all that remains is the grief and the blame that encase me like a shield – or a barrier. Sometimes, I think it's the only thing still holding me up.

The husband puts a hand on her back and tells her to breathe, but she jerks away. I shake my head, thinking it was ever thus: a man who believes he can maintain control and calmness, even when it comes to labour… and a woman who knows he hasn't a clue. She screams as he tries to touch her again, and something in her voice drags my mind back to that night in the sea, their bodies circling round each other in the waves. I push the memory away, watching as he manoeuvres her into the car, and they drive off down the lane. Towards their future… towards their family.

Towards the life I turned my back on.

Sadness waves into me, and I get to my feet and stare at the sea, breathing in its salty scent. Then I kneel down and yank more dandelions from the garden.

CHAPTER SIX

Ali

The rickety cottage walls vibrated as someone knocked on the door, and Ali's eyes flew open. *Jon.* Oh, thank God. After Meg's last night, she'd shoved the onesie under her pillow and fallen asleep, determined to enjoy every minute of this pregnancy, despite everything. But now her husband was here, and they could treasure this time together, just like they had before – even *more* than they had before. Her heart beat fast, and she threw on a robe, eager to see him. It had only been a day since she'd left, but it felt like years had passed.

As she raced to the door, her mind spun backwards to the moment they'd first met at a children's birthday party. Desperate to earn extra money in the last year of her physics master's degree, she'd been working at the weekends for Mad Lab, a company that ran science parties for kids. This party had been the worst: she'd never come across a parent so demanding. She'd tried telling herself it was simply a mother wanting the best for her daughter, and that it was admirable she cared so much. The only thing that calmed Ali down, though, was the thought of a new bottle of vodka chilling in the freezer for the post-party session she knew she'd need. She'd been almost, *almost* out of there when she'd felt a tap on her shoulder. Sighing, she'd turned around, questioning what else this mother could possibly demand.

For a second, she'd frozen, thinking she'd dreamed this man up. It was like someone had plucked the vision of the perfect bloke from her mind and set it down in front of her. His nut-brown hair was slightly long and untidy in a cool arty way, and his deep brown eyes crinkled up at the corners. He was solid but not overly muscled, and most importantly, he was taller than her – a rare thing, given she was almost five nine.

'Hi,' she'd said, shaking herself back to reality. If this man was at this party, then chances were he was the father of one of these kids. Unless... hope darted through her, and she had to stop herself from checking his ring finger. Maybe he was a *single* dad? 'What can I do for you?'

'Have you finished your show?' he asked. 'I mean, not that I want you to be done. It was great,' he added hastily, his cheeks flooding with red. Ali couldn't stop a smile – his embarrassment made him even more endearing. Too many men she'd met lately had been so far up their own ass, she'd sensed they wouldn't even be mortified if they soiled their trousers.

'Yes, I'm done. I'm packing up to leave now,' she'd said.

'Okay, good.' He smiled again, and she noticed for the first time that he had a guitar strapped to his back. *Even better.* 'Not that it's good you're going. I mean—'

'It's okay.' Ali grinned, wanting to put this poor man out of his misery. She loved his bumbling words, so at odds with his confident, open appearance.

'I wrote a song for the birthday girl, and I wanted to play it for her. But of course I didn't want to step on your toes,' he explained, swinging the guitar around to his front.

Ali's eyebrows rose as her heart sank. 'The birthday girl?' She reached into the recesses of her mind to try to find the name. After doing so many parties, they all kind of melded together. 'Florence? Is she your daughter?' She should have known he was too good to be single. But married to the mother from hell? *Shit.*

She must not be all bad to snare someone like this, Ali thought, although even after knowing this man for a matter of seconds, she struggled to picture the two of them together.

'Oh crikey, no.' Ali's heart lifted when he shook his head. 'Steph's my sister. I'm Florence's uncle.' The man met her eyes, and Ali noticed for the first time that the brown was flecked with shards of green. They were beautiful, the kind of eyes you could stare into for hours.

God. What the hell was wrong with her? Ali prided herself on not falling prey to men's bullshit. But this wasn't bullshit, she realised. This was just him.

'I'm Jon.' The man stuck out his hand, and Ali took it in hers, a rush of warmth going through her. She felt her cheeks heat up and cursed her pale complexion.

'Uncle Jon!' A voice cut through their conversation, and Jon swung towards it.

'Showtime,' he said, with that easy smile. 'I hope she likes it.'

'I'm sure she will,' Ali had replied, but he was already gone.

She'd watched through the foliage as he'd plucked the guitar and sung in a rich, raspy voice, a lilting song that somehow managed to be cool and cheesy at the same time. Judging by the rapturous applause and the way Florence threw her arms around her uncle, it'd been a definite hit.

Ali had gone back to her flat for a date with her vodka bottle. She'd tried to put Jon out of her head, but the song he'd written for his niece floated through her mind for days. She'd been about to go for a long walk through the wilds of the Heath in a bid to clear her head for once and for all when her mobile had rung.

It had been Jon, and her life had changed from work to home to work again to one filled with laughter and love... one filled with Jon. It'd taken a while for her to really trust him – to know that he wouldn't disappear like her father had; that she could rely on his presence in her life – but gradually, as time went on, he proved to her he wasn't going anywhere.

She'd been right, she thought now, twisting the handle. Jon might have had a wobble, but he *wasn't* going anywhere. They—

'Ali?' A woman's voice floated through the door, and Ali's heart crashed to the floor. That wasn't Jon. That was *Meg*. What was she doing here so early in the morning? Hell, what was she doing here at all? Last night had been better than expected, but surely, they hadn't graduated to unannounced visits already.

Maybe it was an emergency? Maybe Meg needed milk for the baby or something? Ali gulped in air, fighting through the disappointment that dragged at her heart – at her body – making her head pound like she'd been on a bender. An image floated into her mind of her and her best friend from university, Sapna, downing pitcher after pitcher of watery draught, then singing at the top of their lungs as they lurched back to the house they'd rented with four other students. At one point, they'd collapsed in a stranger's front garden and lain there, laughing and chatting for hours as the starry sky spun above them. Ali had loved that feeling of freedom; of wild abandon. The only other time she'd experienced that had been here at the cottage when she'd streaked across the sand towards the endless horizon.

Ali swung open the door. 'Morning,' she said, blinking into the light.

'Oh my goodness, I'm so sorry,' Meg said. 'I didn't mean to wake you up.'

'That's okay,' Ali responded, her tone the exact opposite of her words. She eyed her neighbour, wondering how someone with such a young baby could look so perky in the morning. What was her secret? Endless cups of coffee? Not when she was breastfeeding, though – Ali had heard enough from mums at birthday parties to know that was a no-no, although it didn't seem to stop them downing copious amounts of Prosecco. Until she'd started working at Mad Lab, Ali had never known kids' birthday parties could be such boozy affairs, although she wasn't knocking it. 'What time is it, anyway?'

'It's almost eight,' Meg said. 'Sorry, sometimes, I forget that people without kids think that's early! I brought you over more baby clothes.' Meg held up a bulging carrier bag, and Ali's heart sank. She shouldn't have accepted that bag last night – she didn't want to make friends here. She only wanted to be with her baby.

'Oh, that's okay. I can't take all your things!' Ali managed a smile, thinking dropping off baby clothes hardly necessitated an early morning wake-up call. Couldn't it have waited until noon? She was exhausted, and the longer she slept, the better it would be for both her and the baby.

'No, really. I insist.' Meg stretched out her arm until Ali had no choice but to take the bag. 'I don't have long before Michael has to go to the studio and I need to get back to grab Jem, but I've always wondered what the layout of this place is like.' Meg bit her lip. 'I did come round once to borrow some milk, but…' Her voice trailed off, and Ali hid a smile, imagining Gran's reaction to any intrusion.

'Did my grandmother even answer the door?' Ali asked.

Meg nodded, to Ali's surprise. 'Oh yes, she did. You know, she—' An expression Ali couldn't identify flashed across Meg's face, then she shook her head. 'It doesn't matter.' She crossed the small lounge towards the kitchen. 'It's very… rustic.'

'That's one way of putting it.' Ali watched with incredulity as this near stranger wandered uninvited through the cottage. Maybe this was a country thing? In London, she rarely crossed anyone's threshold even if they did invite her in.

Meg went to the room at the back, then returned to the kitchen. 'You know, this place has a lot of potential. That back room… if you clear out all the rubbish and make one of the walls all glass, it'd be amazing. You could do the cottage up and rent it out, as an Airbnb or something. You'd make a fortune.'

'Maybe.' Ali would agree to anything to get this woman out. 'Well, look, thanks for bringing this over.' She held up the bag and stepped back, trying to signal it was time for her visitor to leave.

'My pleasure. *Oh!*' Meg lifted her eyebrows. 'I just had a great idea! Why don't we make the room at the back into a nursery for the baby?' She swung towards it, enthusiasm radiating from her. 'I mean, I know you won't be here full-time, but if you have something set up, then you won't need to drag all the baby gear when you do come down.' She made a face. 'And believe me, there's a lot of baby gear to drag. We can paint it, I'll bring over some things we don't need any more – a Moses basket and all that – and before you know it, you'll have a wonderful place all kitted out for the baby! It'll be so easy for you and your husband to pop down for a weekend or the holidays, and when you're not here, it will be good enough to rent out.' She paused. 'What do you think?'

Meg's milky skin flushed in excitement, and Ali swallowed at her words. *You and your husband to pop down for a weekend. A wonderful place all kitted out for the baby.* All that sounded perfect, but…

She turned to scan the dingy back room, images of the nursery she and Jon had planned back home flooding through her mind. Pale green walls like the first shoots of grass in spring, curtains the same shade as summer sunshine, and a mobile over the baby's cot playing Guns N' Roses, of course. She and Jon had talked for hours about it, even if they'd yet to get started. Creating a nursery here, with someone she barely knew, felt… well, it felt wrong. She shouldn't be doing this with a stranger. She should be doing this with her husband.

She held Meg's gaze, doubt seizing her. *Would* he still want to? Would he help prepare for their baby, here or at home, even if—

'*Oh.*' Her eyes widened in surprise, and she slid a hand to her stomach. What was that? Was that… was that a kick?

'You okay?' Meg's brow was wrinkled with concern.

'My baby kicked.' Happiness and wonder flooded through her. 'I've never… never felt that before.' The baby kicked again, and she started to smile.

'It's crazy, isn't it?' Meg put a hand on her shoulder. 'That first time… it's so special. It's like the baby inside is real now, a little person in her own right. Oh, I'm so happy I was here with you! Will your husband be upset he wasn't here for it, though? Michael was practically tethered to my side so he wouldn't miss anything.'

Ali dropped her eyes, disappointment and hurt flooding through her that Jon had missed this – that he'd allowed his fear and confusion to keep him from experiencing this precious milestone… that the knock on the door this morning hadn't been him, and that he still wasn't here. Anger flared, and she glanced up at Meg again. Yes, she should be designing a nursery with her husband, but he wasn't around. Meg might be a stranger, but she was someone who understood. She was someone who would never abandon her baby, not even for one minute.

She was *here*.

'You know what? I think creating a nursery is a great idea,' Ali said, forcing a smile. She wasn't going to wait around for Jon – their daughter wasn't. Time was marching on, and hadn't she pledged last night to make every minute count? And even if she and Jon never came here with their baby, preparing a nursery in a place that had meant so much to her grandmother seemed right… a way to help Ali focus on what was really important.

'Oh, fantastic! I think Michael has some paint left over from Jem's nursery, if you don't mind the same colour. It's a lovely light grey, and it'll look really nice here. I'll have a root around and see if I can find it. And—' Meg strode into the back room again, grimacing at the piles of bin bags and assorted junk, everything from a rusty rake to a dusty fake miniature Christmas tree. 'I'll come over later today to help you clear all this stuff out, if you like? Any heavy things we can get Michael to help.'

'That sounds great.' Ali couldn't help smiling at Meg's enthusiasm.

'I'll bring Jem with me, if you don't mind,' Meg said. 'Michael's been swamped working on that huge commission, and she pretty much sleeps all afternoon. When she's awake, she'll watch the mobile for hours. Easiest baby in the world, except at night.' Meg made a face. 'Right, now go lie down again and have a bit of a rest. I'm so sorry I woke you up! I'll come back in a few hours, okay?'

'Okay. Thanks.' Ali closed the door to the cottage and walked over to the back room, resting the last thing on her mind now. Her baby had kicked. She had strength; she was alive. She deserved to be seen and heard as much as she could, with people who cared. She deserved a place in the world, to show her she *was* wanted.

And if Jon wasn't here right now to do it, then Ali would. With Meg's help, they could create something truly special. Working together with another mother who knew how treasured every baby was – who got the importance of every first, no matter how big or how little – would buoy her up and keep her away from the yawning pit of uncertainty and upset.

And Ali would grasp onto that with both hands. She'd grasp onto anything right now, no matter how tiny, to stay afloat.

CHAPTER SEVEN

Ali

Ali hauled a bag of rubbish across the kitchen and placed it outside the front door, eager to clear the back room before Meg returned so they could plunge right in to painting. She was reaching for another bin bag when her mobile buzzed. *Jon?* Her pulse quickened, and she grabbed the phone, but it was only her boss, Sarah. Ali clicked open the message and breathed in, resolving to stay focused on the nursery.

> *Hope all okay. Take this week off, but we need you back for the Centala meeting next week. Critical you're there.*

Ali stared at the phone, her mind spinning. Centala was a big client she'd been working with for the past year, and they'd be wrapping up the account in the next week. Ali had worked hard on her final report, proud of everything she'd done for them. But now all of that – Centala, her job, Sarah – seemed so far away, as if it was part of another life… a life that included her husband and their baby as one perfect unit.

A life she couldn't let herself think of right now.

She shut off the phone, feeling like a weight had been lifted. No more disappointments; no more intrusions. She'd get as much of this nursery done as she could and focus on nothing but her baby.

A few hours later, Ali was sweaty and aching, but the room was almost bare. It hadn't been as bad as she'd thought. Most of the stuff was already packed away in bin bags. One more corner to clean out, and then she was pretty much done. She took a breath and started sorting through stacks of old beach towels, cracked buckets and… She sat back, staring at a carrier bag with 'Andy' written on the side. These must be her father's things, although she'd never in her life heard him called 'Andy'. Even her mother called him Andrew – among other names after the divorce. Ali opened the bag and lifted out old beach clothes, the once-bright colours now faded and yellowed. A stripy T-shirt, a pair of shorts… she couldn't imagine her tall, solid father had ever fit into these things. Actually, it was hard to even picture her dad as a boy.

She tilted her head, realising that she'd never seen a photo of him when he was young. He never talked about it either – never talked about his childhood or his parents – but then it wasn't as if Ali really talked to her dad, anyway. The familiar dull ache returned when she thought of how he'd exited her life and how she'd longed to have her father back again… longed to have a proper father, full stop.

Swallowing back the lingering hurt, Ali set aside the bag, then pulled down another. Her brow furrowed as she noted the word 'Ben' scrawled across the front, and she opened it up to pull out more kids' clothes – a bit smaller than the ones in her father's bag. She sat back, her mind whirling. Who was Ben? A family friend, maybe? Someone who used to come down for summers with the family? She shrugged. Whoever it was, these things were destined for the bin. Why had Gran saved this stuff, anyway?

As Ali stood looking at the meagre pile of objects in front of her, she realised how little her gran had in her life – and how little Ali knew about her. How long had she lived in this cottage by the sea? Why had she decided to leave London and her family and come down here alone? Why *had* she treasured her solitude so much? Ali had never asked, but she wished she had... even if Gran probably wouldn't have told her; she wasn't big on sharing her thoughts. But being alone in this cottage on the cliff, miles from her life in London, Ali felt a yearning to understand more.

'Hi! I'm back!' Meg's cheery voice cut through the silence, and Ali heaved herself to her feet. 'I brought Jem.'

Ali crossed to the door and smiled at Meg, then glanced down at Jem nestled in her carrycot. Her black lashes grazed her rosy cheeks, and the same rust-coloured hair as Meg's curled finely against her head. God, she was gorgeous. 'Come in, come in,' she said in a whisper, beckoning them inside. Even in her ripped jeans and old T-shirt, Meg somehow managed to look pulled together.

'Oh, you don't need to worry about waking her up.' Meg grinned down at the baby. 'Once she's out, she sleeps like the dead. It's getting her out that's the tricky bit!'

Meg set the carrycot carefully onto the floor. 'Judging by the pile of things out front, you've been busy. I thought you were going to take it easy!' She wagged a finger at Ali. 'Don't worry – I understand. When I was pregnant, I couldn't sit still for longer than a second even though Michael kept telling me to rest and relax. I was so excited to get things ready for Jem.'

Ali nodded. 'I've managed to clear out most of the stuff from the back room. It's quite a bit bigger than I remembered, actually.'

'Right, let me have a look.' Meg pushed past her and surveyed the space. 'Wow, yes, it does look so much bigger without all that junk in it. You can put a cot there, and a change table over there...' She touched the wall. 'If you like, I can do a mural here? I can show you the one I did in Jem's room. I mean, I'm not a professional, but I did go to art school and I love to paint. Let me know if you have a theme in mind, or any idea, or—' She stopped. 'Tell me to shut up, if you like!'

Ali smiled, touched by the idea. 'That sounds great. Let me have a think about some themes, okay? Let's finish clearing the room and do a first coat of paint.' Even that would require a shedload of work, stripping old wallpaper and dealing with what looked suspiciously like yet another damp patch. Meg's usual life would probably suck her back in long before any of this was sorted. Even if she did make it look easy, Ali knew that taking care of a baby was pretty much a full-time job.

'You went to art school?' Ali asked, interested to know more about this dynamic woman who seemed so full of life. 'Do you still paint?' What a great couple they made: Michael with his furniture design and Meg with her artistic abilities. Making beautiful things must have been what drew them together.

'Not for a while,' Meg said, her voice drifting over her shoulder as she peeled off a strip of wallpaper. Thankfully, it came away from the wall easily. 'Although I'd like to get back into it soon. I really miss it.'

A sharp ring cut through the air, and Meg crumpled up the piece of wallpaper into a bin bag. 'Oh, that must be Michael.' She grabbed the phone, and Ali tried not to listen as she told him she was fine, she was with Ali, and Jem was sleeping.

'He likes to check in and see how we're doing,' she said when she hung up. 'He misses us when he's tucked away in the studio. With its own little kitchen and bathroom, he could practically live out there. He always comes home as soon as he can, though, which is so nice. Most men can't wait to get away!'

Ali nodded, thinking that Jon was a real homebody too. She tugged at another strip of wallpaper, wondering what he was doing right now. Had he been able to find his keys without her help each morning? Did he still hum that little tune as he got into bed at night? What was their flat – their world – like without her? She forced the questions from her mind and ripped the paper from the wall.

The two of them continued to work on the room for the rest of the afternoon, making good progress despite downing tools each time Michael called. And he called a lot: wanting to know if he needed to run to the shops for dinner, then if Jem had enough nappies, and then to say he'd finish working around six. Had the man never heard of texting? Ali wondered.

Actually, he kind of reminded her of Jon, who lived in a constant state of disorganisation and couldn't be bothered to type out words when he could say them in a tenth of the time. And although the interruptions sometimes drove her mad, she'd loved how her husband's voice punctuated the silence of her day. The warmth would wrap around her heart, keeping her company inside while the numbers on the screen stimulated her mind. Sadness waved through her, and she let out her breath.

Meg put a hand on her arm. 'You okay?' Her face was sympathetic, and Ali felt tears coming to her eyes.

'I'm fine,' she said, blinking them away. Focus on the baby, she reminded herself. Focus on the baby, and nothing else.

'Just remember I'm right next door if you ever need me,' Meg said. 'I'm always up for baby chat! And whatever else you want to talk about, but I have to warn you that I'm way out of the loop when it comes to Netflix and all that. We don't like to have the TV on when Jem's awake, and once she's asleep, I'm pretty much knackered.'

Jem let out a squeal, and Meg looked at her watch. 'Oh yikes, it's almost five. I'd better get home and get this one fed before Michael comes back to put her down.' She scooped up the carrycot, then glanced over at Ali. 'Do you want to pop by later for supper? It's only leftovers, but you'd be more than welcome.'

Ali shook her head. She'd enjoyed Meg's easy company – her upbeat chatter and grand plans for the space had been exactly what Ali needed – but she was bone-tired now and ready to collapse. The room had been scrubbed, and they'd stripped the ageing wallpaper. Ali had been pleased to see that the damp patch on the wallpaper hadn't gone through to the wall beneath it. They'd made great progress, but she was more than finished for the day.

'Thanks, but I'm going to flop on my mattress from hell and go to sleep, I think,' she said, rubbing her aching back.

'I know, it's so hard to get comfortable when your body is being pushed out of shape,' Meg said sympathetically, 'and I'm afraid it'll only get worse.' She paused. 'Listen, we have an old pillowtop mattress topper which we used before we got a new mattress. I'll have Michael bring it over for you tomorrow.'

'Oh, that would be fantastic.' Ali would give anything to escape Gran's bed of pain.

'Great.' Meg jigged a drooling Jem. 'I'll see you tomorrow, then.'

'Tomorrow, perfect. And thank you. I can't say thank you enough.' Maybe for Meg this was just a fun project, but for Ali it was so much more.

'It's my pleasure,' Meg responded. 'Besides, it's partly selfish. I love doing this kind of stuff, and I really can't wait to get started on the mural.' She smiled again, then went out the door.

Ali wandered into the bedroom and lay on the bed, yawning as Jem's cries and Meg's coos floated through the air towards her. Had Gran lain here too, listening to this baby? she wondered. Had she thought of her own children, like Ali was thinking of hers? Ali put a hand on her stomach, and her baby kicked in reply, as if she wanted to burst out and join them.

'Not yet,' Ali whispered, her eyes closing. 'Stay safe inside as long as you can. But know that we're making an amazing room for you – a room you'll love. Here, where your great-grandmother lived, and where your mother came when she was young. This place is your safe space now too, as much as it is mine.'

CHAPTER EIGHT

Violet

June 2018

The baby is here. I realise neighbourly etiquette dictates I should visit and bring a gift, but I'm hardly a normal neighbour. Besides, the last thing I want is to see its pink mouth opening in a sleepy yawn; its tiny fingers stretching as if trying to catch the air. Despite my reticence, though, this baby seems determined to make its presence known to me, announcing its arrival with a cacophony of cries… all day and all night. It's stiflingly hot, and although I try to close my windows to block out the wails, I can't. The noise is an unwelcome intruder, invading my space even when I'm asleep.

A few times lately I've awoken to find myself standing in the back room, gazing down like I expect to see a child there… like the debris of the past few decades has been replaced by two twin beds, piles of comics and sandy shoes by the door. Of course it hasn't, and I chastise myself as I crawl back to bed. It's been years since a child has been inside this cottage, not since Ali used to stay for the summer holidays. And if I'm being honest, I didn't even want her to come. Yes, she's my granddaughter, but I didn't want that responsibility. I *shouldn't* have had that responsibility. I only relented the first time because Andy dropped her off unannounced, and then every summer after because Andy said she'd begged.

Those weeks with her were torture... pure, unadulterated torture. Not because of her: she was a great girl, clever and curious, but astute enough to know not to bother me too much. We got on easily, the days passing one after the other without argument or fuss. She loved it here; loved the silence and the peace. I could see the difference in her within an hour of arriving – it was as if a coil inside had relaxed, the same way I used to feel when I got here. But I can't relax any longer. Not now, not ever.

I was constantly on my guard. Not just for her, but against myself. I shouldn't enjoy being with her. I shouldn't be happy. I shouldn't get used to having company. I kept myself tightly wound, going through the motions... engaging my body but not my soul – as much as possible, anyway; I slipped up a few times. I told myself I'd keep her safe, but I wouldn't let her love me. I didn't deserve it.

And then she had an accident. I close my eyes, remembering what happened. She'd grown too old for me to cage her up indoors every time I had to take my eyes off her, and she'd gone out to 'play' in the front garden... mooching around, looking bored, whatever it was teenagers did. I'd gone inside to make us supper when I heard a scream. It cut through me, terror pouring in, and I raced to the front of the cottage to see Ali on the grass, cradling her leg. The tyre she'd been swinging on had crashed to the ground – the slender branch it was tied to couldn't support her weight any longer. Her face was contorted with pain, and I could see by the way her limb was turned that it was broken. I helped her into the car – she'd grown so tall, but she was so light – and drove her to hospital, trying my best to distract her while my heart pounded in fear.

As the doctor bandaged her up, I called my son to tell him what had happened and asked him to come collect her. I suppose he could hear in my voice how shaken I was. He told me not to worry, saying that Ali should have known she was way too heavy for the swing. It wasn't my fault. Then he stopped talking, and I knew what he was thinking; what he was remembering... another time, years earlier, when that exact same phrase had been uttered. And I knew then that no matter how old the child – no matter how far from the water – accidents could happen. *Would* happen, and I couldn't do this. I had to be alone.

That was the last time Ali came for a summer. I don't what Andy told her. Maybe she didn't ask to come back; she was getting too old to be cooped up with me for weeks, anyway. Although she and my son came for visits every once in a while, I didn't encourage it. I didn't want a reminder of how I couldn't keep my loved ones safe. It was better to close myself off completely than risk hurting them.

Perhaps that's why I willed Ali this cottage: I want her to have a piece of me that I could never give her when I was alive. I hope she comes here when I'm gone. I hope she brings her children and gives them the idyllic summers that I took away from her... that I took away from my own family.

I'm lying in bed one afternoon trying to rest when there's a knock at my door. As usual, I ignore it and hope that whoever it is will get the hint and leave. But they don't, because there's another knock, and then another. I lever myself up, anger churning inside, ready to let loose on whoever's disturbing me. I don't take interruptions kindly.

'What...' My words fade away when I spot the woman from next door with a newborn curled against her chest. I can't stop staring at the baby, who can't be more than a week or two old now. I'd forgotten how small they are, and how they fold their legs up under their bodies like little amphibians. The way they hunch against you like your heartbeat is the only thing anchoring them in this new body. How thin their skin is, and how delicate the folds of their eyelids are. The whorls of hair on their rosy scalp.

'I'm sorry, I'm sorry,' the woman is saying, and I tear my gaze away from the child. 'I'm so sorry to disturb you. But we have no milk, and I can't go to the shops. We need the milk for tea, and—'

'It's okay,' I say, cutting into her babbling. She looks absolutely exhausted and hollow-eyed, in the way that most new mothers are. It might be a very long time since I've had a newborn, but it's hard to forget that particular brand of fatigue, where your brain seems disconnected from your body and even minor daily details feel like huge obstacles to overcome.

But despite the woman's obvious tiredness, she looks neat and smart. She's wearing a crisp blouse and those awful jeans that are more like tights than trousers. Her auburn hair curls softly around her face, and she's even sporting a slick of lipstick. A smile touches my lips as I remember that, no matter how tired I was, the simple act of tidying myself up made me feel human again.

'I've got a whole jug in the fridge that you can have,' I say, even though that means I'll have to make a trip into the village tomorrow. It's a task I dread even at the best of times – never mind the height of the summer rush – but I want to get her out of here.

'Oh, thank you, thank you.' Her gratitude makes me feel like I've offered her much more than milk, and something inside me softens. Some mothers put such pressure on themselves to get everything right that even not having enough milk can be over-whelming. 'I'll bring you some more when I'm next in the village.'

'That's okay.' The baby starts stirring in her arms, and I reach into the fridge and grab the milk, desperate to get her and the baby out of here. 'You have other things to worry about now. Looks like your little one is ready for a feed.'

'This baby is always hungry!' She shakes her head as she gazes down at it. 'I don't think I've got the hang of breastfeeding yet. I thought babies just *knew* how to latch on, but...' A tear leaks from her eye, and she swipes it away. 'Oh God, I'm sorry. I don't know why I'm telling you this.'

I meet her eyes, an image of my son coming into my mind – the way he'd look up at me after having his fill of milk, all droopy-eyed and content before flopping his head down on my arm and swiftly sleeping before I could even burp him. It was hard, yes, but it was wonderful.

'You'll get it, I'm sure,' I say sharply, shoving aside the memory. 'And if not, then don't worry. That's why formula was invented.' I edge towards the door with the jug in my hands, trying to make it clear that this conversation is over.

'No, I can't give the baby formula!' Her eyes are wide. 'I *have* to breastfeed. It's best for the baby.'

She sounds like she's parroting someone, and I curse all those antenatal instructors who yammer on about the benefits of breastmilk until mothers would rather their breasts were chewed off than resort to formula. It's not fair to mother or baby.

'You also need to do what's best for you,' I say, sighing internally as I realise she's not going to leave easily. 'It's still very early days. Things don't have to be perfect – do what you can to get through this time, and remember to take care of you too.' She nods, and my mind flips back to the time when countless people said a similar thing to me: to take care of myself; to be good to myself. Perhaps, at first, that was why my husband thought I was staying here in the cottage: that I needed some time alone, time away to take care of me.

But that wasn't it at all. I wasn't being good to myself. I was punishing myself. Every bit of me longed to be with my family, but I couldn't. It was better for them if I wasn't. Eventually, even though the grief remained, the longing lessened… mostly.

She reaches out to take the jug. 'I'm Meg, by the way.'

'Violet.' Saying my name aloud sounds strange. I can't think of the last time I introduced myself to anyone – the last time I met someone new. It seems odd to say, but I don't really think of myself as a person any more… as an individual, a member of society. I've lived alone for so long that I'm just me.

'Nice to meet you. I'd better get back before…' She looks down at the baby as if it's a ticking time bomb, then turns to go. I watch her slowly make her way towards the house and open the door. Her husband appears in the doorway and ushers her inside. His eyes meet mine, and I jerk out of sight, not wanting to make any more connections today.

I turn to stare at the sea, trying to calm my churning emotions. It's been a long time since I talked to anyone like that – a long time since I cared enough to try. Not that I care now, of course: the woman wouldn't *leave*. I glance around the cottage again, thinking things feel different somehow, like the air I'm breathing has changed. The thought unnerves me, and I throw every window wide open and gulp in fresh air, telling myself that everything will be back to normal soon.

CHAPTER NINE

Ali

'Ali? It's Michael.'

Ali jerked up, wiping her mouth. She'd been fast asleep on the scratchy, boxy sofa in the tiny lounge. How long had she been out? She blinked at the clock on the wall. Eight o'clock? God, she must have really been tired. She'd collapsed after Meg had left a few hours ago, closed her eyes, and that was the last thing she remembered.

'Ali?' A loud knock jolted the door, and Ali hurried towards it. She swung it open, taking in Michael holding a large white bundle. For a second, Ali thought it was Jem, before she blinked again and realised it must be the mattress topper Meg had told her about. Thank *God*.

'Hi,' she said, struck again by Michael's good looks. He wasn't her type, but she could see objectively that he was a very handsome man. 'Thank you so much for bringing that over.'

'No trouble at all,' Michael responded in an easy tone. 'Want me to come in and set it up?'

'No, no, that's okay. I'm sure you need to get back to Jem and Meg.' The cottage was a disaster zone. After his immaculate house, her mess was the last thing she wanted him to see. 'You can leave it here.' She gestured inside the door.

'It won't take a minute,' Michael said, brushing aside her objection. 'Meg would kill me if I didn't!' He was already in before she could say no more forcefully, and Ali sighed. He was obviously one of those people who'd rather pull out their fingernails than leave a pregnant lady to their own devices. But actually, now that she thought about it, she really didn't have the energy to haul a heavy piece of foam onto the bedframe.

'Okay, thanks.' Ali relented, moving aside. 'Would you like a cup of tea?' She didn't want to prolong the encounter, but it was the least she could do.

'Yes, please. That'd be great. Milk, no sugar. Thank you.' Michael strode into the bedroom, and Ali went to the kitchen and filled the kettle, thinking that she should have stripped the bed for him. There was something so intimate about him touching the fabric she'd slept on for the past few nights. It'd been years since any man but Jon had been in such a personal space. Even though she'd been drawn to him from the start, it'd taken ages before she'd let him in… before she'd trusted him with her body and her soul.

'I'm not like your father,' Jon had told her one night, a few weeks after they'd met. He'd asked her to go away with him for the weekend, but Ali had said no. She wanted to – oh, how she wanted to – but she'd still needed to take him in small doses; needed to give herself space to step back again. Too much time together and she might never be able to pull herself out. Too much time and she might never be able to recover if he left.

Understandably, Jon had been upset when she'd turned him down. His grin had faded, and he'd stared at the ground. Panicking that she might lose him, Ali had taken his hand and tried to explain in a halting voice just how much she liked him, but that she needed to take things slowly. He'd asked why, and Ali had told him about her father's many broken promises and how she'd closed herself off tightly after that.

Jon had squeezed her hand. 'I love you,' he'd said softly. 'I'll be here for you, and I won't hurt you. And I'll keep trying to prove that to you for as long as it takes.'

Ali let out a breath now, trying to push down the pain the memory stirred up. She put a hand on her stomach, reminding herself of her earlier words to her daughter. This was a safe space. No darkness would touch it.

'Okay, I think I've got it arranged properly here,' Michael called from the bedroom. 'Give it a try – see how it feels.'

'Er, okay.' Michael edged out of her way and into the kitchen to give her space in the tiny room, and Ali lay down. The soft surface enveloped her body, and she closed her eyes. After sleeping on what felt like a board with springs digging into her, this was absolute paradise. She only opened her eyes when she heard Michael rustling around in the kitchen.

'Just getting my tea!' he called when she sat up. 'Hope you don't mind me making myself at home. How is it?'

'It's perfect,' she said, coming into the kitchen. 'Milk is in the fridge if you want any.' It was good to see a man who took care of himself – she was hardly going to complain.

'Right, then, let me make a few adjustments,' he said, setting down his mug and striding back into the bedroom. 'We don't want it to slip off in the middle of the night!'

Ali could hear Michael struggling with the topper for a few minutes. 'All done,' he called.

'I never realised how close this cottage is to our house! I heard Jem crying.' He walked back into the kitchen. 'I hope she hasn't been waking you up. We'll try to close her window at night from now on.'

'Oh, don't worry,' Ali said, waving a hand in the air. 'I'm going to have to get used to it!' She smiled and brought a hand down to her bump again.

Michael smiled, too, then tilted his head. 'Did your grandmother ever say the noise bothered her or that we were keeping her
up? I hope not. I'd hate to think we were inconsiderate neighbours.'

'I'm sure Gran wasn't bothered.' Ali didn't want to say that
she wouldn't have known if her grandmother *had* been bothered,
seeing as how they'd hardly talked.

She fidgeted under Michael's steady stare, hoping he couldn't
read her mind.

'Did you know that she used to be a GP?' Ali said to fill the
silence. 'She loved kids.' The words came out before Ali even
paused to wonder if they were true. *Did* her gran love children?
Truthfully, Ali had no idea. She didn't seem to have minded having
Ali around, but… Ali's mind flipped back to the irritated look on
Gran's face that first summer Dad had dropped her off. *Had* she
minded? As a child, Ali had always taken her grandmother at face
value. The silence, leaving Ali to her own devices for hours on end,
the way she'd disappear into herself – that was just Gran, and Ali
never once thought it might have been because of her presence.

'It's a shame we didn't get to know her better. You must miss
her,' Michael said, and Ali felt tears come to her eyes.

'I really do.' She shoved her earlier thoughts away. She and Gran
had understood each other; they had got on well those summers
together. And living in this space where Gran had spent so much
time, Ali felt closer to her than ever now.

'She didn't have much, did she?' Michael glanced around the
cottage. 'Not many people live with so little these days.'

'She always said she came here to get away, so why would she
bring the world with her?' What had she been trying to escape? Ali
wondered now. Was there a reason behind her silence and isolation?

'She didn't keep any diaries or anything, did she?' Michael
asked. 'It would be fascinating to read her accounts, if she did.
I'm really interested in local history, and she must have seen a lot
of changes in this area.'

Ali shook her head, wishing Gran had left something like that behind. 'No, nothing that I've found. There was a lot of junk in the back room, though. Meg and I spent the day clearing it out.' The bag of kids' clothes flashed into her head, and she made a mental note to ask her father who Ben was the next time she spoke to him.

Whenever that was.

Silence fell again, and then Michael hit his head. 'I almost forgot! I've got one more thing for you. Be right back.' He ducked out of the cottage and across to his house, leaving his tea on the table. What on earth had he gone to get?

'Meg wanted to give you this.' He came back inside carrying a Moses basket and stand in his arms. 'It's hard to believe Jem was tiny enough once to fit in here! They grow so fast. And like Meg said, we can't wait to have another little one… the sooner the better. I'd love to have a big family. I know most men don't get broody, but I do! This is such a great place to raise kids too.'

Ali nodded, thinking if her own idyllic childhood summers were any indication, Michael was right. She'd have loved to have grown up here. The open spaces and clean fresh air were the ideal location for the perfect family life she'd envisioned – a far cry from the three-bedroom flat she'd shared with her mum and the au pair in the very centre of London, a stone's throw from King's Cross. It might be upscale now, but back then, the area was full of bedsits, druggies and prostitutes mixed with the up-and-coming yuppie couples who were ready to buy but couldn't afford a nicer area. Ali had stepped over homeless people and bumped into drunks, and she'd had recurring nightmares that one of them was going to break in and steal her away.

Ali's mother had worked at the nearby university and said the location was giving Ali a real-life education, so she wouldn't grow up to be like the ignorant kids she was teaching, who thought everyone had a cleaner and couldn't even make toast for themselves. Her mum wore the location of their flat like a badge of honour, refusing to move even when she could afford better. It was why Ali had settled in the confines of Crouch End as soon as she'd had a choice, where most of the streets looked like they'd been curated by *Good Housekeeping*.

'Where shall I set up the Moses basket?' Michael asked. 'I told Meg it might be better to wait until you've painted and everything, but she was adamant I had to bring it over now, to "fully realise the vision" or something like that. She's so excited to help out with this. She did a great job with Jem's nursery, and I'm sure she'll make this a wonderful space too.'

Ali smiled, loving how he supported his wife. She'd always thought you could tell a lot about a marriage by how each partner spoke about the other in their absence. What was Jon saying about her now? she wondered. Had he told anyone what had happened? Surely anyone he spoke to would help him see what was right.

She jerked as she realised Michael was waiting for an answer. 'Could you put it in the corner there?' She pointed into the back room.

Michael nodded and started setting up the basket, fiddling with the stand to get things right. 'I don't know why they make these things so complicated,' he said, grimacing as he tightened a screw. 'Right, there you go.' He got to his feet. 'I'd better go back and give Meg a bit of a breather. Hopefully, she's managed to get Jem settled again.'

'I love that you're so involved,' Ali said. 'In this day and age men should be, but in reality, I'm not so sure they are.' She'd heard an endless litany of complaints from mums at birthday parties, and the very fact that it was mainly mums at the parties seemed to confirm what they said. She'd aired her doubts to Jon a few times before they'd started trying for a baby, but he'd always reassured her he wanted to pull his weight – and more. She'd believed him wholeheartedly. Why wouldn't she?

'Jem is my baby too. Only thing I can't help out with is breastfeeding, and I would if I could!' Michael smiled. 'Anyway,

I always told myself that when I had a family, I wasn't going to be anything like my parents.' His face twisted. 'They were way more interested in their own lives than mine, that's for sure. Shipped me off to boarding school as soon as I turned seven! Meg and I both know the damage absent parents can do. Having a dedicated mother and father... that's the best gift you can give a child.'

Ali nodded, her gut clenching as his words swirled around her. She desperately wanted that for her baby – for her to have the family Ali never had. Michael was right: it *was* the best gift you can give any child. But she couldn't do it alone. She needed Jon. She needed him to fulfil his promises; to be there for them. To be a father, a real one. He would... wouldn't he?

What if he didn't?

What if he never came?

'Thank you.' Ali forced the words through the panic and fear sweeping through her. After waving Michael goodbye, she hobbled into the bedroom, barely able to move with the emotions pressing on her. She lay down on the mattress, hoping the cushiony softness would pull the protection of calmness and peace around her and her daughter once more. But still the questions echoed in her head, and she thumped the bed in frustration and anger. God, if only she could silence her brain as easily as she could silence the mobile!

As she drew the duvet over her body, the sound of Michael gently singing to Jem drifted from the window above. His earlier words filtered into Ali's mind: how he was eager to give his wife and child everything he could – eager to protect them from the loveless childhood he'd had. His weren't just empty words either. Michael was living them, playing a very active role in his child's life as a father while still being a solid husband, if the affection between Meg and him was anything to go by.

Many people in Ali's life had let her down, but Michael was proving that plenty of men did step up... that the family she wanted could and did exist. She closed her eyes, the peace she'd longed for finally descending. Like Michael, Jon was a good man too. He wasn't her father – he kept his promises. He would do right by them.

He'd come when he was ready. He'd join them in this perfect place she was making for their daughter… for their family.

CHAPTER TEN

Ali

'There.' Meg stood back, hands on hips, surveying the room in front of her. 'Do you know what? I think we're actually finished! Well, except for the mural, anyway. I can't wait to get started on that. It'll really make this space something special.'

'It's special already,' Ali said, crossing the room to stand beside Meg. It was as if the woman had reached into her mind and pulled out the picture-perfect space she'd envisaged: dove-grey walls, a beautiful basket nestled in the corner, a whitewashed floor with faux-lambskin throws. A matching change table and a beautifully crafted rocking chair completed the room. Ali could imagine herself with the baby curled into her, moving back and forth rhythmically as the waves crashed outside. And Meg was right: the colour was perfect. Even if they did have to do three coats to make the scarred walls look halfway decent, the hard work had definitely been worth it.

'I can't thank you enough,' Ali said, watching Meg clean the splatters of paint from her arms. Her neighbour had worked tirelessly over the past few days, moving between her baby and painting, barely pausing for a rest. She must be one of those people who didn't need sleep because Ali knew for a fact that she hadn't got much last night – the noise from Jem's bedroom had woken

Ali too. She'd jerked awake to the sound of voices, wondering for a second if she'd left the radio on. But… she'd sat up, cocking her head. Was that Meg's voice? And Michael's?

She'd rolled across the downy pillowtop and put her feet on the floor, squinting at the old digital clock Gran kept by her bed. The red had glowed and then slowly separated into numbers: 2:24 a.m. Ali had lifted the curtains and peeked up at Jem's open window. True to his word, Michael had kept Jem's window closed most nights, but it had been so warm last night that a fresh breeze was needed.

Meg had been clutching Jem to her chest. Michael's arm was around her, and he was staring down at his baby with all the love and tenderness only a father could have for his child. Longing swept over her, and she'd picked up the mobile, her fingers hovering over Jon's contact. God, she missed him. A week had passed now, and despite her earlier certainty, he still hadn't rung. Should she call and see how he was doing? Tell him their daughter had kicked?

But what if he wasn't ready yet? She couldn't take more of the words he had uttered – the words she still didn't believe could be true. She didn't want any of that to invade this place.

He *would* come, she'd told herself. Then she'd put the phone down and closed her eyes, comforted by the light streaming from Jem's room.

'It's no trouble.' Meg flashed her a bright smile now. 'It's been really good to have something to throw myself into, and I'm so excited to start planning out the mural! When I was painting, I used to love that feeling of time standing still; of losing yourself.' A wistful expression came over her. 'I miss that.'

Ali nodded, thinking she could definitely relate. If she was working on a new project, she'd stay at the office for hours, absorbed in the numbers. Sarah had always admired her focus, saying that no one was better than Ali when she was 'in the zone'. She jolted, remembering the Centala meeting in a couple of days.

There was no way she could walk back into that world without Jon, but if he didn't come by then…

'You still need to let me know your ideas.' Meg wagged a finger at Ali. 'Then I'll do a bunch of sketches so you can see my plans before I start painting. And don't worry – it'll be something you can easily paint over if you want to change it when she's older.'

'That all sounds perfect.' Ali smiled at Meg, trying to imagine the child inside her as a living, breathing girl with opinions of her own. A face flashed into her head – a little girl with shaggy brown hair, a mischievous grin and Ali's bright blue eyes – and she grasped onto it, wanting to keep the picture in her mind as long as she could.

She washed the paint off her hands at the kitchen sink, thinking that she'd really enjoyed the past few days. She'd never been one to have a large group of friends, preferring to hang out with Jon or on her own. In fact, she hadn't had a close friend for years – she needed time to let her guard down like she had with Jon, and life had been too busy to make that connection. But with Meg, it was different. Ali's pregnancy and their work together on the nursery had given them common ground straight away. There were none of those awkward silences or 'getting to know you' questions that Ali usually dreaded.

Meg had been great company, babbling on about her pregnancy, the birth (way too many details, but Meg seemed to want to share) and how wonderful it had been to make a life with Jem at the centre of it and a husband to help out. Ali hadn't been sure at first if she could handle hearing all of that, almost opening her mouth more than once to ask Meg to stop. But the more her neighbour talked, the more Ali found herself enveloped in a world where husbands didn't let you down, pregnancies were perfect, and the future was full of love and light. It was exactly what she needed to keep her thoughts away from any threatening darkness.

And Ali had enjoyed getting to know Jem better too. She was so sweet, gurgling and kicking whenever Ali grinned at her. The soft weight of her in Ali's arms was so calming and grounding, instantly lifting Ali's spirits. Babies were simply *magic*, and Ali couldn't wait for the moment she'd meet her own.

A knock on the door made them both jump.

'Oh, that's probably Michael,' Meg said. 'I wanted him to come by and see the back room, now that we've finished. He's been super busy, but he always makes it back in time for dinner and the bedtime routine.'

Ali nodded, thinking that Michael must have been busy because he hadn't been calling or checking in nearly as much. Still, his commitment to be there every night – even in the middle of the night, if last night was the norm – was commendable.

Meg crossed to the door and swung it open. 'Oh!' she said, sounding surprised. 'Hello. Can I help you?'

'I'm looking for Ali. Is she here?'

Ali heard the voice, and everything went bright, as if someone had switched on a light inside of her. It wasn't Michael.

It was Jon.

He was here.

Finally.

She rushed to the door and flung herself into Jon's arms, breathing in his fresh clean scent… the scent of *home*. His arms tightened around her, and she drank in the warmth of his body, never wanting to let him go.

'I'll give you two some time,' she heard Meg say as she slipped past them and out the door.

'How are you?' Jon pulled back, and Ali smiled up at the face she knew so well… a stranger no more, now that he'd come. Memories flooded through her mind: the way he'd looked at her when they'd first met. His smile when he'd slid the ring on her finger in the registry office, whispering that he loved her. No one had been there except Sapna and Jon's best mate to witness, but they couldn't have cared less. They'd only needed each other and the vows they'd made.

How he'd hugged her so tightly when she'd told him she was pregnant.

And the way his eyes had pinched shut, how he'd rubbed his face, when he'd said he couldn't deal with this baby.

But he hadn't meant that, she told herself, happiness bursting through her. Those words *hadn't* been true. The doubt, the hurt… that was behind them. They would be parents now, together. A family.

'I'm fine, now that you're here. I'm so glad you came.' She ushered him into the cottage, excited to show him everything she and Meg had done. God, he looked awful, as if he hadn't slept in days. She went to the kitchen and flicked on the kettle. 'I'll get you a cup of tea, and then we can—'

'Ali.' She swung around to see him standing in the nursery, one hand on the Moses basket. His face was tight, and his eyes were red and glazed with tears. Her heart dropped. He couldn't be that upset she'd done this without him, could he? Maybe she should have waited, after all.

'I thought it would be nice to have a nursery here,' she said quickly. 'In case… in case…' Her voice broke, and she swallowed. 'But there's still some bits and bobs to finish. You and I can do it together if you want.'

But Jon was shaking his head. 'Ali…' His voice was soft now. 'I thought giving you space might help you…' He drew in a breath. 'We can't do this together. Not the nursery, not the baby.' He turned towards her, away from the nursery. '*I* can't.'

Her gut clenched, her breath bursting out as if he'd punched her. The current of darkness started to suck at her, to pull her back into black water. She stepped towards him, into the nursery. 'But why are you here, then? I thought you'd come to say you were wrong. That you can do this. I thought that with time... you'd say you were ready.'

Jon held her gaze. 'I wanted to talk to you. You had your phone turned off, and I got worried.' He looked down at the Moses basket, then back up at her again. 'I thought I was ready. I really believed I was, you know that. But...'

She shook her head, thinking that when it came right down to it, was *anyone* ever ready... ready for all the joy, tragedies, love and heartache life could throw your way? No one could predict the future, but the important thing was knowing that no matter what, you were a family. You didn't reject those who needed you; those who depended on you. You stayed strong... you stayed together.

'She's just a baby,' Ali said. '*Our* baby. No matter how afraid you are, or whatever doubts you have, think of that.' She put one hand on his arm and the other on the basket, as if she could connect them all together.

Jon was silent for a minute, and they stood there, in the place she'd made for their child, as the waves crashed in the background and the sun streamed in through the window. It was every inch the peaceful image she'd pictured in her mind... if only her husband wanted to be a part of it, to give her child that gift of dedicated parents, like Michael had said. But the silence stretched on, broken only by the shrieking of the kettle.

Then Jon stepped away, and a coldness washed over her. She started to tremble, wrapping her arms around herself to try to keep warm. He wasn't going to change his mind. He wasn't going to be there for her when she needed him most.

She ran her eyes over the nursery, desperately trying to block out the image of the tiny room filling with water, of the waves sweeping the Moses basket with their wailing baby out to sea. Of Jon taking her arm, holding her back as she tried to swim after it—

'Come home, Ali,' he said. She blinked, realising the wailing was the kettle, not their baby. 'I'll stay somewhere else. But please, come back to London – you'll have to some time, anyway. You can't stay here forever.'

Ali moved back. *Home*. Home was him… the husband she'd thought she'd known. But that person didn't exist any longer, and nothing was right. She couldn't crawl into the bed they'd assembled together. She couldn't sleep under the silky duvet they'd bought on a trip to Portugal. She couldn't look into the room they'd earmarked for the nursery or stare at the prints they'd picked out for the walls.

'No,' she said, straightening her spine as an idea hit. 'No, I don't.' She didn't have to go back… ever. Like Gran, she could make a life here. Here, where her daughter had a place in the world already.

'This is my home now,' she said. Calm enveloped her, and she crossed the room to take the kettle off the hob. Instantly, the room was silent, and she breathed in the peace.

Jon stared at her. '*This* is your home? What are you talking about? Ali, you can't stay here. That's crazy! It's the middle of nowhere, and the cottage is practically falling down. What about your job? And what about the…?' His eyes locked on her belly, and rage ripped through her. He couldn't even say the word?

'I'll be fine. *We'll* be fine. You got what you wanted. You don't have to deal with the baby.' She went to the door and yanked it open, gulping the fresh sea air as if it could cleanse this scene from her mind. 'So… leave.' Jon winced, and she could see the pain in his eyes. Good, she thought. He deserved that.

'This is not what I wanted,' he said, his voice shaking. 'You must know that. It's just—'

'*Go!*' The force of her shout stunned even her, but she couldn't let him stay any longer in the place she'd been building for her daughter – a place where she was loved and wanted, without any doubt or hesitation. Ali thought once again of Jon saying he'd prove that he wasn't like her father, and anger surged through her.

'Everything okay?' Ali and Jon turned to see Michael coming up the pathway towards his house next door. He crossed the grass into Ali's front garden. 'I heard the lady tell you to go. So maybe you should think about leaving now.' His tone was friendly, but his eyes were hard. 'Or should I call the police?'

'He's leaving,' Ali said, her voice calm now even as rage vibrated inside. 'We're finished talking. Right, Jon?'

Jon held her gaze, and Ali's mind flipped back to the night she'd left – the night she'd come here. More time had passed, but still nothing had changed. And now she knew nothing would. She could see by the look on his face he saw that too.

There was nowhere they could go from here. Nowhere together, anyway.

Jon paused, looking back and forth between Ali and Michael, then nodded. 'Okay. I'm going. Please, stay in touch. *Please.*' He touched Ali's arm before she could move away, then turned to go. Ali and Michael stood, watching in silence, as Jon climbed into the car and drove away.

'Thank you,' Ali said finally.

'That's what neighbours are for. You all right?' Michael looked at her, concerned.

Ali let out a breath. The worst had happened… Jon had let her down. He hadn't changed his mind, like she'd been so desperate to believe. All his words, all of his promises were empty. When it came right down to it, he wasn't strong enough to hold them up.

But even with all the pain and anger churning inside, Ali was still standing. She *was* strong enough to do this on her own – to be that dedicated parent and her daughter's whole world, like Michael and Meg had said.

'I am,' she said. She put a hand on her stomach, and the baby kicked. 'We are.'

Meg stepped out from her house and crossed to the cottage. 'Was that your husband? He's gone already?'

Ali paused, thinking she might as well tell Meg the truth about Jon. After what Jon had said, there was no going back. And Michael would be sure to tell his wife that he'd seen them arguing; seen Ali shouting at Jon to go. If she and Meg got even closer, it'd come out, anyway. Better to do it now and get it over with, then she could focus on her baby once more.

'Yes, that was my husband.' Ali swallowed. 'I came out here to get away from him. I'm... I'm leaving him.' She didn't want to say more; didn't want to linger on what had just happened.

'Oh, I'm so sorry.' Meg touched Ali's arm. 'What a difficult time for you – I can't even begin to imagine...' Her voice trailed off and then she shook her head. 'But you know what? You and the baby are better off being somewhere you're happy. Babies know, believe me. They can sense it.'

Ali nodded. That was exactly why she was making her home here now. 'I'm going to move here... permanently.'

'Ah! That's brilliant news!' Meg clapped her hands. 'I was afraid you'd take off after I finished the mural and I'd never see you again. I can help you with everything when the baby comes too. I swear I'm a natural with newborns!' She grinned. 'Oh, we're going to have so much fun! Right, let me get you a cup of tea and then I reckon you could do with a nap. You've probably been doing too much, and seeing your husband didn't help matters, I'm sure. I'll make certain he doesn't bother you again – I'll come out as soon as I see his car. And if he won't listen to me, Michael will tell him to go again. Believe me, he can be scary when he wants to be.'

Ali smiled, trying to picture Michael as scary. 'That'd be great. Thank you.' And Jon would be nothing up against the whirlwind of Meg, that was for sure. If a fight broke out between the two of them, she knew who she'd place her bets on.

'Right, let's get you tucked up in bed, and I'll bring you the tea.' Meg bustled Ali over to the bed, helped her in, then pulled the duvet around her.

As Meg turned the kettle on and clattered around the kitchen, Ali let her eyes close. She'd meant what she'd said to Jon: this was her home… a sanctuary now and in the future. Here, in the place that had sheltered her grandmother, with neighbours – friends – next door to watch out for her… the same people who had watched out for Gran too.

Sleep crept over her, and she let herself drift off.

CHAPTER ELEVEN

Violet

June 2018

I slump to the floor to catch my breath, surveying the jumble of objects in front of me. I've spent hours trying to sort out the back room, and I'm nowhere close to finishing. Thanks to my endless weed-pulling, I'm not in bad shape. My back isn't what it used to be, though, and combing through the junk of the past fifty-odd years is no mean feat. Most of it is from time spent here with the kids: old board games, yellowed comic books, jumbled swimming costumes and bags of old summer clothes… all things that meant nothing at the time but came to mean so much that I could never bear to get rid of them. I might not have returned to that life – the busy life of a wife and mother – but that didn't mean I never missed it. Sifting through its remains was too painful; too much of a reminder of what I gave up. It was enough to know those things were here.

But now… now, I need to do something to remind myself that life is gone forever. Because ever since seeing the woman next door and her baby a couple of weeks ago, things *haven't* been normal. The longing I thought I'd pushed down has flared up. It haunts me day and night, as I lie in bed listening to the infant crying. I can't wait any longer: I need to act. I need to shut off that world for good.

I shove another bag of clothes into a bin bag, then reach down to grab another. The plastic handle cracks and the contents spill onto the floor. I scoop them up, my fingers touching something that feels like fur. I shake off the clothes and out comes Hasty, the very originally named bear from Hastings. He's a little crushed, but thanks to the fact he was packed away in a chest for years, then buried inside this plastic bag away from eager hands, he looks quite good: his brown fur is soft, his little black eyes are shiny, and the jaunty sea captain's outfit he's wearing is still perfectly intact.

I hold him close, memories flooding into my mind before I can stop them. My son had spotted the teddy in a souvenir shop on a trip into Hastings and saved up his meagre pocket money for ages. When he had enough to buy it, he'd nagged and nagged me to drive into town until I'd finally relented. I'd never seen him happier than when he'd held the teddy in his arms at long last, and that summer, the bear had pride of place on his bed. He'd loved it so much.

Can I really throw it away?

I sit back and hold the teddy out, my reflection shimmering in his black eyes. For a second, it feels like I can see my son there too. I think of the newborn curled against its mother's chest, and an idea filters into me. Maybe I can give the teddy to the baby next door? My son never had a chance to play with this bear, and he deserves to be loved. He deserves to have someone clutch him joyfully. By giving him to another child, oddly I feel like I'm doing something for my son too.

Of course, that means having to pay the neighbours a visit, and that's something I'm still not keen to do. I don't want to make connections; I don't need more disruption in my world. But doing this feels… right.

I give my wispy hair a quick brush, check that my hands and fingernails are clean after all that rummaging around in the back room and slip on my shoes. Outside, the sun beats down. The bear is hot in my hands and in the few short steps to my neighbours' front door, I'm sweating. I'm about to knock when I hear a voice – a *loud* voice – coming from the window above me… the unmistakable sound of Meg shouting at her husband.

I freeze as her voice gets louder and words slice through the heavy air, and I can't help thinking of the cries I heard that night in the sea. 'You need to give me space!' she's saying, and I can hear the ragged desperation in her tone. 'I can't *breathe*. Please, give me some space. Just for a second.'

I can't hear her husband's response, only his low rumbling tone, but whatever he's said, it doesn't calm her down. The sound of something crashing echoes through the air. The husband's voice rumbles again, and I can't stand here any longer.

I make my way back to the cottage, the bear still in my hands. I can't hear Meg's pleas any more, but I feel like they've followed me home, curling through my head and battering my brain; pushing their way into the place I've locked myself away in. I remember the time I begged for space – begged my husband to leave me alone – but I know this is nothing like that. As a new mother, she does need help, even if she thinks letting her husband pitch in is admitting that she can't do it all on her own. She's not me… she doesn't deserve to do everything alone.

But none of this has anything to do with me. All I want is to give the baby that bear, then retreat back into my shell. I put on the kettle, breathing slowly in and out until its whistle blocks everything else from my mind.

CHAPTER TWELVE

Ali

Booming thunder jerked Ali from a deep sleep, and she turned onto her side. Wind whipped around the cottage, bushes banged against the thin walls, and the windows shook in their frames. Lightning flashed, illuminating the scarred ceiling. Ali shivered and pulled the duvet around her, too lazy to get up and close the window she'd left open. This cottage would definitely need some improvements now that she was going to be here permanently.

She closed her eyes, trying to go back to sleep. She hadn't meant to doze all afternoon, but she'd sunk into a deep and dreamless slumber. The decision to make this place her home had been a calming tonic – like she had finally shut the door on the pain, fear and doubt that had lurked at the back of her brain despite all her efforts to banish them. Even ringing her boss Sarah to say she was quitting had been much easier than she'd imagined. Sarah had been anything but impressed, but Ali had simply ended the call, then turned off her mobile once more. She wanted nothing from her old life any longer.

The longer Ali listened to the wind, the louder and stranger the noises seemed to become. She lay still for a moment, wondering if the sounds she was hearing were real or if the storm was playing tricks on her. Snatches of voices flew on the breeze towards her, then high-pitched cries – human or animal, Ali didn't know. She shivered at the eerie noise, the hair on her arms standing on end.

A loud banging rang through the air, like something nearby had fallen over, and Ali sat up in bed, her heart pounding. What was that?

Calm down, she told herself, bringing a hand to her stomach where the baby was kicking like crazy. It probably *was* something falling over, that's all. Every inch of her protested the thought of going out in the storm, but the last thing she needed was some piece of debris to come flying through the cottage window in the wind. Back at home, she'd curl up with Jon during the thunder and lightning storms that lit up the city sky. He'd stroke her hair, gently poking fun at how she jumped at each thunderclap.

But he wasn't here now. She had to deal with this herself, like her gran had done. And if Gran could, so could she. She'd better get used to it if she was going to stay here alone. Shivering, Ali rammed on a sweatshirt over the T-shirt she'd slept in. The storm had broken the heat of the day and the air was cool and clammy, going straight to her bones, as Gran used to say.

She opened the front door of the cottage, then closed it firmly behind her so it wouldn't fling open again in the wind, as she surveyed the garden. Everything looked okay – Gran had long since chopped down the tree where she'd broken her leg swinging on the tyre. In fact, according to her father, Gran had chopped it down the very next day, as if it had somehow been the tree's fault and not hers for being too silly to realise the branch wouldn't hold her weight now that she was older.

Had that been her final summer with Gran, or had there been one after that? Ali squinted, trying to remember, but nothing came to mind… nothing except the endless, lonely summers that had followed.

Everything seemed fine out front, so Ali went around the side of the house towards the back. Lights were on both upstairs and downstairs next door – the storm must be keeping them up too. She scanned the back of the property, relieved that nothing seemed damaged or out of place.

Ali was about to go inside the cottage again when she spotted Meg pulling the front door of their house closed with a loud clap. Maybe that was what she'd heard earlier, Ali thought: the door banging in the wind. It made sense, given nothing else seemed awry. Meg must have been up with the baby anyway and gone to secure it.

Ali went back inside, heart beating normally now that she knew what had happened. And seeing Meg and the lights next door in the middle of this dark night helped too. Gran may have been on her own, but Ali wasn't. She thought of Michael telling Jon to go; of how Meg's eyes had lit up when Ali said she'd be staying. They'd help her if she needed them.

They'd already helped, more than they knew.

CHAPTER THIRTEEN

Ali

Light filtered through the blind, and Ali slowly opened her eyes. Every muscle in her body ached with fatigue, but she swung her legs over the side of the bed with a sense of purpose. The wild wind had stopped, the sky was bright blue, and it was a new day: the first day of her life as a permanent resident at Seashine Cottage. She strode into the middle of the lounge, staring at the small space. There was an endless list of renovations she could start on: new kitchen units, better windows, fresh flooring… Ali bit her lip as she thought of her current jobless state. Maybe she'd better stick with the basics. If Gran could put up with an antiquated kitchen, then Ali could too.

Her eyebrows flew up as she glanced at the digital clock on the bedside table. God, it was almost ten thirty! She'd actually slept in – the mattress must be working its magic. But where was Meg? She'd been so excited to talk to Ali about the mural. Ali couldn't wait now to get started, to really make this place her home. She peeked through her bedroom window and up at the house, where the window was closed, and the blind was still down. Perhaps they were having a rare lie-in, too, after the storm.

Ali puttered around the kitchen for a bit, listening to the radio and staring out to sea, then thought up a few ideas for the mural.

Finally, when it was almost lunchtime and there was still no sign of Meg, she decided to head over. A late morning was one thing, but Ali knew they must be up by now. Hadn't she been told a million times that babies didn't sleep in?

She shoved on her shoes and went out the front door, an image from yesterday filling her mind: Jon standing right here, unable to even say the word 'baby'. Anger flashed through her then fizzled away, replaced by relief and the feeling that she was free.

She turned to stare at the ocean and inhaled the salty air, then cut across the grass to Meg's. Inside the house it looked dark and still, but the car was in the wide gravelled drive, so they couldn't have gone too far. Actually, now that Ali thought about it, she didn't think she'd ever seen the car *not* there. They seemed to be homebodies, like Ali and Jon had been. She glanced down the drive to the studio, noticing the door was still tightly locked and there weren't any lights on inside. Usually, Michael was working away by this time. Maybe he was taking a bit of a break and they'd gone out for a walk? Ali closed her eyes for a second, turning her face up to the sun. The weather was beautiful this morning.

She'd see if they were in, anyway. She rapped on the door, listening for any noise in response. The faint sound of Jem's crying filtered through the wood, her wails rising then falling like the crashing waves, and Ali lifted her eyebrows. So, they *were* home. Maybe Jem was poorly? Was that why Meg hadn't come over like she'd planned? Ali bit her lip as the crying continued, wondering whether to knock again. If Jem was ill and Meg was trying to get her to sleep, the last thing she wanted to do was interrupt.

She was about to go back to the cottage when the door opened, and Meg appeared.

'Oh, hello!' Her hair was tousled, and her cheeks flushed, but her eyes looked as bright as ever. 'Come in, come in! Sorry, I was trying to get Jem down for her nap.' She cocked her head, visibly relaxing when the cries went quiet. 'Oh, thank God. She was up all night teething and that storm didn't help. What a wild night!'

Ali nodded. 'I heard your front door banging. Did any rain get in? Hope there wasn't any damage.'

'Nothing damaged except our full night's sleep!' Meg said, opening the dishwasher and unloading the dishes. 'Michael had an early start this morning, and we barely got any rest.'

'He's in the studio now?' Given how quiet it seemed, Ali had thought he wasn't there.

Meg bent down to grab the cutlery, her long hair falling over her face. 'He's gone to visit his parents at their holiday home in Spain, trying to drum up some new business with the expats.' Her voice sounded funny, coming upside down.

'Oh.' Ali raised her eyebrows, a little surprised. In all the time they'd spent together, Meg hadn't ever mentioned this trip. But then, there was a lot Ali hadn't mentioned either. 'How long is he gone for?' With how committed he was to Meg and Jem, Ali guessed he wouldn't want to be away too long. But business was business, and he'd need to support his family.

Meg shrugged. 'We'll see. As long as it takes to get a few more commissions, I guess.'

'Are you okay here on your own?' Ali asked. Michael was so hands-on that Meg was sure to feel his absence keenly.

'Of course I am,' Meg snapped, banging some plates on the counter. 'Sorry, sorry,' she added hastily. 'I'm just really tired. It was a long night.'

Ali nodded, thinking that was the first time she'd ever heard Meg say she was tired. Meg reached up to put away some glasses and Ali's mouth dropped open. 'Meg, oh my God! That cut on your arm! Are you okay?' There was a huge red gash on her arm, crusted with blood.

'Oh, that. I scraped it on the side of Jem's change table last night. Lethal corners in the dark,' she said, grimacing. Jem's cries started up again, and Meg sighed.

'Look, why don't you go see to Jem and I'll finish here,' Ali said. 'Then we can pull together some lunch and if you're not too tired, talk about the mural?' That was sure to cheer her up.

'That sounds brilliant!' Meg said. 'Actually, I did a few quick sketches last night. I can't wait to show them to you.'

'I can't wait to see them,' Ali said, making shooing motions with her hands. 'Now go!'

A few minutes later, Jem was silent once again, and Meg came back downstairs with a sketchpad in her hand. Ali was stunned at Meg's creativity and artistry. She'd come up with one brilliant idea after another, from little birds flying across the wall spelling out the word LOVE to a fanciful underwater scene with mermaids. From the quick drawings she'd produced, her talent shone through.

They'd finally agreed on fluffy white clouds with fairy castles and turrets, a fantasyland that evoked a sense of both calm and wonder – and of safety and protection, exactly what Ali wanted. She couldn't wait to have that vision on the wall of the nursery.

'Come on, now that Jem is sleeping, let's take this plan and see how it might work in the cottage. I'll bring the monitor just in case.' Meg grabbed the monitor and sketchpad, then went to the door, shoving her feet into flip-flops. Surprisingly, the sun had disappeared completely, and rain was splattering from the sky with such ferocity that it bounced off the gravel. The two women hurried across the grass and into the cottage, laughing together as Ali scooped up a few of Gran's scratchy towels to dry off.

'We look like we've come straight from the shower!' Meg said, wiping her face. Her hair curled in ringlets and her face shone. 'Right, let's take a…' Her voice faded away as she stared into the back room, where water was pouring from the far corner of the ceiling down the newly painted wall. 'Oh my God.'

Ali's heart lurched as she crossed the small space, looking up at the sagging, damp ceiling that seemed close to collapse. As she stood there, taking it all in, huge chunks of plaster fell to the floor, leaving nothing between her and the leaden sky. Water dripped onto her upturned face, mingling with the tears pooling in her eyes. The nursery was ruined... all their hard work was gone, washed away.

The baby gave a flurry of kicks, as if she knew her mother had somehow let her down, and Ali shook her head. What was she going to do now? It wasn't only the nursery: the cottage was uninhabitable. Just yesterday, she'd decided this place would be her home. But...

'Look, you'll come stay with me,' Meg said, taking her arm. 'At least until you call someone and see what the damage is, okay? Michael's away, anyway, and it'd be so nice to have your company.' She turned to face Ali. 'What do you say? We can stay up late, talk about babies... it'll be brilliant. Come on, say yes. Please?'

Ali met Meg's hopeful gaze, turning the idea over in her head. There was no way she could go back to London, not now. And she did like being with Meg... with her cheerful banter and love for all things baby, she'd wrap Ali even further in her perfect bubble. Anyway, it wouldn't be for more than a day or two, while the roof was repaired, and then Ali could come back here and start over – make the cottage and the nursery fit for purpose once again. It was hard work, sure, but she'd do it a million times over if she had to.

Ali nodded, shivering in the damp space. 'Okay. Yes. And thank you.'

Meg threw her arms around Ali and gave her a huge hug. Ali stiffened at first in surprise, then let herself relax into the embrace. She may not know Meg very well yet, but she'd been right about one thing: Meg *would* help if she needed her. 'I'm so sorry about the roof, but I'm sure it'll all be fine. And we'll make the nursery even better.' Ali smiled, thinking how Meg was echoing her thoughts.

'Come on, let's go back to mine. You can call a roofer, and I'll make you a nice hot cuppa. Everything will be okay.'

Ali nodded, her eyes raking over the ruins of the nursery. Then she turned and followed Meg into the warmth of the house next door.

CHAPTER FOURTEEN

Ali

After a calming cup of tea and a quick call to a roofing company, Ali headed back through the pouring rain to the cottage to gather a few things for her stay at Meg's. Hopefully, she wouldn't need to be there for too long, but despite her pleas to the roofer that it was an emergency, he'd responded there was no way he could make it out today or tomorrow – he was so busy, he wasn't sure when he could come. Apparently, Ali's cottage hadn't been the only home damaged in the storm.

She went straight to the bedroom, trying not to look at the wrecked nursery. Everything will be okay, she told herself, repeating Meg's earlier words like a mantra. They'd do the nursery up again, even better this time. This place would be a home once more.

Right, now where was her holdall? The faster she could pack, the faster she could leave without having to think about the damage here. Ali cast her mind back to that first night she'd arrived from London, desperate to get away. She'd put her things in the drawers and shoved the bag… to the back of the shelf in the wardrobe? Ali opened the rickety wardrobe door and stood on tiptoes, rummaging blindly around on the top shelf. But instead of touching the canvas, her fingers grazed something soft and furry. What the hell? She grabbed it and pulled, almost afraid to see what it was. Relief flooded through her when she realised it was a teddy bear.

Ali sat down and ran her fingers over it, a memory surfacing in her mind. She must have been about eleven, and she'd been bored – so bored that she could still remember the crushing sense of these four walls closing in as her muscles twitched with energy. Normally, she loved the empty space of the day she could fill however she wanted, but it had been rainy and grey and she couldn't think of anything inside to do.

Despite the rain slanting through the air, Gran had been sitting out back with a cup of tea, staring at the ocean. Ali knew better than to disturb her. Gran had never said anything, but Ali could see that when she gazed off into the distance like that, she wasn't here… she was somewhere else. Nothing bugged Ali more than being told by her mother to come back to earth when *she* drifted off. She wasn't about to do the same thing with Gran.

She'd flopped down on the sagging bed and turned onto her side, her eyes falling on an old wooden chest in the corner. Last summer, when she'd been 'young and silly' like her mum always said, she'd pretended that chest had been buried on the beach by pirates. She'd even tried to open it, but it was locked. She'd asked Gran if there was treasure inside, and Gran had merely shaken her head without saying anything. Ali had contented herself by spinning more tales. Maybe it was gold, or diamonds, or maps to find more treasure.

What *was* inside there? she'd wondered as she stared at it again. Probably nothing too exciting, but at least opening and going through it would give her a few minutes of fun.

Ali had sat up, thinking about where she could find the key. Gran always kept her keys in a little jar on the kitchen table – would it be in there? She'd yawned and padded into the kitchen, grabbing the key ring and taking it back into the bedroom. Crouching down beside the chest, she'd tried each key in turn, her heart pounding. She'd felt like some kind of adventurer on a search for gold!

A *dumb* adventurer, she'd thought, her heart sinking when she had come to the last key and it hadn't worked. But maybe… She'd tilted her head. Maybe Gran kept the key in her bedroom? Ali had never been inside her room, but she'd glimpsed a jewellery box on the tiny bedside table – she remembered being surprised that Gran even had a jewellery box since she never wore any. Ali had glanced out the window. Gran was still sitting there, her back to the cottage. Ali's pulse had raced. Did she dare go into Gran's room and search for the key? Gran wouldn't want her in there – though she'd never told Ali it was off limits, Ali could sense that space was sacred. But she'd come too far in her quest to stop!

Ali had crept into her grandmother's cramped bedroom, then opened up the satin-covered jewellery box. Instead of the mess of necklaces and bracelets like her own mother's box, there had been nothing except the faded and torn satin lining, as if someone had swept everything away. The pirates had already plundered, she'd thought, lifting the insert in case they'd forgotten something.

A key! She'd grabbed it and raced back out to the chest. It had to work. She could feel it! She'd twisted it in the lock, and… bingo! The chest had clicked open to reveal… a stack of blankets and one teddy bear, dressed in a sea captain's outfit.

Ali had sat back. Oh well. No gold or hidden maps, but the bear was cute enough. Why had Gran locked it away? She must have forgotten it was in there.

Ali had been so absorbed in taking off the bear's cute little outfit that she hadn't noticed Gran moving from her perch by the sea and coming inside again.

'What are you doing?' Gran had grabbed the bear from her grasp, and Ali had jumped. It wasn't so much her grandmother's presence that had shaken her – it was the angry tone and the harsh look on her face, something Ali had never seen before. She'd dropped the bear and run into the back garden, tears streaming from her eyes. Gran was the one person who never yelled at her. She may not like hugs and cuddles, but she was never mean. How could she snap at Ali just for playing with a stupid bear? Okay, so she shouldn't have got the key from Gran's bedroom, but…

She'd been sitting in the rain, her knees up against her chest to try to stay warm in the salty chill, when Gran sank down beside her. They'd sat in silence for a minute or two, Ali still trembling with sobs.

'You're so sensitive,' her mother always used to say, shaking her head so that Ali knew it wasn't a compliment. But Gran seemed to understand her in a way her mother never did… until now.

'I'm sorry,' Gran had said, both of them gazing out to the waves breaking in the ocean as rain dripped down their cheeks. 'That bear, well… it's a special one. I packed it away to keep it safe.'

'Was it Dad's?' Ali had asked, and Gran had shaken her head.

'No, it belonged to…' Gran had sighed. 'I'm sorry I snapped at you,' she'd said, before Ali could ask who had owned it. She'd put a hand on Ali's back, and Ali could feel the warmth seeping through her thin T-shirt. 'Come in for some tea? Camomile for you, though, young lady.' She'd smiled, her eyes crinkling up at the corners, and normalcy had slid over them. Ali had never questioned any more, and she'd never tried to find that teddy again. The next day, the chest had been wide open, and the contents had disappeared.

Now, Ali wondered if the teddy had something to do with the bag of clothes she'd found… the bag belonging to a boy named Ben. Who was he? Was he the little boy Gran had mentioned? And why was she keeping his things – things that were so precious she couldn't even bear to let Ali touch them?

Ali sat down on the bed and picked up the teddy, running her fingers over its soft fur. What had it been doing in the wardrobe?

Was that where Gran had put it after Ali unlocked the chest? It had been special to Gran, after all. Maybe she'd wanted it close.

Ali stared at the bear, an idea filtering into her head. Gran hadn't wanted anyone to play with it back when Ali had been young, but the reason behind that was lost now, buried in the past. Gran was gone, too, and it felt right to pass this teddy on to the family who'd kept an eye on her; who'd tried to help her. It was a small way of extending the connection between them.

Ali stuffed her bag full of clothes and toiletries, put the teddy on top, then closed the cottage door and went back across the garden. She knocked on the door, and Meg swung it open, her hands encased in Marigolds.

'Hi!' she said, ushering Ali in. 'Jem's asleep' – she pointed to where the baby was peacefully slumbering in the corner of the kitchen – 'and I thought I'd better tidy up for you.'

'I'll put my bag down and then come help,' Ali said, even though her cleaning skills were probably nowhere near Meg's immaculate standards.

'No, no, no.' Meg waved a finger. 'You sit and relax, whatever you like. Actually, why don't you go up and have a little nap? The guest room is right beside Jem's. It should have everything you need, but let me know. Hope Jem won't bother you too much in the night.' Meg grinned. 'I guess you'll have to get used to it anyway!'

'That's fine. Thank you so much. I'll try not to be in your hair for very long – hopefully, the roofer can fix the leak before Michael comes home.'

Meg shrugged. 'Don't worry. It's good to have you here. No rush.'

'Well, thanks again,' Ali said. 'Right, I'll go up, then.' Meg nodded and turned back to the sink, and Ali jerked. 'Oh! I almost forgot. I have something for Jem.' She fished the teddy from her bag and snuggled it gently under the sleeping baby's arm. Jem's eyelids fluttered and she nestled against it. Warmth flooded through

Ali at the sight of the baby cuddling something that had been so special to her grandmother.

'Oh, you didn't have to do that.' Meg turned from the sink. 'What did you—' Her words came to an abrupt halt when she spotted Jem with the bear. 'Oh, wow. So cute.' Something about her tight tone made Ali think she didn't quite mean it, though. Maybe you shouldn't give a baby so young such a big soft toy?

'Might be better for when she's older,' Ali said quickly. 'But it is really cute, isn't it? My gran had it for years – it was really special to her. I remember trying to play with it when I was young, and she wouldn't even let me touch it.'

Meg eased the bear out from under Jem's arm, holding it carefully. 'That's really kind of you,' she said, although her tone didn't quite convey that sentiment. Ali bit her lip, wondering if maybe giving an old toy was some kind of faux pas. 'Thank you.'

'Well, I'll go up now,' Ali said, hoping she hadn't offended Meg. After everything she'd done, that was the last thing Ali wanted. She padded up the stairs, her hand gliding along the solid oak bannister. Light shone in the windows upstairs, making the polished wooden floor glow, and Ali paused for a minute, drinking in the serenity.

She peeked into the first bedroom on the right, guessing from its spacious size and large bed that it was the master bedroom. The checked duvet and clean lines of the furniture made it seem modern yet warm… exactly like the couple who slept here. What would someone think if they gazed into her and Jon's room? Ali wondered. An image of their dingy duvet and rickety bed frame, tilting from missing too many steps during the dodgy assembling process, rushed into her head. Based on that, anyone could see they weren't solid.

Perhaps she should have known they weren't as unshakeable as she'd thought? She'd chosen to believe Jon's words that he'd never hurt her; that he'd always be there. She'd *wanted* to believe him. She knew he loved her, but she also knew that love wasn't enough.

People had to be strong too – they needed to have that strength in themselves to 'deal'; to be there. Otherwise, when you hit hard times, everything would collapse, like the bed that hadn't been put together properly.

Ali continued down the hallway to the guest bedroom and sank onto the bed, nearly groaning in relief at the softness of the mattress. Through the open window, her cottage next door looked dingy and tiny, and she could see the hole in the roof. Her stomach twisted at the damage inside, but it was fixable. The roof could be repaired, the nursery repainted… the vision would still be intact.

And in the meantime, she had somewhere comfortable and peaceful to stay, at the heart of the perfect family.

CHAPTER FIFTEEN

Ali

Ali wandered down the staircase and into the lounge, yawning. It was gone midnight, and she was wide awake. She really had to stop napping in the middle of the day. She'd meant to sleep for only an hour or so earlier, and somehow, she'd conked out for three! After the cottage, where everything rattled and the bed – even with the pillowtop – was only just about comfortable, Meg's home was like a five-star hotel.

'Oh, you're still awake!' Ali said as she came around the corner into the lounge. She'd assumed Meg had gone to bed as soon as Jem was down… that she was knackered after being with the baby all day, like she'd said earlier.

Meg glanced up from where she was sitting, glass of wine in hand, watching the telly. Ali tried her best to hide her surprise at the drink. She'd had the impression that all alcohol had been banished from the house. Where had Meg got that wine? And how could she drink if she was breastfeeding? Ali wasn't judging. She was simply… curious.

'Come join me.' Meg patted the sofa beside her, then looked down at the glass in her hand. 'Sorry to be drinking in front of you; hope you don't mind. It's been so long! I finished Jem's last feed, and I thought I'd sneak one in while Michael's gone.'

Ali shook her head. 'I don't mind at all.' She'd never been a big drinker anyway, apart from the mandatory post-party vodka.

Meg gulped her wine. 'You know, I can't even remember the last time I had a glass. Even before I got pregnant, I didn't drink a lot. Michael always said too much made me crazy!' She tapped her head and flashed Ali a grin. Ali smiled back, thinking it was hard to imagine Meg as crazy. She was energetic, yes, but she always seemed to have it together.

'So… now that you're planning to stay, you're going to have your baby at the hospital in Hastings, right?' Meg asked. 'It'd be so much easier than having to go back and forth to London for appointments, and anyway, you can't do a two-hour journey when you're in labour! Well, you could, but it'd be bloody uncomfortable.' She made a face. 'I nearly broke Michael's leg, I grabbed it so hard on the way to hospital. I told him it was a small price to pay compared to what I was about to go through!'

Ali smiled back absently at the image of the two of them, holding hands in the dim light while Meg pushed, full of joy and excitement as they awaited the birth of their beautiful daughter. She couldn't imagine a more perfect tableau… miles away from the scenario that awaited her when the time came. She'd envisioned a scene similar to Meg's so many times that it was almost impossible to picture anything else. Ali took a breath in, pushing away the pain that threatened. No matter how different it might be, she'd get through it.

'You said you're about twenty weeks? So you'll have another appointment in a month or so, right? Plenty of time to sort it out.'

Ali nodded. Meg was right: if she was staying here, she wouldn't be able to have the baby in London. She didn't want to, anyway. This was where she'd be spending the rest of her pregnancy. These were the people she wanted around her. When the time came for her next antenatal appointment, she'd book into the Hastings hospital.

'Tell me how you and Michael met,' Ali said, eager to replace all thoughts of London with the warmth of this family. 'Have you guys been together long?'

'Oh, yes. Ages. We're high-school sweethearts, actually. I know that sounds so cheesy, but it's true.' Meg took a sip of her wine. 'Neither one of us really fit in in secondary school.'

'Does anyone?' Ali shook her head, thinking of her own wretched adolescent school days. She'd gone to an all-girls' grammar school and she'd been painfully shy and self-protective, holding herself tightly. It'd taken her ages to feel comfortable enough to let down her guard, and she'd eventually become fast friends with Sapna, another girl in her tutor group. Although they couldn't have been more different if they tried, something about them had clicked.

Sometimes, Ali really missed her best friend – well, *ex*-best friend. They'd been so close, going to the same university and even moving in together after graduation while they both got started on their careers: Ali as an analyst for a consultancy firm, and Sapna working all hours as a junior doctor. Even though they'd both got their own places after a few years, they'd remained close. Sapna had been the one to encourage Ali to keep seeing Jon when her doubts had threatened to overwhelm her, saying that she could see he was a really good bloke and that he'd be perfect for Ali. She'd even been a witness at their tiny wedding.

But then a few years ago, Sapna had started dating a married man… a consultant from the hospital, who had a daughter the same age as Ali when she'd discovered her father's affair. Sapna hadn't known he was married at first. After finding out, she kept trying to break it off, but somehow, she always seemed to end up back with him. Ali had finally snapped, telling Sapna to stop seeing this man for good or their friendship was over. She hadn't really meant it – she'd only wanted to give Sapna some extra motivation to end the relationship. Her friend would do the right thing, Ali was certain.

When a month had gone by but Sapna still hadn't rung, Ali had decided that enough was enough. Surely, Sapna must have told the man where to go by now! She'd dialled Sapna's number, but Sapna didn't answer. She didn't respond to any of Ali's text messages or her voicemails or even her knocks on the door. Ali realised that there was only one conclusion: Sapna was still seeing the married man.

When she'd told Jon that she couldn't believe Sapna would do this, he'd met her eyes.

'Not everyone is as strong as you,' he'd said, and her mouth had fallen open. *Strong?* She'd never thought of herself that way. What did he mean?

He'd shrugged, saying that sometimes, people made mistakes. And when emotion was involved, it was harder to correct it – harder to do what you knew was right, or what was needed. If you gave someone time, though, they might just come through in the end.

She'd nodded, mulling over his words. Maybe he was right, but she couldn't stand by her friend while she ripped apart a marriage... while she damaged a little girl, the same way Ali had been damaged when her father had left. She'd called Sapna one final time and left a voicemail saying that she missed her and to ring if things changed... hoping that Jon *was* right and that her friend would come through. Then Ali had hung up, her heart aching.

Sapna had never called, though. Over the years, Ali had thought of her often. *Was* she still seeing that man? If not, why hadn't she rung? Did she think Ali had been too harsh with her ultimatum?

Ali shifted on the sofa now, Jon's words ringing in her head. *Not everyone is as strong as you. But give someone time and they might just come through in the end.* She let out a breath, swallowing down the bitter taste in her mouth.

'Ali?' Meg's voice interrupted her thoughts.

'Sorry.' She glanced up, jerking herself back to the present. 'You were telling me how you and Michael didn't fit in.'

Meg nodded. 'This is a small place, and it wasn't cool to be into art and drawing, like I was. I'd rather spend time working on a painting than drinking down on the beach. And Michael had been kicked out of his boarding school, and he was super posh. All the kids were mocking his accent and how clever he was. Like me, he started taking refuge in the art room. We never really spoke until one day, a group of boys barged in when I was working on a painting. They began harassing me, you know, like teen guys do. I wasn't scared at first, but then...' She swallowed. 'They started pushing me around. Thank God Michael came in. He grabbed an art knife and told them to leave me alone. They must have seen that he meant it because they couldn't get out of there fast enough. They never bothered me again.'

'Wow.' Ali raised her eyebrows at the dramatic story. 'Knight in shining armour.'

Meg nodded. 'He really was. From that moment on, he was always there for me. Always.' Her face twisted and she traced a heart on the condensation in her glass, then scribbled it out and met Ali's eyes. 'You shouldn't have got me started! You probably don't want to hear this now.'

Ali smiled. 'It's fine.' She and Jon may not have had what it took, but it was nice to hear that two people could make a commitment to each other and stick to it for so long – that high-school sweethearts existed apart from rom-coms and fairy tales. Michael and Meg were real-life evidence it was possible.

'So... do you want to talk about what happened with your husband?' Meg asked, her tone tentative. 'I'll completely understand if you don't.'

Ali shook her head. Rehashing the horrific scenes was the last thing she wanted. All of that was behind her now, and that was how it should stay.

'Whatever it was, I'm sorry.' Meg reached out and squeezed Ali's hand. 'But I have to say, I think it's so brave of you to leave; to do this on your own. I really admire you.'

Ali's eyebrows flew up. Meg, this woman who seemed to have the perfect life, admired *her*? 'Well, I didn't feel like I had much of a choice, you know? It's like you said: babies know.' She tilted her head, thinking that while she'd been wrong about Jon, he'd been right about her. She *was* strong enough to do what was right… for her and the baby.

Meg nodded, her hand still on Ali's.

Jem started crying, and Meg drained her glass, then plonked it on a coaster. 'Right,' she said. 'Time for your first lesson.'

Ali cocked her head. 'First lesson? What do you mean?'

'Baby lesson, of course!' Meg smiled. 'How to settle a crying baby. Believe me, this is one skill you'll definitely need. Come on.' Before she could say anything, Meg took her hand and pulled her up the stairs, where the soft crying had escalated to full-on wails.

'Right, now, different things work differently for different babies. You'll need some time to get to know your own little one, but here's what works for Jem. We try not to pick her up because she gets super upset when we put her back down again.'

Ali went inside the room. Meg's words twisted around her heart, mingling with the baby's cries. *Time to know her little one.* She needed time. God, how she needed it.

'We crouch down here and reach into the cot, then pat her chest.' Meg slid gracefully onto the soft, carpeted floor and started patting Jem's chest. The crying got softer but didn't stop and Meg met Ali's eyes. 'Sometimes, it takes a while,' she said, 'but she *will* stop. The important thing is that she knows we're here for her. Always.'

Ali nodded, her eyes filling up.

'Okay, you try,' Meg whispered, gesturing for Ali to draw her hand into the cot. Ali gently tapped the baby's chest, feeling the soft, solid weight beneath her skin. Jem's eyes shifted onto hers, staring up at her as she continued her rhythmic tapping. It was almost hypnotic, and Ali held her breath as Jem's eyelids slowly sank shut.

'You see?' Meg whispered. 'You're a natural!'

Ali couldn't move; couldn't speak. All she could do was stare at Jem, watching as the baby fell under the spell. Her own baby kicked, and a yearning rushed into her, so strong she could feel it vibrating in every cell. She wanted this so badly: to take care of her baby, to be its whole world, the same way Jem was looking at her now. She wanted to be the natural Meg claimed she was. She wanted to learn – to fulfil the promise she'd made to her child… and to become a mother, in every sense of the word.

They were about to creep from the room when her eyes caught something on a shelf to the side of the cot. Squinting in the dim light, she could see the unblinking lens of a camera. Was that some kind of fancy monitor system? If so, it looked pretty high tech.

'Does your monitor have a camera too?' Ali asked Meg as they slowly backed out of the room. 'I thought I saw one in there.'

'Oh, that.' Meg closed the door softly behind them, and they crept down the corridor. 'No, it's not part of the monitor. It feeds through to the studio. Michael had it put in when he went back to work, a month or so after I had Jem. He had another big job that he had to get started on, but he wanted to make sure me and Jem were okay, and to feel like he was right there with us. He misses Jem so much when he's not with her.'

'That's so sweet.' God, Michael really had meant it when he'd said he was committed to his family. 'How is he doing, anyway? He must miss you guys.'

Meg nodded. 'He's okay. Right, want to go back down and chat some more?'

Ali shook her head, her mouth stretching in a yawn. 'I think I'll go off to bed.' Putting Jem down had made her sleepy, too, and given her a warmth and contentment that she wanted to keep close as long as possible. 'Good night.'

Meg smiled. ''Night. It's so good to have you here.'

Ali touched her belly. 'I can't think of anywhere else I'd rather be.' It sounded so clichéd, but right now, she really couldn't.

CHAPTER SIXTEEN

Ali

The next few days passed in an easy haze as Ali and Meg fell into a comfortable routine. Ali would get up, put the coffee on and start breakfast, keeping everything warm until Meg appeared with Jem. They'd spend the day playing with the toddler, then chat after supper until the sky darkened. Meg would pour herself a glass of wine after producing another bottle from goodness knows where, and Ali's eyelids would slowly feel heavier until she couldn't resist the call of bed any longer. She still didn't understand how Meg could appear so *alive* in the morning after staying up so late, not to mention consuming all that alcohol… If she wasn't used to it, surely she'd have a killer hangover? With all the crying Jem was doing lately, Meg was up and down all night too. But she seemed to be functioning admirably well, particularly without Michael on hand to help.

Ali had asked a few times when Michael might come back, but Meg had only said he was still working on securing new business and that it'd probably take a bit more time. Ali had to admit she was in no rush for him to return – with Michael gone, there was space for her to spend time with Meg and Jem without feeling like she was in the family's way. And the longer she could stay here, the more she could pull that feeling of warmth around her… the more she could learn to be the mother her baby deserved.

It was as if every new skill brought her daughter closer, moving Ali even further from the pain of her family's collapse. Ali couldn't thank Meg enough for her patience and positivity. It was beyond comforting to have someone like her on hand, and Meg was a fantastically thorough teacher. From winding to feeding to changing nappies, Ali had already learnt so much.

Okay, time to get some lunch on. Ali headed to the cupboard, thinking how different it was that here, she'd fallen into the role of the cook. Back home, it was Jon who'd taken over kitchen duties after Ali's one attempt at making spaghetti had ruined a pot by burning the pasta and sticking to the bottom. The flat had reeked for weeks afterwards, and Jon had all but banned her from the kitchen. But with Jem teething and Meg spending most of the late morning trying to get her down for her nap, the duties fell mainly to Ali. That was fine. Actually, it was more than fine. Apart from learning how to take care of a baby, she was learning to cook.

She groaned at the sight of the empty cupboard, flinging open more doors to look for something to eat. Neither of them had been in the village to pick up any food, and the kitchen was like Siberia. Ali stood on tiptoes, trying to reach the top cabinet to see if anything edible might be lurking there. A black lens, similar to the one she'd spotted in Jem's bedroom, stared back from the top. She gripped it and turned it around, looking to see if it was functional. Like the one in the bedroom, this one was turned off.

She tilted her head. What was that doing here? She could understand a camera in Jem's bedroom – there was nothing as beautiful as a sleeping child, and it was always good to have an extra set of eyes in case the baby woke up when Meg was showering or something.

But one in the kitchen too?

It seemed a little much… to Ali, anyway. She wasn't sure she'd like Jon watching her every move with their child, monitoring her actions like she maybe couldn't be trusted on her own. But

Michael wasn't watching Meg, she told herself. He was watching Jem. He'd been adamant that he hadn't wanted to miss a thing, and he obviously stood by his words. And maybe it was comforting for Meg to know that even though Michael was busy working in the studio, he was still looking out for her… for them.

The ringing of the landline interrupted her thoughts.

'Meg?' she called. Ali waited for a response, but there was only silence. That was odd – Ali had thought she was in the lounge. Jem cooed in the high chair beside Ali, having stubbornly refused to succumb to sleep, and Ali turned to the baby.

'Where's your mummy gone, hmm?' Jem loved to sit beside her and watch her cook, a little sous-chef in training. Ali adored their cooking time together, even putting on a funny voice as she assembled their meal, pretending to be on TV as Jem giggled and clapped her chubby hands.

'Meg?' she called a little louder, but there was still no response. Shrugging, she scooped up the receiver. 'Hello?'

'Is this Ali Lawton?' A man's voice came down the line, and Ali's brow furrowed. Who was that?

'Speaking.'

'This is A1 Roofing,' the man said. 'I'm sorry to take so long to get back to you, but we can come out today and assess the damage to your cottage. If it's not too bad, we might be able to do the repairs too – or at least a temporary fix to tide you over.'

'That would be great,' Ali said slowly, a mix of emotions inside. She'd have to go home some time, of course. She and Meg might get along well now, but she didn't want to overstay her welcome. And Michael would be back at some point, too, eager to spend time with his family… without her here. She swallowed, sadness filtering through her that this neat little trio was coming to an end. If it were possible, she'd want it to last forever.

'We'll be there after lunch.' The man checked the address with her, then hung up.

Ali replaced the receiver, looking around to tell Meg the news. Where on earth was she?

Maybe she was having a nap, Ali thought, although that'd be a first. Gingerly, she unstrapped Jem from the high chair and picked her up, glancing out the window at the brilliant blue sky.

'Oh, there she is!' Ali spotted Meg down the lane by the side of the studio.

'Look, there's Mummy!' Jem started kicking her legs and reaching out her arms, clearly excited to see her.

'Come on, let's go say hi.' Ali slipped on her shoes and headed down the bumpy pathway towards the studio. She breathed in the salty air, tightening her arms around Jem as she bounced her up and down.

Finally, they reached the studio, but Meg was nowhere to be seen. She must have gone inside, Ali thought, noticing the door was open before bending over to catch her breath. God, that short walk had really taken it out of her. She might be pregnant, but she hadn't thought she was *that* out of shape. She put a hand on the wooden door of the studio, about to open it wider when Meg appeared on the other side.

'Oh my God!' Her hand flew to her mouth. 'You scared me!' She stepped out, then slammed the door closed, snapping shut the huge padlock.

'Sorry. We didn't mean to startle you,' Ali said, following as Meg grabbed Jem and walked away. 'We saw you out here. Jem was dying for a cuddle, and I've got some news.'

'Michael wanted me to put this lock on the door to make sure no one could get in. He told me to make sure the house doors are always locked too.' She looked at Ali. 'Did you lock it now?'

Ali shook her head. 'No, sorry. I was only coming out to see you.' She bit her lip at Meg's panicked expression. 'But I promise to from now on.'

Meg laughed, but it sounded far from relaxed. 'I know it seems a little over-the-top, but he's so rarely away that he wants to make sure we're safe.' She continued quickly down the pathway without asking Ali what her news was. Had she even heard? Ali forced her legs faster to catch up.

'So... you talked to Michael? How is he doing?' She grinned. 'You can tell him that I'm going now that my roof is fixed. It's safe for him to come home!'

Meg swung towards her. 'Talked to Michael? What do you mean?'

Ali's brow furrowed. 'Well, you said he asked you to put that lock on, so...'

'Oh yes, sorry.' Meg swiped her hair back, and Ali was pleased to see the mark on her arm was healing. For a while there, Ali had wondered if it needed to be looked at. 'God, this heat. It's making me go a little scatter-brained today. Michael's good. He misses us, you know. Sends his regards and all of that!'

They went inside the house, and Meg turned to face her. 'You're not really going, are you? Look, whether your roof is fixed or not, you can still stay here. You know that, right? Michael's not going to be back for a while, and I love having you around. Jem loves you too. It's like having a sleepover every night!' Meg went into the lounge and collapsed onto the sofa, with Jem now sound asleep on her shoulder.

'I never really had a best friend,' she said with a wistful expression, tucking her legs underneath her. 'I never had someone to chat to, to laugh with... someone I just got on with. Apart from Michael, of course.'

Ali nodded, thinking of Sapna. She'd been a firm fixture in Ali's life, the only real friend Ali had had for years. Ali had missed her so much: missed the easy way they'd giggle about anything, the history and life they'd shared. Sitting on the sofa each night with Meg talking about everything from nappy brands to the best breast pads reminded her of that camaraderie – albeit with very different topics of conversation!

'Growing up, it was only me and my mum,' Meg continued. 'She worked really long hours – usually night shifts – and we didn't have any family around. She'd make me supper as soon as I got home from school, then lock me in and go to work. Sometimes, I'd be so terrified I'd crawl under the bed as soon as it got dark and stay there until she got home again. I was afraid to even move. It made me want to be there for my child, in a way my mother never was. I can't imagine leaving Jem like that.'

'Wow, that's tough.' Ali's heart lurched at the thought of Meg as a little girl left home alone all night. Then Meg's face morphed into her own, and sadness curled in. Ali might not have been alone physically – a rotating bevy of au pairs had been there to watch over her – but she'd felt lonely, as well. 'My mum was gone most of the time too.'

'It *was* tough.' Meg nodded, as if she knew Ali got it. 'I couldn't go out after school to play dates or clubs, and even on the weekends, Mum would be working. And when I was old enough to go out on my own, then, well… I'd grown used to setting myself apart from people; delving into my art. The only time I did have a group of friends was when I went to art school, and then… it doesn't matter.' She waved a hand, then smiled. 'That's why it's so nice to have you here – and why I want you to stay! Please say yes.' She paused. 'With Michael gone, I feel… safer with you here. You know?'

Ali nodded. She *did* know. She felt safe here with Meg too.

'Thank you,' she said, reaching out to hug her friend. 'I'd love to stay.'

CHAPTER SEVENTEEN

Violet

June 2018

Rain slices from the sky. For the first time in a very long while, I stand behind the window and gaze out, wanting to see a sign of life – wanting to see movement next door. I need to hand over the teddy and put everything else out of my mind. But the window I can see from my bedroom is firmly closed with the curtains drawn and the front door has remained resolutely shut all day – I know because I've been watching. I could go over, I guess, but the last thing I want is to wake up the baby. By the sounds of things, that whole family needs sleep.

I'm sweeping the kitchen floor for the millionth time when there's a knock on my door. My eyebrows fly up when I spot Meg through the window. Oh, good. The very person I wanted to see. I shake my head at myself, thinking I can't remember the last time I actually *wanted* to see someone.

'Come in!' I say. It's been a while since I've said those words to anyone. 'I'm afraid I don't have any milk, though.' I'm out of practice making jokes and banter, but I need to diffuse the nervous energy I feel flowing from her. Even though she's standing perfectly still, the air around her is almost vibrating, coming out in waves to envelop me. Her eyes fix on me, her gaze so intense I take an instinctive step backwards.

'I don't think I can do this,' she blurts out before I can ask if everything is okay. 'Nothing I do is right. Nothing works. The baby just cries and cries…'

My heart sinks as I realise this won't be a quick visit. As much as I want to give her the teddy and get it over with, I can't leave her like this.

'Sit down,' I say softly. I flick on the kettle, sympathy running through me as I remember my own feelings of being overwhelmed when Andy was placed in my arms. 'You know, lots of new mums feel that way at first. It's such a huge responsibility, but you can do it. You *are* doing it.' I nod towards the baby, now dozing comfortably against her chest. 'Look – no crying; happy and thriving. That says it all, and that's down to you. You've been there day and night.' I know that's true because I've heard her with the baby at all hours.

'Not because I wanted to,' she mumbles, and a faint buzz of alarm rings inside me as I recall her words to her husband, pleading with him to give her space. I'd thought then that she wanted him to back off, but maybe… maybe she meant that she wanted space from the baby? The constant care for a newborn can be relentless, and perhaps she has a touch of the baby blues. How old is the baby now? I try to remember, but time is a blur.

'Have a seat,' I say again, gently propelling her towards my saggy sofa. 'I'll bring you a cup of tea. Sometimes, a good cuppa can change the world.' If only, I think, but I know it's comforting to hear that.

But she doesn't move. 'It's… it's just…' She gulps in air, and I remember overhearing her say that she can't breathe.

'Look, it's okay to want some time away,' I say. 'Everyone needs a break. Sometimes, even an hour or two on your own will make you feel like a new woman.'

'I wish I was a new woman,' she says, staring out to sea. 'I wish…' Her voice fades away and my mind flips back to that night, at the two bodies twisting and turning in the waves, grasping and pulling. What *was* happening? I wonder. I shove the question from my mind, telling myself to stay out of it. She has a husband. She has family. I'm not the person she should be talking to.

I grab two mugs from the cupboard, then sit across from her. 'Does your husband know how you're feeling?' I ask. She nods and relief slides through me. If he's aware, then he'll keep a close eye on her. I don't need to worry… not that I would, of course.

'Meg? Where are you?' His voice filters through the thin cottage walls, and we both turn towards it. If the proof is in the pudding, then he's definitely watching out for her. The knowledge makes me feel calmer; more certain she'll get help if she needs it.

'Thanks for offering me tea, but I'd better get back,' she says. 'I'm sorry to bother you. I—' She shakes her head. 'God, you'll think I'm such a nuisance.' She smiles, but it doesn't reach her eyes, and my heart aches for her.

'It will be okay,' I say, because I know that sometimes, when you're in the thick of it all, you think you'll never emerge. And although things might be different, you *will*. No one was waiting for me when I started my new life, but she has a baby and a husband by her side. 'Your husband is there for you, and I'm sure you have lots of friends to support you. But if you ever want to talk, I'm here too.' The words fly out, and I wish I could take them back, but it's too late. She won't need me, though, I'm sure.

'Thank you.' She meets my eyes and pushes back her chair, and I can see that she really does mean it… that somehow, despite my reluctance to get involved, I have made a difference. An unfamiliar little glow flickers inside as I walk her to the door.

I watch as she crosses the garden towards her husband. He puts his arm around her and the baby, ushers them both into the house, and closes the door behind them. I head back inside and lie on my bed, listening as they put the baby down for a nap. They'll be okay, I tell myself. Once things settle into a routine, they'll find their rhythm. Everything will be fine.

It's only when I shut my eyes that I remember I still haven't given her the teddy.

CHAPTER EIGHTEEN

Ali

'There. You did it!' Meg high-fived Ali as they stared down at the collapsed buggy. It'd taken five tries and countless barely smothered swear words before Ali had managed to wrestle the reluctant contraption from the standing into the collapsed position, but finally she'd succeeded. They'd just returned from their now-daily walk along the winding trail that ran along the top of the cliffs. It was such a beautiful day that Meg had even packed a picnic. Laughing at Jem's shocked expression when she bit into a crisp for the first time and trading tales about nappy-changing nightmares, Ali had almost felt like everything was right with the world.

'You're a real expert now!' Meg said with a smile. 'I knew you would be.'

Ali grinned back, thinking that, while she might not be an expert, with every day that went by and with Meg's help, she was gaining confidence and getting closer to fulfilling the promises she'd made to her daughter: that she wouldn't let her down, and that she'd do everything she could to be the best mother possible… practically and emotionally.

Michael still wasn't home – Meg said he was desperate to return, but that he was talking to a major Spanish furniture supplier now, in a series of critical meetings. In the meantime, Ali was savouring the feeling of companionship she had with Meg... something she hadn't experienced in ages. Even when it came time for Ali to return to the cottage, Meg made it clear she wouldn't be on her own, chattering on about all the things they could do together. Michael would take up his place at home eventually, but they'd still be good friends.

Ali *would* miss their night-time chats, though, even if she was starting to wonder at the amount of alcohol Meg was getting through. But after months of not drinking, could Ali really blame her for splurging? She was sleeping longer in the mornings, but Ali didn't mind. It gave her a chance to practise her skills with Jem.

They'd only been back from their walk for a few minutes when a pounding on the door made them both jump. Meg grabbed Ali's arm, her eyes wide. 'Who is it?' she called out, her voice shaking. Ali stared, bewildered by her response. What was she so scared of?

'Um, I'm looking for Ali Lawton? She's not in the cottage next door, and I was wondering if you'd seen her?'

Ali took a step back in surprise at the voice. *Sapna?* What the hell was she doing here? Ali yanked the door open, standing at the threshold.

'Ali, hi. Thank God I found you.' Sapna shuffled from one foot to the other, her face pale and anxious. Despite the time that passed, she looked remarkably similar: corkscrew sandy hair, bottle-green eyes and that wonky smile she'd always said she was going to have fixed. Once, Ali had known everything about her, from how her boyfriend kept begging her for anal to her favourite takeaway. Now, she knew nothing.

'You're looking well,' Sapna said, although Ali knew she looked anything but. Sapna had always said to start any conversation with a compliment. Clearly, some things never changed.

'What are you doing here?' Ali stared, unable to anchor this part of her past in Fairview, at Meg's door. Memories crowded into her head: how they'd go out for 'dinner only' but somehow end up drunk at one in the morning, careening through the empty streets of London towards home. When Jon had asked her to marry him, and Ali had said yes in a heartbeat, then called Sapna in a panic from the grungy loo of the pub. The time Sapna had thought she was pregnant and spent half her pay packet on pregnancy tests, taking one after another until she was finally convinced she wasn't.

They'd supported each other through years and years of trivial details and major life events, and Ali had relied on her like no other person until she'd met Jon. Their friendship had been built on decades of knowledge and shared history, the kind of things that bound two people together no matter how much things changed – no matter what had happened.

Or so Ali had thought. Hurt flooded through her again that after everything, their friendship had faltered over a relationship – a relationship that had been wrong from the very beginning. Had Sapna realised that now? Was she still with that man?

Why hadn't she ever called?

'I… I wanted…' Sapna swallowed. 'I—'

'How did you know I was here?' Ali interrupted, shoving away all thoughts of the past. It didn't matter now why Sapna had never rung.

'I talked to Jon. He called me last night.'

Ali stiffened, drawing in her breath. Jon talked to Sapna? Why?

'Ali…' Sapna touched Ali's arm, and Ali jerked away. She'd missed Sapna so much, but their friendship was part of another life. 'He's worried sick. You must know how worried he is for him to hunt down my number and call.' She attempted a smile, and Ali remembered how they used to joke that Jon couldn't find anything unless it was right in front of him, blinking with a neon sign. 'He didn't know who else to talk to.'

Ali shook her head, seething now despite her efforts to stay calm. How could Jon do this? He knew how much she'd agonised over the ending of their friendship. And he'd seen how much she'd missed her friend, both in those early days when she'd smarted with anger and later on, when sadness at how quickly their relationship had dissolved had sunk in. Did he remember his words that not everyone was as strong as her and that if she gave Sapna time, she might come around in the end? Had she?

Had *he* changed his mind? Was he hoping that by sending Sapna now, Ali would let him in again too? Before she could quash it, a rogue bit of hope darted through her. She stared at her old friend, wondering how much Jon had told her… wondering what he'd said. That he didn't want the baby… or that he did?

'He's been trying to call, but your phone is off.' Sapna's eyes were steady, but Ali could tell by the way she was twirling her hair that she was nervous. The small familiar gesture made her feel like maybe they did still know each other, after all. Her heart twisted.

'He said you'd gone to your grandmother's cottage. I went there, but everything was dark and closed up. So, I decided to come here and ask if they'd seen you, and here you are.' Her eyes locked on Ali's belly, then swept up to her face.

'Yes,' Ali said. 'Here I am.' They stood facing each other, as if in a stand-off where no one knew quite what the goal was. 'So… what does he want?' Her heart was pounding, and she couldn't hold back the hope now ballooning inside. Maybe he *had* needed more time. Maybe—

'Just to check you're okay.' Sapna's voice was soft and gentle, and Ali's gut clenched like she'd been punched. *Just to check you're okay.*

'Look, I'm on your side. Not that there are sides in any of this.' Sapna paused, and Ali could see how hard it was for her to find the right words. *Were* there any right words for this situation?

'Men can't really understand how we feel, how we can love something so strongly, so soon,' Sapna said finally. 'They don't carry the baby inside of them. They don't have that physical connection like we do.'

Ali blinked. Sapna was speaking as if she'd been pregnant; as if she'd had a child. Had she? Sadness filled Ali as it hit her once again that as close as they'd been, she knew nothing about Sapna's life now.

Sapna looked at her as if she would understand, but Ali shook her head. How could Sapna use that as an excuse? Maybe men didn't have a physical connection with their children during pregnancy, but if they'd promised to be there for their family, then nothing should change that. Nothing should make them question that… question a future together. Look at Michael, for God's sake. He was so committed to his family that he'd even installed cameras so he didn't miss one second. Ali was sure he was strong enough to face anything to keep his family safe.

Sapna started twirling her hair again before glancing down at Ali's belly. 'I can't pretend to understand how you must be feeling right now. I have no idea how hard this must be. But I do know that whatever he might have said – no matter how stupid or hurtful – Jon loves you. He wouldn't have bothered to call me otherwise, to reach out to me after what happened between us.' She waited for Ali to respond, but silence stretched between them.

'I understand why you're angry at him, but he's worried about you,' Sapna said. 'You can't stay here alone. Come back to London, Ali. You can… you can stay with me until you're ready to talk to Jon. I'd love that. Love to be friends again, if we can. I'm so sorry things ended the way they did between us. I never wanted to lose you. I was… well, I suppose I was afraid to let you down, to disappoint you. You made it clear how you felt about me and Eric together.'

Ali held her gaze. 'Are you still with him?' She wasn't sure why she was asking, but part of her wanted to believe Jon was right: that maybe somehow, people *could* be strong enough in the end.

Sapna blinked and looked down. 'We're married.' Ali's eyes widened as Sapna held up her hand, pointing to a diamond ring – princess cut, what she'd always wanted.

'And the daughter?' Ali had never forgotten the man had a daughter the same age she'd been when her father had his affair.

Sapna shook her head. 'Eric doesn't see her. But not because he doesn't want to. Her mother won't let her.'

'Right.' Ali stepped back. All of this time had passed, and yet nothing was different. Sapna hadn't stopped seeing that man – she'd married him, tearing apart the family in the process and hurting a little girl, like Ali had been hurt. And Jon… Jon hadn't changed his mind either. What an idiot she was, hoping he had… hoping he *would*. How many more disappointments did she need?

Ali caught her breath as she realised that Sapna and Jon were more similar than she'd thought. They were like her father: people who didn't understand what promises were; people who let anger, fear and emotion weaken and break the bonds. People who *did* disappoint those who loved them. Time wouldn't change – hadn't changed – a thing.

And Ali wasn't like that. She wasn't, and she never would be. She was like Meg; like Michael. These were people who understood commitment, unwavering despite any obstacle. *That* was real love.

She straightened her spine and faced Sapna. 'I'm not going back to London.' Her voice was loud and strong, and she had never felt more certain. 'And I'm not alone. I have friends here. True friends.' Her friendship with Meg might be new. It might not be built on years of shared history, but its foundation was something much stronger – not only pregnancy and baby talk, but shared ideals, shared values. Sapna flinched, but Ali couldn't stop. 'People who care. People who are keeping me safe and helping me do what I need to for my child.'

Before Sapna could even respond, Ali closed the door and locked it firmly. Meg touched her arm, then peered out the window in the door. 'She's going. You okay?'

Ali nodded. 'I meant what I said, you know.' She thought back to their first meal together when Meg had been so excited about

Ali's pregnancy, reminding her that the most important thing was her baby. Meg had pushed her forward, towards the light and away from the darkness, keeping her above water. Ali owed her everything. 'You are a real friend. I can't thank you enough.'

Meg propelled her into the lounge and onto the sofa. 'You're helping me too. Just by being here. Just by...' She shook her head. 'You know, I was thinking. Why don't you stay with me until after the baby is born? That will give you all the time you need to fix the cottage up – and do any other renovations it might need. You can make it into a really great place.'

Ali tilted her head. Hadn't she been thinking she'd like to stay here forever? She'd love to, but... 'Don't you need to talk it over with Michael?' A few days was one thing when her husband was travelling, but for a stay that could be potentially months?

Meg shrugged. 'He won't mind. He loves all things baby, as I'm sure you've noticed. And he'd be only too happy to help. So? What do you say?'

Ali nodded, warmth rushing through her. 'That would be great. Thank you so much. You know, you're so lucky to have someone like him.' Ali touched Meg's arm. She flinched, and Ali realised she was touching her injury. 'Oh, sorry! I was thinking earlier how much better it looks. Does it still hurt?'

'A bit, but it is getting better.' Meg smiled. 'Right, let me get Jem down for her nap. You sure you're okay?'

Ali nodded. She was moving forward now, building a new life for her and her baby with people who understood the meaning of commitment... people with whom she really did connect.

Maybe her daughter wouldn't have a dedicated mother and father, but she would be surrounded by those who wouldn't waver, no matter what. And if that wasn't true family, then Ali didn't know what was.

CHAPTER NINETEEN

Ali

'Morning! Good sleep?' Meg flashed Ali a bright smile as she padded down the stairs the next morning, then turned and stuck out her tongue at Jem. The baby laughed, and Ali's heart melted. There really was no better sound. 'Listen, I've got an idea. After last night and all you've been through, I think you could really do with something to cheer you up a bit.' Meg's eyes sparkled.

'Something to cheer me up?' What did her friend have in mind?

'Yup! Why don't we go out?' Meg radiated excitement, and Ali's brow furrowed.

'For a walk?' It was another beautiful day, and lately they'd been walking for miles. Surely, Meg couldn't get so excited about that, though.

'*Out* out, silly!' Meg nudged her arm. 'A meal, maybe, up in Hastings. Get back into civilisation a bit!'

Ali nodded slowly, trying to hide her surprise. Since Michael had been gone, they'd only left this little area to venture into the village for groceries. Ali had thought that Meg was happy to chill around here – even *with* Michael, hadn't she said they rarely went out? Why the change now?

Meg laughed at Ali's expression. 'Don't worry, I really do mean just a meal, maybe at a pub or something casual. I'm not going to drag you clubbing or anything!'

'Thank God for that,' Ali said, trying to remember the last time she had gone clubbing. She'd never been a big fan, even in her younger years. The thumping music, the wet sticky dancefloor, the jostle and the push for drinks at the bar… and even worse, having to get dressed up in a ridiculous outfit like some show pony, trying to catch the eye of the opposite sex who'd barely even make an effort before asking if she wanted to go back to theirs. No thank you.

'So?' Meg eyed her hopefully. 'You up for it?'

Ali paused, turning the idea over in her head. She loved pubs, actually: the quiet hum, the clink of glasses and the jovial laughter floating through the air. She used to go to loads with Jon, back when he was still trying to make it onto the circuit as a singer after teaching all day. He'd be playing in the corner, and she was more than content to sit there on her own, listening to his husky, melodic voice.

Right now, she'd prefer to sit at home and perfect putting Jem to sleep, but maybe a meal out would mark the start of this new world, with people who wouldn't let her down. Besides, it was the least she could do for someone who'd helped her so much. And after all, wasn't that what friends did – go out with each other? After losing Sapna, she'd really missed their long dinners out.

'That sounds perfect,' she said, grinning as Meg punched the air. For the rest of the day, Meg was buzzing with excitement, throwing herself into getting ready for their meal as if her life depended on it.

It was amazing how different she looked, Ali thought later that night, her eyes sweeping over her friend's black corset-style top, ripped black jeans and spiky-heeled ankle boots. She'd piled on the eyeliner and her hair was swept up in a messy, loose topknot. It was a total transformation, miles from the fresh-faced Boden-style woman Ali had met that day on the lane. Despite the niggling unease when she stared at this stranger, trying to piece her together with the person she'd come to know, Ali would be the first to say she looked incredible. No wonder Michael was so in love! It was a rare woman who could pull off wholesome mum and hot chick.

Ali fluffed her hair up, thinking she wasn't radiating either. Right now, she was more sloppy than sexy; more weedy than wholesome. She looked passable in the dusky pink top Meg had loaned her and a pair of maternity jeans that were actually comfortable. Huge, but passable. But she'd never complain. She'd never mind being big because that meant her baby was growing. It meant she was doing what she should to keep her baby safe.

Even Jem was decked out in her finest frock with a little pink cardigan, although Ali bet that would stay clean for all of five minutes. Her pastel freshness was a complete contrast to Meg's goth chic.

'Right, are we ready to go?' Meg asked a few minutes later, checking her lipstick in the mirror. The dark red made her pale smooth skin look flawless, and Ali felt even dowdier in comparison. 'I've thought of a perfect place, a really relaxed pub with great food. Not too busy, but with enough atmosphere. You'll love it.'

'Sounds good.' Truthfully, right now Ali wanted nothing more than to take a nice warm shower and crawl under the duvet, but Meg was so excited there was no way she could even think of aborting the trip.

Meg strapped Jem in the back of the car, then climbed in the front beside Ali, got out the keys, and started the engine. She flicked through the radio stations, then selected one with dance music, opening up the car window and singing along to lyrics Ali had never even heard before. Jem watched her mother with wide eyes, gurgling and cooing as Meg grooved to the rhythm.

'God, this feels so good,' Meg said, as she pulled away from the house. 'It's been ages since I've driven. Ages since I've been anywhere!' She glanced over at Ali. 'You don't mind if I have a couple of drinks, do you?'

Ali shook her head. 'No, of course not. But...' She bit her lip, thinking that she wasn't exactly keen to drive home in the dark on unfamiliar roads, even if Meg was by her side. But saying that after everything Meg had done for her felt wrong. 'Won't Jem need to have another feed after supper, though?'

'What, are you keeping tabs on me now?' Meg's angry voice echoed loudly in the car, and Ali looked over at her with surprise. What on earth? 'I'm sorry,' Meg said in a softer voice, putting a hand on Ali's arm. 'It's been so long since I've been able to relax a little – to think about something other than Jem. I love her with all my heart, you know that. But...'

'It's okay.' Ali shifted in her seat. Meg was such an involved mother that it was understandable she'd need a break every once in a while. She was only human. 'I'm happy to drive home if you like. Just relax and enjoy tonight. You deserve it.'

Meg flashed her a bright smile and continued down the winding roads towards town. After the quiet and peace of Fairview, Hastings seemed bright and noisy, the streets full of people. Ali recalled coming here with Gran once. It was rare she could even get her grandmother to leave Fairview – to leave the confines of her land and cottage – but Ali had begged Gran to take her to the fair in town. After saying she couldn't stand one second more of Ali's whining, Gran had finally succumbed.

Funnily enough, Ali couldn't even remember the fair now. Her only memory of the trip was splashing in the waves, then coming back to Gran's tiny car, all sandy and hot. She'd told Gran that she had more fun with her than her parents, then pleaded to stay with her. Gran had smiled and patted Ali's head, saying grandmothers had all the best bits of parenting and none of the worst, and that if Ali lived here, she'd have to see her bad side too. Gran had made a face like an ogre and started growling, but Ali still hadn't believed she could ever be horrible – at least not as angry as her own mother seemed to be sometimes. Gran could be quiet and maybe a little impatient, but the only time Ali had seen her truly angry was when she'd grabbed the teddy that day.

It was funny that after all of her begging and pleading to stay, Gran's home was her own now – that she was staying there for good. What would Gran make of Jon and how he'd failed her? Ali wondered. What would she think of Ali coming here?

Meg drove through the town centre and then up a narrow street towards a pub decorated with bunting, teeming with punters who spilled out into the street. Ali paused, thinking that if she closed her eyes now, she could almost hear her husband singing the very piece he'd written when he'd proposed. She'd been sitting there, drifting off as usual, when something in his introduction to the song made her sit up and take notice. What followed had been a song which had touched her unlike anything she'd ever known. The words gripped onto her heart, making her feel more loved and cherished than she ever had before. What she and Jon had was special, she'd believed. They knew each other in a way no one else ever could.

'You okay?' Meg touched her arm, her face full of concern.

'I'm fine.' Ali smiled, forcing her thoughts from the past. Who needed love songs from a man who watched his wife walk out the door when she needed him most? All that was behind her now. 'Come on. Let's go.'

'Wow!' Meg stared at the building in front of them as they got out of the car. 'This place has changed! I mean, when I used to hang out here, it was good – great food and all that. But now… it's got popular, by the looks of things.'

So much for a quiet meal in a cosy corner, Ali thought, eyeing the packed interior with a sinking heart. They'd be lucky if they could even find a place to sit, let alone eat. And with a baby in tow, it wasn't exactly going to be a relaxing night. At least they wouldn't stay long, if at all.

'When did you hang out here?' Ali asked, curious. With Meg's story of how she'd been an outsider and never had many friends, Ali hadn't pictured her as a pub regular.

'Oh, when I was in art school,' Meg said, opening up the back door to get Jem. 'What do you think, hey Jem? Ready for your big night out?'

Jem kicked and gurgled, and Meg smiled. 'Of course you are! Come on, let's go in.' She heaved open the pub door and the noise hit Ali like a wall. She tucked her hair behind her ears and smiled self-consciously as she scanned the people. Amidst the artsy, cool young crowd, a pregnant lady and a mother with a baby stood out like sore thumbs, even if that mother was dressed to fit in. Still, no one even turned to look at them as they threaded their way through the noisy room towards what Ali prayed was a dining area at the back. Her heart sank again when she realised there was indeed a dining area, but it was very posh – and already stuffed with patrons.

'Hello.' A woman with a tiny nose ring that sparkled in the light smiled at them, then made googly eyes at Jem. 'Do you have a reservation?'

'A reservation?' Meg's eyebrows flew up. 'You never used to need to book to eat here.'

'Well, you do now. Most days, anyway. Ever since we were featured on Great British Pubs last year, we've been overrun. And I'm afraid we're fully booked tonight. You can try your luck getting a table for bar food out front.'

'Come on, let's do that,' Meg said, turning to scan the room. It was impossible to even *see* tables, there were so many people.

'Meg… there's no way we're going to get a table. It's way too busy! And what about Jem? And a high chair?'

'Of course we're going to get a table.' Meg grinned. 'We have a secret weapon.'

Ali furrowed her brow. 'What?'

'You!' Meg pointed to Ali's stomach. 'You're pregnant! You'd have to be a complete tosser not to move to let a pregnant lady sit down, never mind a woman with a baby.'

Ali nodded, thinking there were plenty of tossers on London transport who had done precisely that: denying her a seat on packed Tube trains even when she'd shoved her 'Baby on Board' badge directly under their noses. She'd loved that badge; loved the secret thrill of belonging to a club, trading glances with other pregnant women as they passed by.

'Come on.' Meg took her arm and propelled to the front of the pub, stopping in front of a group of lads occupying a prime table right by the window.

'Excuse me, would you mind moving? My friend here is having some contractions, and we need a comfortable place for her to sit and relax.'

Ali tried to keep her face neutral. Contractions? At twenty-two weeks? Did she look *that* big? She tried not to grin as the clearly clueless men immediately jumped up and scrambled to their feet, almost knocking over their pint glasses in the process. 'Of course, of course,' one said. 'Please, sit down.' Ali smiled at him, thinking she was probably old enough to be his mother.

'Great, thanks!' Meg chirped, swinging her legs into the padded booth. She handed Jem over to Ali. 'Would you mind holding this one? I'll go get some menus so we can order.'

'Sure.' Ali bounced Jem on her lap, the noise swirling around her ears. This might not be the ideal place to bring a baby, but Jem was clearly enjoying it, swivelling her head back and forth, taking in everything with wide eyes.

Ali spent the next few minutes jiggling Jem, trying to keep her entertained because once she started straining to escape from Ali's arms, all hell would break loose. Granted, it was so noisy here that no one would hear her cries, so that was one thing in this place's favour. Right, where the *hell* was Meg? How long did it take to grab a few menus?

Finally, she spotted her friend threading through the crowd towards their table. 'Sorry that took so long,' she said. Her cheeks were flushed, and her eyes sparkled. 'It's absolutely manic up there. I'd forgotten what it's like to be out on a Friday!'

'Meg? Is that you?' A female voice cut through the noise, and Ali turned to see a woman about her age hovering by the booth. The woman's arms were covered in tattoos and her long blonde hair spiralled down her back, only somewhat held back by a colourful bandana. Everything about her screamed 'artist'. 'Oh my God, I haven't seen you for ages! I thought you dropped off the face of the earth! Here, budge over. We need to catch up!'

'Oh my God! Caro!' Meg screamed and threw herself at the woman. They hugged, then Meg pulled back. 'Ali, this is Caro. We went to art school together.'

'Hi,' Ali said, trying to extricate her fingers from Jem's clutch to shake Caro's hand.

'Nice to meet you,' Caro responded. 'And who's this lovely thing?' she asked, looking over at Jem. Ali waited for Meg to answer, but she seemed like she was somewhere else, so Ali said: 'This is Jem.' Jem reached out to Caro's hair and gave it a yank, and Caro laughed.

'That's me told, then.' She turned to Meg. 'So how the hell have you been? What have you been up to all these years? You look fabulous, by the way,' she continued. 'Really well.'

'I've been great!' Meg said in a bright tone. 'Busy being a mum to this one here.' She reached over and took Jem from Ali's arms.

'Oh my God, this is *your* baby? She's so cute!' Caro's shriek could have broken glass, and Ali tried not to wince. 'You always used to tell us you didn't want kids!'

Ali tried not to show surprise. Meg hadn't wanted kids? She'd thought Meg was one of those women who'd pined for motherhood since birth. At least, she seemed cut out for it. And hadn't she said she wanted ten children? But people changed their minds, she told herself. Jon certainly had.

'Well, life happened.' Meg smiled and stroked Jem's head. 'And it's been wonderful.' She looked up at Caro. 'How about you? Any children? Didn't you say you were going to have a farm and your kids would help out?'

Caro laughed. 'Oh yeah, I'd forgotten about that. Well, I'd still raise a brood on a farm, but my wife Jill – she's around here somewhere – convinced me I wouldn't like shovelling manure, after all. I stayed and opened a gallery in the Old Town. Come have a look some time! And if you're still painting, I'd love to see some of your work.' She turned to Ali. 'This woman here is so talented. She would have won all the awards at school if she'd only stuck around long enough! Have you seen any of her paintings?'

Ali shook her head, thinking the mural didn't count.

'Ask her to show you.'

'I will.' Ali wondered why, if Meg had been so talented, she'd left the school and given up painting. It couldn't have been because she'd got pregnant, because Jem was only a year old. Why had she stopped?

'Listen, a bunch of us are heading to a party down by the water now. There'll be a ton of people there – some great contacts if you're interested. I always thought you'd make it big in the art world, and if you're still producing work like you did back in school, I know lots of interested people. Not to mention it'd be a great chance for us to catch up properly!'

Jem let out a squeal, and Caro shook her head. 'Oh God, I'm sorry. Of course you can't come to a party with a baby! What was I thinking? Doesn't matter, I'm sure we'll run into each other another time.'

Ali waited for Meg to agree and say that they were going to have a meal then head home, but instead she turned to Ali.

'Would you mind taking Jem back?' she asked, as surprise flashed through Ali. Meg was actually going to the party? 'She's exhausted, anyway. I'm sure she'll crash out in the car. You'll be okay, right? You can grab something to eat on the way home? Probably be faster than trying to order here.'

Her eyes met Ali's, and Ali could see how much she wanted to go with Caro. This party was more than a chance to relax and have a little fun, Ali realised – it sounded like a huge coup and a great way to jump-start her career. Meg had been saying how much she'd missed painting and that she'd love to get started again. And while the last thing Ali wanted was to drive home on her own, after everything Meg had done for her, she could hardly say no. Besides, entrusting your daughter – one you had never used a babysitter for or been away from for long – to someone else was a big deal, and the fact that Meg trusted her gave Ali a warm glow inside. She was ready to go home, anyway.

Ali nodded. 'Okay.'

'Oh, thank you, thank you.' Meg's excitement made Ali smile despite her exhaustion.

'Take good care of this little one. I know you will.' Meg planted a kiss on Jem's head, then handed the baby to Ali. 'Call me if there's any trouble. Here are the keys.' She shoved a heavy fob at Ali. 'The house key is on there too.' She linked arms with Caro. 'See you later!' she called out over her shoulder as they pushed through the punters.

'Wait!' Ali yelled, and Jem started crying at the sudden noise. 'How are you going to get back?'

Meg shrugged. 'Uber? I'll be fine, don't worry. Bye!' And with that, she disappeared into the crowd with Caro.

Ali watched her friend go, then nuzzled the top of Jem's head. 'Guess it's just you and me,' she whispered. 'And you,' she said, sliding her hand down to touch her belly. A smile lifted her lips. 'Come on, guys. Let's go home.'

CHAPTER TWENTY

Violet

July 2018

It's been quiet for the last week or so – no baby crying, no arguments and no surprise visits from Meg. Peace seems to have descended, and I pray that she is better able to cope now. She's lucky to have a husband who can be there all the time. My own husband went back to work the day after I'd given birth, leaving me alone and in pain with a screaming infant. That's how it was in those days, and I'm so pleased that things have changed for the better.

The warm glow that I was able to give Meg some kind of helping hand at the start of a new life has made me feel something I haven't for ages: useful, that I can do something right, despite all the mistakes in my past. It's a feeling that lifts me up, letting a tiny slice of light into this dark prison I've locked myself into. My gaze falls on the teddy waiting patiently on the sofa and a bit of sadness stirs inside. Once I hand him over, I'll have no reason to speak to Meg. The door will be closed again; the light blocked out. But that's a good thing, I remind myself. Talking to my neighbours – talking to anyone – isn't a habit I want to get into. My world is *here*.

I turn from the window, staring at the scarred walls. The cottage hasn't been touched since it was built, except for the bare essentials:

winterising so I could stay all year, new windows when the old frames started to leak, patching the roof almost every spring. Once I decided to make this my home – once I left my family in the city – I couldn't make any improvements. It felt like I didn't deserve it; like I should let this place crumble away until the edge of the cliff finally reached out and swallowed it up… taking me with it.

And so, the floor is cracked and scuffed, and the kitchen cabinets hang off the hinges. The bed is like a personal torture device, the springs digging into you with every move. The cottage walls are dark and stained, and the toilet needs to be flushed at least twice to make it work.

I hear a door slam and I peek out the window to spot Meg putting a squalling baby – I still don't know if it's a boy or a girl – into a car seat, then climbing behind the steering wheel. My heart drops when I see her face, and I know instantly that, despite hoping everything next door is now fine, it's clearly not. Her expression is vacant, and she's moving strangely, like she's struggling under a heavy weight. I pray that she's going to the doctor, but she's really in no condition to drive – not like this. Where on earth is her husband?

I can take her wherever she's going. I put on my shoes and step outside, but I'm too late: the car is flying down the lane, dust rising as it goes. It crests the hill, and I shield my eyes and wait for it to turn right towards Hastings, but instead it just… disappears.

I shake my head. That lane runs parallel to the cliff edge and comes to a dead end. She couldn't have gone further, but she definitely didn't turn off. I know I'm getting old, and my brain is more unreliable every day, but I haven't imagined this. The dust is settling now, and the air is clear. But the car is gone.

I hurry as quickly as I can down the road, my muscles protesting and my heart beating fast. What happened? Did she stop the other side of the hill? Or… I shake my head against the image of the car, ploughing through the field at the end of the lane, then making a turn and gliding towards the cliff edge. My heart beats faster as fear fills me, and I urge my legs forward. *Please God, no. I couldn't bear it if Meg and her baby…*

After what feels like forever, I reach the top of the small hill and see the sun glinting off something metallic at the side of the road, right before the turn. With my heart in my throat, I hurry closer, relief flooding through me when I spot the car in the shallow ditch. Oh, thank God, thank God.

But how did it end up there? I rush down the hill and over to the car, picking my way through the long grass and bushes. It's tilted slightly to one side, but everything else looks fine. It's not the car I'm worried about, though. I kneel down, cursing the pain in my knees, and look inside. I can hear the baby crying – that's always a good sign – but Meg… well, what I see chills me to the bone.

She's sitting in the front seat, perfectly still. Her eyes are open wide, and she doesn't appear to have any injuries. But she's staring straight ahead, blinking, as if she's not even there.

I knock gently on the window. 'Meg? Are you okay?'

She starts and turns towards me, then opens the door. I take her arm, help her out, then sit her down on the grassy bank, telling her to rest. Then I go to the car and get out the baby, all sweaty and red, from the car seat. I hold out the child for Meg to take, but she keeps her arms crossed in front of her.

'What happened?' I ask. She was so driving fast, and in her state… another shiver goes through me.

'I don't know. I'm not even sure how the car got in the ditch.' Meg stares up at me, like she's trying to remember. 'I just had to get away. I just…' Her voice trails off, and she glances towards the house, then down at the baby in my arms.

I remember her words that she needed space, and I hold the baby tighter. It's obvious she wasn't thinking rationally because, in her bid to escape, she took the child with her. Unless she'd planned to do something… something to the infant and herself?

The chill grows into fear as I think once more of the night I saw her in the ocean when she was heavily pregnant. I never made sense of it, but I never really tried. Now, I'm starting to wonder if that strange struggle in the water with her husband was because she wasn't coping then too… because she was trying to escape. Not many women know it, but sometimes depression can start in pregnancy.

'I'm never going to feel better, am I?' Her voice is dead, as if she's given up. 'I'm never going to be okay. It's going to be like this… forever.'

I shake my head, reaching out to take her hand. 'It's *not*. I promise you.'

But she looks at me like I have no idea. I bite my lip. I'm not helping her at all. Perhaps I didn't help before either, I think as my heart sinks.

'Have you been to see the doctor?' I ask. If my suspicions about that night in the water are correct, then hopefully she's seen someone. If not, she needs to. 'There is medication you can take that will make things better. You don't have to do this on your own.'

'Medication,' she repeats in that flat voice. 'I'm breastfeeding. I can't take any medication. My husband says it's bad for the baby.'

'Well, he's right. Some over-the-counter medications can be, especially when you're pregnant. But this wouldn't be a painkiller, this would be something you need.' I pause, choosing my words carefully. Despite that night, her husband must not understand how critical the situation is now. Sometimes, it's easier to pretend everything is okay. I've seen it a million times in my patients. 'And like I said before, you can always use formula. Your health is as important as the baby's.'

She doesn't say anything, and I sigh inwardly. I need to get through to her. As much as I don't want to involve myself in other people's lives, I can't ignore this. I want to, but I… can't.

I'll talk to her husband, I decide, and make sure he understands – make sure she visits the doctor to get the help she desperately needs. She obviously respects his opinion, and if he tells her she needs to take the medication, I'm sure she will. It's for their own good… as a family.

I take her arm. 'Come on. Let's get you home. Are you okay to walk?' I scan her body to assess any injuries, but she's wearing a long-sleeved shirt so I can't see any.

She nods. 'I'm fine. Well, mostly.' We go the mile down the road slowly, and finally we reach the door of her house.

'Thank you.' She meets my eyes. 'And please… please don't tell my husband about this. *Please*.' Fear flashes across her face, and I know she's thinking how worried and scared he'd be if he found out. But he *should* be worried and scared – he needs to be. 'I'll go back and get the car. He doesn't have to know.'

I hold her gaze, guilt needling me. Because I know that I will tell him: he does need to know. I don't want to lie, but I'm not keen to upset her even more now, so I give a tiny nod and tell myself it's for her own good.

She needs help, and the sooner she gets it, the better it will be for everyone.

The sooner I can go back to my life alone.

CHAPTER TWENTY-ONE

Ali

Ali's eyes flew open at the sound of Jem crying. God, was it morning already? She heaved herself up, wondering why Meg wasn't going to the baby. Lately, Ali had been the one to get Jem up in the morning, but Meg must be itching to give her daughter a cuddle after she'd missed putting her down last night.

But the crying continued, so Ali made her way down the hallway to Jem's nursery. Peeking into Meg's room, she saw that the bed was still made, and the blinds were wide open. She stood for a second, trying to absorb the fact that Meg hadn't come home last night. A mix of worry and anger swept through her. Was her friend okay? She must have lost track of time. Maybe it had been too late to get an Uber, or perhaps she'd stayed over at Caro's. She probably hadn't wanted to wake up Ali or Jem by calling the landline, and Ali's mobile was still off.

Ali scooped up Jem and went downstairs, her mind replaying last night. The baby had fallen asleep within a minute of the car starting, and Ali had had to use every last bit of her concentration to follow the roads home. At times, she'd felt like the only person on earth as she'd twisted and turned under the starry sky, the trees casting strange shadows on either side of the road. She'd shivered as she turned into the lane, squinting at a dark shape moving across the fields away from the house. What was that? She blinked and it disappeared, and she laughed at herself as she parked in front of the house. She'd obviously been up *way* too late. Jem was still fast asleep, and she'd lifted her gently in her arms and carried her up to the house, scrabbling in her pocket for the keys Meg had given her.

The key fob had been heavy in her hand, the metal engraved with letters. Ali had drawn it closer, eyebrows rising when she spotted the letters MICHAEL. Why would Michael leave without taking his keys with him? Meg must have her own set of keys, surely, so there was no reason to leave them here for her. And wouldn't he need his house key?

Must be an extra set, Ali had thought as she put the key in the lock and went inside. Up in the nursery, Ali had undressed a sleeping Jem and pulled on her onesie, placed her into her cot, then crawled into her own bed. Lying there in the dark, the silence wrapped around her as Jem slept peacefully in the next room, Ali could almost believe for a moment that this was her life; her world. Just her and the baby, in a house full of love.

The feeling stayed with her the next morning as she got Jem dressed, fed her breakfast and took her out on the back deck to enjoy the fresh morning air. She and Jem had moved on to playing blocks in the lounge when Ali heard a car pull up the drive. She hauled Jem onto her shoulder and clambered to her feet, disappointment and relief mingling inside when she spotted Meg in the car. She took Jem to the door and pulled it open, reminding herself that this wasn't her world; that Jem wasn't her baby. Her own child was tucked up inside of her, waiting for the day they'd finally meet.

Meg was climbing out of the passenger's seat, cheerily waving goodbye to Caro. Ali expected her to look like something dragged through a hedge backwards – she certainly would, if she'd stayed out all night – but Meg appeared as fresh and alive as ever.

'Hey!' Meg bounded up the stairs. 'How are you guys?' She reached out for Jem, bouncing her in her arms. 'Hey, gorgeous. I missed you! Did you have a good sleep?' She grinned at Ali. 'Thank you so much for taking care of her. I can't say thanks enough! I had such a great night. I met loads of people. Some might be interested in buying my pieces! Caro said they're big buyers, and if I have something to show, she'll consider representing me at the gallery. I only need to paint them now! I'm starving. Come on, I'll make us all a huge fry-up.' She pushed inside the house.

Ali blinked, trying to take in the torrent of words. 'That's fantastic news!' she said, coming into the kitchen where Meg was cheerily singing to Jem as she cracked egg after egg into a bowl. God, how hungry *was* she? 'What did Michael say? He must be so excited for you!' Ali assumed that Meg had called her husband as soon as she'd left the party. If Ali had a big coup like that, wild horses couldn't have kept her from sharing the news with Jon. When she'd told him about a big project Sarah had put her on, he'd whisked her out for a meal at their favourite pub down the street. He'd let her natter on and on about her work, although she knew he couldn't understand a word of it.

'Oh yes, he's really happy for me,' Meg said, whisking the eggs as if her life depended on it. 'Of course.' Ali nodded, thinking she wouldn't expect anything less. Michael loved Meg with everything he had, and it made sense he'd support her with getting her painting career on track. That was what committed husbands did: be there for their partners.

'Hope scrambled is okay. Then Jem can have some too.'

'That's fine.' Ali watched as Meg turned up the heat on the hob.

'I'm sorry to have abandoned you last night,' Meg said, from her place at the stove. 'Especially after going out was my idea. And then I dumped Jem on you and asked you to drive home in the dark… that was pretty shitty of me. It was just—'

Ali put a hand on her friend's arm to stop her talking. After everything Meg had done and all she had given her, it was the very least Ali could do. 'Please don't worry. I was ready to come home, anyway, and Jem was out like a light before the car engine even started. We enjoyed our time together this morning too.'

Meg turned to face Ali, her features soft. 'I knew I could trust her with you. Thank you.' She gave Ali a quick hug, then turned back to the eggs. 'Right. Who's ready to eat?'

CHAPTER TWENTY-TWO

Ali

'Ali! Come look at this!'

Ali hauled herself off the bed from where she'd been resting. What did Meg want to show her now? Her friend had been on a high ever since returning from the party yesterday morning, excitedly drawing sketch after sketch, then calling Ali to come see. If Ali had thought she was energetic before, that was nothing compared to her current state. She padded carefully down the stairs to see Meg standing in the middle of the room, surrounded by boxes.

'Look what the delivery man brought!' Meg chose one and ripped it open, revealing a huge set of oil paints. 'And what's inside here?' With a look of excitement on her face that rivalled a kid at Christmas, Meg tore open another box to reveal a stack of canvases, then an easel, then more oil paints, some brushes... Ali gulped as she caught sight of a receipt tucked into the box. *Yikes.* Who knew art supplies cost so much? This was almost Ali's monthly salary, and she made a good living. Michael's business must be doing very well indeed.

Though, of course, there was every chance that this was Meg's money. Perhaps she had some savings, or... Ali shook her head, thinking what a bad feminist she was for assuming the money was Michael's. Her mum would shake her head, saying she'd failed to combat gender stereotypes in her daughter. Ali sighed, thinking of how her mother had always seemed so strong; so able to do anything. When Ali was young, one of her favourite photos of her mother showed her at a protest, her mouth wide open as she shouted out something, carrying a sign demanding equal pay for women. Her mum had looked like some kind of superhero, and Ali had stared at that picture for hours, praying that when she grew up, she'd be like her mother.

But after Ali's father's affair and the resulting divorce, her mother had changed. She'd still been strong, but something about that strength seemed fuelled more by anger and bitterness than inner resilience. She hadn't been around much, but whenever she was, she'd mutter how Ali's father had turned out to be nothing but a weak specimen of a man, and how she shouldn't have believed it was possible to find a good man in the first place. Ali had rolled her eyes at the familiar refrain. When she'd found Jon, she'd felt sorry for her mother and how much she'd missed out on.

Was it possible her mother had been right, after all?

No, Ali told herself. Her mother was crazy, and Ali wasn't going to let herself become twisted and bitter – she wasn't going to let what happened with Jon affect her feelings towards her daughter. Because that's exactly what it had done for Ali and her mother. It had pulled them apart; created a distance that had grown so much it was impossible now to bridge.

And wasn't Ali here in a household with living proof that not all men let you down?

'Are you planning to open an art school?' Ali joked, pushing the thoughts from her mind. 'You certainly have enough supplies!'

'Oh…' Meg tilted her head, surveying the pile in front of her. 'I may have gone a little overboard last night. To be honest, I can't even remember clicking on half this stuff! I was so excited. That's what credit cards are for!' She laughed. 'It's been ages since I've painted, and after talking to Caro, I really can't wait to start again.

I missed it so much.' She met Ali's eyes, and Ali thought how she looked like light was streaming from her.

'Why did you stop?' Ali asked, wondering if she should probe but curious to discover the reason.

'Well...' Meg started opening up another box. 'Painting isn't something you can dip in and out of – at least not the kind of painting I do. It's all-absorbing; it sucks you in.' She shrugged. 'I didn't want it to be just a hobby, so I figured if I couldn't do it how I wanted to, I wouldn't bother.'

Ali nodded, thinking that although that explained why she hadn't painted since Jem was born, it didn't explain why she hadn't worked for the years before that. If Meg was as talented as Caro had said, something big must have happened to make her stop. But Meg didn't ask many questions about Ali's life or her past, and that was how Ali liked it. Perhaps they should keep it that way. Anyway, what did it matter? Their lives right now were infinitely more important than anything in the past. They didn't need to know every little thing about each other to be friends.

'Okay, I'm going to organise this stuff in the lounge,' Meg said, lugging a box across the floor. 'The light there is perfect for painting.'

She spent the rest of the day setting up an easel in a corner of the lounge and arranging her art supplies in a cabinet she'd bought. Ali didn't mind – she was happy playing with Jem, enjoying the little girl and getting more experience for when her own time came. Jem seemed content, and Meg's words from yesterday floated through her head: that she knew she could trust Ali. Ali was honoured and touched that her friend felt that way. Still, the same feeling of unease when she'd seen Meg all dressed up the other night nagged her. If painting really was that absorbing, how could her friend start again now, with a toddler by her side? Toddlers weren't known for their ability to entertain themselves or wait patiently to be fed... or wait patiently for anything.

But Meg knew all that, Ali told herself. She was probably just eager to expel this first creative burst of energy. She couldn't expect to sustain total absorption. She wouldn't want to, anyway, because that would mean barely spending any time with Jem. And no matter how much Meg loved painting, Ali knew beyond a doubt that Jem was the centre of her world.

Come suppertime, Meg was sitting down at the easel, a paintbrush in her hand.

'Pasta's ready!' Ali called, but Meg didn't budge. 'Meg?' Ali said again, not wanting to disturb her but thinking that she must be starving. But Meg merely raised a hand and told them to go ahead, so Ali and Jem had dinner alone.

After tidying up the kitchen and setting aside a plate of food, Ali poked her head into the lounge again. Meg was in the same place, still staring at the easel.

'Do you want to put Jem down?' Ali asked softly.

Meg looked up for a second, as if Ali was speaking in a language she didn't understand. Then she nodded. 'Oh yes, of course. Thank you.' She stood and stretched, holding out her arms for Jem. Ali watched as they went up the stairs, then scooted over to have a look at the easel. Sympathy flooded into her when she noticed it was still blank. It must be hard to get back into something after being away from it for so long, even if you had missed it.

When Ali came down in the morning, Meg was at the easel once again, painting away despite Jem's increasingly louder squeals in her cot.

'Morning!' Ali said. 'I think Jem's awake. Sounds like she's eager for her feed!'

Meg glanced up. 'She's already had one, actually. I gave her a bottle earlier.'

Ali blinked. A bottle? She didn't even know Meg had any. She'd certainly never seen her use them.

'I was hoping she'd go back to sleep eventually, but she wants *me*. The second I show up, she'll be wanting to feed. It's, well… actually, I'm trying to wean her.'

'Oh!' Ali raised her eyebrows, surprised. The cosy image of that night she'd looked up to see Meg and Michael together as Meg fed the baby flashed into her mind. Hadn't Meg said she'd be happy to carry on for as long as the child would let her? That she loved doing it, and that it felt so natural? And hadn't Michael said how important it was for the baby to breastfeed as long as possible?

Did this have something to do with the painting? Ali wondered. Did Meg want to stop so she could pay even more attention to her work? When you breastfed, you were pretty much on call 24/7. Meg had never seemed to mind, but maybe now… No, Ali told herself. Meg wouldn't stop breastfeeding for one painting!

'If I could, I'd probably go on forever,' Meg said, as if she'd heard Ali's questions. 'But I think it's mostly a comfort thing for Jem now, anyway. She barely drinks anything when I feed her. Michael thought I should carry on, but honestly I think it's time.' She met Ali's eyes. 'It's my body, too, you know? She's my baby too.'

'Of course!' Ali said, surprised to hear there might have been any disagreement. 'You're her mother. You know better than anyone.' Her voice rang with conviction, and she thought of her own situation. It was her body. It was her baby. 'And if you think it's time to move on, then you're probably right.' Ali would trust Meg's mothering instincts with her life.

Meg nodded. 'Thank you. Anyway, we agreed to wean Jem while Michael's away. He's such a big softie that he can't bear not giving her what she wants.' Meg shook her head. 'The crying is awful, I know, but I don't know what else to do. She's going to have to get used to it, that's all.' Meg ran a hand over her face, looking exhausted.

'Have you been painting all night?' Ali asked. 'Why don't you get some sleep? I'll take care of Jem.'

Meg slicked back her hair and turned to face Ali. Her cheeks were red, and her hair curled in sweaty tendrils around her head. The old jeans she was wearing were dirty and torn, and her T-shirt was stained. Yet, Ali thought she'd never looked more beautiful. There was a kind of freedom about her now that Ali hadn't seen before.

'Uh, yeah, I guess I have. Time got away from me.' She turned back to the canvas. 'But that's all right. Who needs sleep?' She flashed a smile. 'Would you mind watching Jem? I want to get this bit right…' Her voice faded as she started working again, and Ali went up the stairs to settle Jem. She could understand wanting to finish what you were working on. Jon always hated to be interrupted when he was writing lyrics or trying to pin down an elusive tune from brain to paper.

But as the next couple of days went on, Ali realised it wasn't only one bit Meg wanted to finish… and it wasn't just an initial burst of creative energy that would soon run dry. Meg's earlier words rang true: painting had sucked her in, pulling her inward and away from the world around her. She hardly slept or ate – she hardly seemed to *need* to sleep or eat – and she barely spent any time with Jem, nodding absently when Ali asked if she wanted her to watch the baby again today. Ali had no idea how her friend was even still functioning, but she understood that Meg was determined to finish this painting quickly to show Caro; to strike while the iron was hot. Once she was finished, she'd step back from her work and normal service would resume once more. Ali could see how much she loved painting, but she must really be missing her baby too. Maybe that was why she was working so intensely: because she wanted to finish and be back with Jem.

Not that Ali really minded taking over. She missed their chats and the easy rhythm of their days together, but she had to admit she was loving stepping into Meg's role with Jem. The little girl was comfortable with Ali, and Ali knew their routine inside out. And with Meg trying to wean Jem off breastfeeding, it was easier for someone else to feed her, anyway. Ali adored the way Jem kicked her feet each morning when she came into the nursery, how her eyes locked on Ali's when she gave her the bottle, the gentle rise and fall of her chest as she dozed in the dim light of her room… taking care of the little girl was everything Ali had dreamed of; everything she had hoped for the future. With every second that passed, it felt like that future was getting closer and closer until she could practically touch it.

And now, Ali was ready. Ready to be a mother. Ready for her own baby, whenever she chose to arrive.

CHAPTER TWENTY-THREE

Ali

'Right, I think I might be done!' Meg pumped a fist in the air and got up from the easel, stretching her lithe body. 'Come on, Jem. Let's celebrate!' She grabbed the baby from Ali, turned on some music and grooved around the lounge, her face beaming. Ali watched, relief and sadness swirling inside – a strange combination that reminded her of how she'd felt the morning Meg had returned home from the party, interrupting her reverie with Jem. Now that Meg was finished with this painting, she'd be back in her daughter's life full force. And while Jem needed her mother, it would feel odd for Ali to step into the apprentice role once again.

But she wasn't an apprentice – not any more, she reminded herself. She *was* a mother, thanks to Meg… thanks to Jem. She'd continue to stay here, soaking up the warmth of this house. All she needed now was her baby.

'I'm going to take the car and get some groceries… and maybe some wine and some treats!' Meg said. 'The pantry is empty. I don't know how you managed to cobble together the last few meals. You're a genius. I'll take Jem with me – give you a bit of a break!'

'Okay.' Ali yawned, every bit of her feeling weighed down. The bigger she got, the harder it became to move even one step.

She went up the stairs, lay down on her bed, and within a minute she was fast asleep.

A couple of hours later, the sound of a car door slamming jolted her awake. She lay there, eyes closed, as the front door opened, and Meg unpacked the groceries. It was so quiet that Jem must have fallen asleep. She turned onto her side, drifting somewhere between consciousness and sleep.

Finally, the need for the loo dragged her from the bed. She yawned and rubbed her eyes, slowly getting to her feet and padding down the corridor. Next door, Jem's room was empty – she must be downstairs. Ali went into the toilet, then down the stairs. Inside the lounge, Meg was working away on what looked like a new painting. Ali scanned the room. 'Where's Jem?'

Meg started, as if she'd suddenly realised where she was. 'Oh, I guess she's sleeping.'

'No.' Ali shook her head, a funny feeling coming over her. 'No, she's not in her room.'

'What?' Meg leapt to her feet. 'Not in her room? Are you sure?' She dropped the paints in her hand and tore up the stairs, panic registering in her every move. She reached the top and turned to look down at Ali. 'Did you keep the door locked when you were here? Did you see or hear anything?'

Ali shook her head, alarm building inside. What was Meg talking about? Did she think someone could have taken Jem? In this sleepy place where barely anything moved, it seemed extremely unlikely.

Meg rushed down the stairs and threw open the front door, running outside in her bare feet. Ali watched, incredulous, wondering what on earth she was doing. She was about to follow and get her to come back in when she heard a faint noise. She paused, straining to make out what it was and where it might be coming from. Her eyes fell on the metallic hulk of the car… was it coming from there? Did she hear *crying*?

Heart pounding, Ali ran to the car and glanced inside. There in the car seat in the back was Jem, mouth open in a wail. God, it must be roasting in there! All those horror stories of children dying in hot cars flooded into her mind, and she frantically tried to tug open the door – any door – but they were firmly locked. Panic building, she streaked up the steps and into the house, scanning the kitchen table for the keys. But the tabletop was empty. Meg was God knows where, and Ali knew she couldn't wait any longer.

She rushed outside and over to the cottage to grab Gran's old rusted shovel, then ran back to the car. Heaving the shovel back, she cracked the pointed corner against the front window furthest away from Jem. The window splintered, and Ali struck it again. Shards of glass flew through the air, and she reached inside and unlocked the door, then hauled Jem from the car. The baby was hot and heavy in her arms, but thankfully her eyes were open, and she seemed alert. Ali felt every muscle go weak as relief poured through her, followed quickly by disbelief. How could someone forget their baby? How the *hell* did that happen?

'Oh my God!' Meg reappeared, snatching her daughter from Ali's arms and holding her close. 'Oh my God. I forgot her. I forgot her in the car.' She held Jem out, scanning her face, then glanced over at Ali. 'She's okay, right? When you got her out, she seemed okay? I mean, she looks fine now, but…' Meg was frantic, the words coming from her like bullets.

Ali drew in a breath, trying to calm her emotions. 'I think we should take her inside, somewhere cool, and get some liquid into her to hydrate her. Then we should take her to hospital and get her checked over, just to be safe.' Anger flared as she stared down at Jem nestling in her mother's arms. Jem could be dead right now if Ali hadn't asked where she was. She put a hand on her stomach, feeling the hard swell as she gulped in more air. Everything was okay. Jem was all right, and so was her baby. For a second, as she'd stared inside the hot car, she'd felt like Jem was her own child – the child she'd give anything to keep safe.

But Jem already had a mother… a mother who really needed to get some rest; to take care of herself and her daughter properly. After this near-tragedy, Meg *must* realise that she couldn't continue painting this way – that she couldn't let it suck her in. Maybe that would mean stopping painting for now; Ali didn't know. But nothing was worth risking the person you loved most in this world.

'Please don't tell anyone about this,' Meg pleaded quietly as they went inside. 'I mean, at the hospital. We can tell them she got overheated, right? We don't need to let them know I forgot. *Please.*' Her eyes looked tortured, and Ali felt her earlier anger drain away. Meg was such a good mother – so loving, so patient, so competent – and she'd taught Ali so much. Maybe she'd been MIA these past few days, but Ali had seen how much she'd missed creating art. To abandon yourself to something you love after years away from it was understandable… especially since Ali had been there to take care of Jem. Meg might have taken it to an extreme, but her absorption didn't negate her absolute love for her daughter.

This was a terrible, once-in-a-million mistake that could have been heartbreaking, but thankfully wasn't. Ali didn't doubt for a moment that Meg would never knowingly put Jem in danger. She'd seen how protective her friend was, always making sure the door was locked. And people did forget their children – caring people, solid people. Hadn't a former prime minister once left one of his kids in the pub? It happened, and of course she wouldn't want to put Meg in a position where she might have to face uncomfortable questions. After this, Ali was sure Meg would refocus on her baby.

'Don't worry. I won't.' Ali touched Meg's arm, and Meg's face sagged with relief.

'Come on, let's head to the hospital,' Ali said, after Jem had cooled down and had some water. Ali went back out and grabbed the car seat from Meg's car, strapping it into her own before sliding behind the wheel. Meg got into the back seat beside Jem, stroking the baby's head and keeping her eyes trained on her at all times. Ali navigated the country roads to Hastings, then pulled into the hospital car park.

Ali opened the hospital door and ushered Meg and the baby inside. She glanced down the corridors, emotions spilling into her. This was where she'd come when her own baby made an appearance. She closed her eyes for a second, picturing herself waddling down the corridor, her stomach contracting. For an instant, Jon's face flashed into her mind before being replaced by Meg's. That was who she wanted by her side.

The A&E was almost empty, and Jem was seen straight away. Her temperature was fine, her colour had returned to normal, and she'd done a wee, which showed she wasn't dehydrated – miraculous after being in a hot car. Ali had never seen anyone look more relieved than Meg when the doctor announced they could take Jem home, chastising Meg only once for keeping her daughter out in the sun too long. Meg had simply nodded and ducked her head.

They were making their way towards the exit when a comfortably padded woman in an NHS uniform called out. 'Meg! Is that you? And oh my goodness, your baby! Look how big she is now. I say it every time: time really does fly!'

Meg turned slowly towards the woman. 'Hi, yes, it is! This is Jem. Say hi, Jem. This is someone who knew you only in my tummy!' She stroked Jem's arm and smiled.

'Everything okay?' the midwife was asking. 'You know how I hate to see my charges back in this place! How're you getting on? Hope you're all right?'

Meg nodded. 'Oh yes, everything is fine. Wonderful, even.'

'And that handsome husband of yours? I don't mind saying, we all swooned every time he came in, even if he is a bit young for me.' She winked at Ali. 'I know that's not professional, and I'm a married woman and all, but you'd have to be blind not to notice it, am I right? Came to every appointment, asked lots of questions and, if I remember correctly, he even took notes! If only every dad was that interested.'

'He's great,' Meg said in a flat tone. Ali put a hand on her arm. She must be completely worn out.

'Well, you give him my best and take care of yourself. And this one.' The midwife tapped Jem's nose. 'Lovely to see you doing so well, my dear. You and this baby are a real success story here. In fact, I'd like to have you in to talk to some of my high-risk patients, if you're up to it?'

Meg nodded, but she looked anything but keen. 'Of course,' she mumbled.

'Great. We've got all your details on file. I'll be in touch!' She scurried down the corridor, and Ali's brow furrowed.

'What does she mean, "a real success story"?' Ali asked. Meg had made everything around her pregnancy seem so easy. Was there more to it than she'd said? Maybe she hadn't wanted to scare Ali by telling her horror stories or something.

Meg didn't answer for a second, and Ali wondered if she'd heard. 'Oh, I think I was one of the first to use their new birthing room or something. They probably want to make everyone feel comfortable using it, even those at higher risk.'

Ali nodded, and they walked in silence to the car, then Meg turned to face her. 'Thank you for being there. I can't say thanks enough. If you hadn't…' She swallowed, then swiped a hand over her face. 'I don't even want to think about that.'

Ali didn't know how to respond. Meg was right: if Ali hadn't been there, the outcome could have been very different. Before Ali could stop it, an image crashed into her mind: Meg's face contorting as she lifted a still, silent Jem from the car, sinking to the ground as she clutched her dead baby… *no*. Ali pushed it away, cradling her belly. She wouldn't think that. It hadn't happened. Everything was fine.

Meg would relax now; recover from the past few days. She'd be the mother Ali had come to admire so much, and the perfect world would be restored again.

CHAPTER TWENTY-FOUR

Ali

Ali lay in bed as thunder boomed. Rain splattered against the window, and a flash of lightning was quickly followed by another clap of thunder. Her mind snapped back to the night in the cottage when she'd awoken during a different storm, alone and terrified. She'd spotted Meg and the glow of her house, then remembered she wasn't alone, after all… that she was safe, sheltered by the love and warmth of the family next door. Ali flipped over onto her side on the soft mattress, thinking it was funny: now she was inside that house, but the perfection she'd craved – the perfection she'd witnessed – had gone missing.

Because despite Ali's certainty that all would be okay, Meg *hadn't* stopped painting. Ali couldn't believe that the horrific events of a few days ago hadn't made more of an impact, but Meg hadn't slowed down. She hadn't paid any more attention to Jem, either, getting up the morning after the accident and sitting down at the easel as if nothing had happened. Ali had scooped Jem from her cot and brought her downstairs, her heart sinking.

'Maybe you should take a break today?' she'd said to Meg, trying to keep the surprise and dismay off her face. But Meg had just shaken her head, telling Ali her last painting was 'shit' and that if she wanted a shot at gallery representation, she'd have to do much better than that. She'd waited long enough, she'd said, and she wasn't going to throw away this chance. Then she'd carried on working with barely even a glance at her daughter, burying herself in her art once more… as if she was eager to blot out the reality of what had happened the day before.

Ali could certainly understand that, but this kind of wild devotion to her work at the exclusion of everything else wasn't right, especially after almost losing her child. Meg *had* said she loved the total absorption of it all, but that was before she'd had her daughter. Ali had seen first-hand how much she loved being a mother; how much she loved her life. But now, nothing else seemed to matter but the painting in front of her. It was as if it had some kind of power over her that she wasn't strong enough to fight, whether she wanted to or not. Ali had asked yet again when Michael might come home, but Meg's answer hadn't changed: not yet.

As long as Ali was there to keep an eye on Jem, everything was ticking along fine. She loved the little girl, but she missed her friend's steadying, positive influence; missed feeling that they were working together… maintaining the vision of motherhood Ali had always wanted. She was starting to feel like she was on that road alone, and everything she'd thought she'd put behind her was threatening to seep back in. Each time she changed a nappy or put Jem to bed, Jon's face flashed into her mind, his words that he'd always be right there echoing through her head. She'd push them out and focus on the baby once more, but, sometimes, the pain and anger hovered around her, like smoke in the air after extinguishing candles.

Ali had not long drifted off to sleep when a giant crash came from downstairs – a crash that definitely wasn't thunder. What the hell was that? She slid out of the covers and pulled on the robe Meg had lent her, tying the knot over her swollen belly.

She padded down the stairs and around the corner into the lounge. The sight that greeted her was like something from a nightmare. Her mouth dropped open, and she stepped back, stunned at the scene. Meg was standing with a carving knife in her hand. Her face and arms were splattered with red, like some kind of tribal ritual gone wrong. The easel was upended, lying on its side, and the lounge looked as if a tornado had ripped through it. And on the floor, with huge, gaping slashes through it, was the painting Meg had been working so hard on.

Meg turned towards her and Ali sucked in a breath. Her gaze was so intense it burnt through Ali, and the hand in which she held the knife was shaking. Ali couldn't tell if the red on her hands was blood or paint, and fear shot through her. There was a huge red stain on the floor, and Ali's heart started pounding. Had Meg hurt herself?

'Are you all right?' Ali asked in a low voice, staying in one place in case coming closer startled her. 'I heard a crash and wanted to make sure everything's okay.' It obviously wasn't, but Ali wasn't about to suggest that.

Meg surprised her by laughing and shaking her head. 'Oh, God, sorry, sorry. I'd forgotten it was so late! I know this looks bad, but' – she held up her hands – 'this is all red paint, and the knife is for ripping the canvas. I tipped over the bottle of wine, then knocked over the easel trying to pick it up quickly. Luckily, I'd already drunk most of the wine, anyway!' She set the easel upright again, then stepped forward and plunged the knife into the artwork, slicing it through the fabric. 'I thought I'd experiment with something different. And oh, it's so satisfying.'

She thrust the knife in again, and Ali shivered. It might be satisfying, but watching Meg gleefully wield the knife with red splattered over her hands, well… that was a little too realistic for Ali. 'I can't wait to show Caro. She's going to love it.'

Ali peered at the painting. The slashes of red practically pulsated off the canvas, fading into swirls of mauves, browns and blacks.

It felt like the colours were looming towards her, reaching out to envelope her.

'It's great,' she managed to say. It really wasn't her style, but she was hardly an art aficionado. The one time she and Jon had ventured to the Tate Modern, they'd spent the whole time wandering from café to café, drinking wine and barely even looking at the paintings. By the time they'd left, the whole thing had been a blur.

'In fact… I wonder if it's too late to show her now.' Meg looked at her watch. 'Just past midnight – she should still be up. If you don't mind staying with Jem, I'll head over there.'

Ali raised her eyebrows. '*Now?* It's late, and you haven't slept properly for days. There's a big storm outside, too, and the car window still isn't fixed. The roads will be dangerous.'

Meg waved a hand in the air. 'It'll be fine. I'm fine. I've driven in much worse conditions.'

'But…' Ali shook her head. 'But you've had all that wine.' She pointed to the empty bottle on the floor, hoping that would help Meg come to her senses. Ali could understand her friend's excitement, but she had to be reasonable. Driving was out of the question.

'It's fine,' Meg said through gritted teeth. 'Besides, I can hold my booze. Don't worry, I'm not going to have an accident this time.'

'An accident?' Ali gulped in air. Had Meg crashed the car before? Was that why she hadn't driven for ages?

But Meg didn't even seem to hear her. 'I'll go get changed, and then—'

She stopped as Ali swiped the car keys from the coffee table.

'What the hell do you think you're doing?' Meg asked.

Ali shook her head, the keys heavy in hand. 'I'm sorry, but I can't let you drive.'

Meg stared at her. 'You can't let me?' she asked, her voice quiet.

'Not in the dark, so late, after all you've had to drink.' Ali was standing her ground, although unease niggled at Meg's sudden calm – and the tiny fact that she was still holding the knife. Ali told herself not to be ridiculous. Meg might have lost herself in her painting the past few days, but this was the woman who'd taught her everything about being a mother; the calmest and most patient person Ali had known.

Ali swallowed, looking down at Michael's name engraved in the heavy metal. 'When is Michael coming back, anyway? Have you talked to him lately?' She hated to ask yet again, but…

Meg stood stock-still with the knife, fixing Ali with her stare. 'Why do you keep asking me that?' she said in a soft tone that made the hair rise on Ali's arms.

Ali shrugged, trying to stay nonchalant. 'No reason. Just wondering. You must miss him?' she said, trying to appeal to Meg's gentle side. 'He's been gone for ages.' She paused, hoping this was working. 'So when *is* he coming back?'

Meg tilted her head, her eyes still lasering into Ali as if she was trying to read her thoughts. 'It doesn't matter.' She drew in a breath. 'Now give me the keys.'

'I can't do that,' Ali said slowly. She wasn't going to let Meg drive in this state. Meg had protected her; kept her safe. Now she'd do the same for her friend.

'Give me the keys.' Meg's voice emerged low and gravelly, and she stepped towards Ali. Ali shook her head and backed up in an effort to keep them from Meg's grasp. But Meg lunged forward and knocked into Ali, ripping the keys from Ali's hand. The force propelled Ali back against the wall, and she let out a little cry, wincing. She froze for a moment, checking in with her body and making sure everything was okay. Relief flooded through her when the baby kicked.

Meg took a step back. 'Sorry,' she said. 'I'm sorry. I didn't mean to do that. Are you all right?'

Ali stared, thoughts flying through her mind. She was all right, and so was her baby. But the fact that Meg, the gentle woman she'd thought she'd known, could react with such physical force was shocking.

'Why don't you go get some sleep?' Ali said softly, not wanting to inflame Meg more. 'Caro will be able to see your work better at the gallery than half asleep at night, right?' Ali swallowed, relief shooting through her as Meg collapsed into a chair. Her actions seemed to have stunned her as much as they had Ali.

'I think you should go,' Meg said, staring down at the floor.

Ali nodded slowly. Meg seemed calmer now, as if the storm inside had blown over. They could talk in the morning. 'I'll go up to bed, but you have to promise me that you'll get some rest and that you won't drive anywhere tonight. Okay?'

Meg looked up, meeting her gaze. 'No. I want you to *go*. Back to your cottage. Wherever. Just… leave me alone. Leave *us* alone.'

Ali's mouth dropped open. 'Back to the cottage? But what about—'

'I don't need someone telling me what to do; watching whether I'm eating or sleeping, waiting for me to make another mistake,' Meg said. 'Believe me, I really don't. I'm fine. We're fine. *Go.*'

Ali stood still as Meg's words swirled around her. She didn't mean them. Of course she didn't. They were friends – real friends, like she'd told Sapna… friends who understood each other; who cared about the same things. She couldn't mean them.

But this wasn't the woman she'd come to know, Ali realised. This wasn't the woman who'd invited her into her home and taught her everything. Somehow, Meg *had* lost herself, drowning in her painting. Ali had no idea how to pull her out again.

'Okay. I'll leave first thing tomorrow.'

But Meg was shaking her head. 'No. I want you to go now.'

'Now?' The thunder had stopped, but Ali could still hear rain falling outside. What state would the cottage be in? Hopefully, the quick repair job had held. She shuddered as if she could feel the cold and damp already.

Meg nodded, and Ali sighed. 'All right. I'll pack my things.'

Ali went up the stairs without waiting for Meg's response, trying to get her head around what had happened. The rage in Meg's eyes, the way she'd pushed Ali, telling her to leave…

Ali might be going, but she wasn't going to abandon the woman who'd taught her so much. She wasn't going to abandon her friend, not when she needed her most; not when Jem needed her most. She shuddered, hoping the little girl would be okay without her around. Her mind flashed back to Meg saying that she'd trust Ali with Jem. She *had* trusted her, and Ali wouldn't fail her now.

She'd call Michael, she decided, throwing a few things into her bag. First thing tomorrow, she'd tell him what was happening and ask him to come home. Ali was sure he'd drop everything to be with his wife and daughter if they needed him, and that was never clearer than right now. He'd come and help get Meg back to her usual self.

He'd put his family back together again.

CHAPTER TWENTY-FIVE

Violet

July 2018

I'm staying busy working in the front garden, all the while keeping an eye out next door for Meg's husband. After yesterday's accident, I knocked on the studio door twice, but each time it's remained closed even though the bangs and whining saw make it clear there's someone in there. But I'm not giving up: I'm determined to get Meg the help she needs… then put this family out of my mind, once and for all.

I snip off a branch from the rose bushes by the front door, unable to believe how they've grown. I planted them as soon as the cottage was finished, eager to decorate my seaside home. Hardy and resilient, they've flourished here. I bend to sniff one now, the scent transporting me back to the first time we came to this place as a family. The builders had rung to tell me they were leaving the site for good. Too excited to wait, I'd bunged Andy and Ben in the car, driven to my husband's office and convinced him to leave, and then we all travelled here together. Bumping down the lane, I cranked open the window and breathed in the fresh salty air – there's nothing like it.

Glancing in the rear-view mirror, I saw that Andy had fallen asleep, but Ben… he was gazing at the sea with amazement, fascinated by the sheer size of it. The sun was glinting off the water's surface, and the light was almost blinding. Ben said he loved the 'seashine' – that's how this cottage got its name. He'd never seen something like that before, and the whole first day all he could do was stare. After the maze of narrow London streets clogged with traffic, I knew exactly how he felt. The vastness was a kind of freedom, stretching out to infinity with endless possibilities.

We pulled up beside the cottage, and I went to the back, gently shaking Andy awake as Ben tumbled out the other side of the car. The first thing he did was run straight for the sea. Luckily, my husband caught him before he reached the edge of the cliff. The memory makes me draw in a sharp breath, and I hunch over, letting the pain swirl inside.

I stand up straight and flex my neck, trying to ease the aching in my shoulders. Maybe I'll take a little break and head over to the studio next door again – hopefully, he'll hear me this time. An image of Meg, eyes empty, staring at the horizon as her baby wails, enters my mind and I shudder. I can't wait any longer.

Just as I'm thinking this, the husband emerges from the house with a bag of rubbish in his hands. Perfect, I think to myself.

'Hello!' I raise my arm, hoping he sees me before he goes back inside.

He turns towards me, his eyes red and ringed by dark circles. My heart squeezes with sympathy. New babies take it out of you, and I'm about to make his heavy load much heavier.

'Hello,' he says. 'Everything okay?' He puts the rubbish in the bin, then goes back up the stairs. I can see how eager he is to return to his family.

I pause, unsure how to start now that I'm here. He knows how low Meg has been, but despite everything, he obviously doesn't realise how serious it is. He can't, or she would be on medication right now. 'I'm worried about your wife,' I begin slowly. 'She had a bit of an accident yesterday, down the road there, in the car. Your baby was in the back seat.'

'What?' The husband shakes his head. 'Meg never said a thing about an accident, and I'm sure I would have known. You must be mistaken.'

'I'm not mistaken, unfortunately.' I pause to let it sink in because I know this news isn't easy. 'Meg isn't sure what happened, but the outcome could have been a lot worse. She said a few things that made me think she's suffering from postnatal depression. She told me you knew she was feeling down, but I think this is more than the usual baby blues. She needs to see a doctor.'

'She doesn't need a doctor,' he says easily, as if he's the expert. Something about his casual flippancy makes irritation curl inside me, and I shake my head. I can understand not wanting to admit there's a serious problem, but this is his wife and child. He was there that night in the water, and now that he knows about the accident... 'Look, I used to be a GP. I've seen plenty of cases of postnatal depression and sometimes, they can resolve with a bit of counselling. But sometimes they don't, and medication is needed. I know Meg is breastfeeding and neither one of you is keen on formula, but for the safety of your family...' I let my voice fade away, stunned by the anger that flashes across his handsome features.

'The safety of my family? Who are you to give me advice on that? Some old biddy living alone with no one nearby – no family to speak of. At least none that can ever be bothered visiting. What do you even know about being a mother?' He snorts, and I step back, stung by his venom. 'Go back to your cottage. Leave us alone. Leave my wife alone. We don't need you – or anyone else.' He disappears inside the house, and the door slams in my face.

I stand there for a moment, frozen, his words ringing in my ears. *What do you know about being a mother?* He's obviously upset

– hearing about the accident must have been a shock; maybe he'd hoped things were getting better. But his sarcastic words are true, and they cut through to the very heart of me. What *do* I know?

I should leave them alone, I think, turning slowly and walking down the stairs. Wasn't that what I wanted, anyway? Wasn't I only helping so I could retreat again?

But… a picture of Meg sitting in the crashed car as the baby screams in the back filters into my head. I can't walk away knowing something terrible could happen, can I?

I cross the grass towards my cottage, trying to push away the image of Meg and her baby in the waves, desperately struggling to stay above water. The baby cries, and they reach out to me as I stand in the shallows, helpless, unable to move. Panic and fear build inside me, and then Meg's face changes into someone else's… someone else I couldn't save.

My son.

I squeeze my eyes shut and breathe in. I'm not trying to block out the memory – I've relived that nightmarish day countless times – but I need to focus. I want to see his face clearly. I need to remember everything, to twist the barb in my soul.

I knew from the minute I awoke that it was going to be one of those days: a rare early-summer morning that was just perfect, with blue skies stretching overhead and no clouds in sight, a soft breeze lifting the humidity, and the ocean rippling with gentle waves ideal for jumping over but not big enough to worry about.

As I sat up, contentment unfurled inside of me. I was here with my boys, and the whole glorious day glittered in front of us. Working only part-time was more than worth it to have days like this. Only Robert's presence would have made it any better, but he'd be coming down tomorrow to stay for the weekend. And, if I was being honest, part of me liked having the boys to myself for a bit. When Robert was around, they hung off him like monkeys, and I was often relegated to the food/drink/laundry departments. Not that I minded… too much. Watching them with their father made me go all warm inside.

The kids woke up, bleary-eyed and yawning, then instantly alert when they saw the sunshine. They rushed through their breakfast and down the cliff path to the beach – at eleven and seven, they were old enough now to go on their own for a bit while I tidied up here, and I knew I could rely on Andy to watch over Ben. He might still be young, but he was mature and acted as my second pair of eyes.

I was finishing up when I heard a shout from below – not a playful yell, like when the kids were racing along the sand, or one of unjustness when one of them was wronged, but one full of terror. I looked out the window to see Andy pointing at Ben, struggling in the sea. I was in the water in an instant, pushing out against the waves slapping my shins, then finally throwing myself into the brine and trying to reach him. Salty water stung my eyes, but I wouldn't close them. I couldn't lose sight of him or it would all be over. It would all be over, and it would be my fault. I couldn't live with that.

Ben threw out a hand to me, trying to grasp on, but the space between us was too big and the current was carrying him even further away. I tried to narrow the distance – tried to battle the waves – but like something from a nightmare, I couldn't even move. I could only watch as he bobbed under the water once… twice… and then…

He disappeared.

I tried to scream his name, but it stuck in my throat. My mouth opened, forming the word, and then water slammed into me and I couldn't breathe. I stayed in the sea, trying to swim, for as long as I could. I didn't want to get out because I knew that once I did, it would mean…

Finally, a man – I never did find out who – dragged me back to the shore. He wrapped a towel around me, but I couldn't stop shaking. I didn't stop for a day, actually. I felt Andy by my side, crying and trembling, but I couldn't turn to look at him. All I could do was stare at the water.

Boats came, scouring the sea. Robert arrived from London, pale-faced and drawn, asking over and over what happened, and I still couldn't move. I couldn't do anything until my son was found.

There was a storm that night, thunder and lightning after the heat of the day. The boats had to come off the ocean, and the coastguard came to talk to me. There was a riptide, probably, and the current had been too strong for my boy to fight. They hadn't found him yet, but they would keep looking.

They never did find him, and I never left. And now, all these years later, I'm still here. Still staring out to sea, where my Ben is. Where he died, and where I died too. After what happened, I couldn't carry on as if nothing had happened. I'd failed my son – I'd failed as a mother – and I couldn't let my family depend on me again… for their own good. I didn't deserve a family, anyway. Until Meg burst through the door that day, I was a hollowed-out shell, grief the only thing propelling me through the motions. No one needed me and even if they did, there was nothing inside me to respond.

But now someone does need me. A family: a mother and her baby. I don't know how, but they've cracked my heart open and made me care. *What do I know about being a mother?* I may not be one now, but they've reminded me how precious motherhood is and how it needs protecting. To my surprise, there *is* still something inside me. I'm not going to let them sink. I'm not going to let them drown.

I'll pull them up to the surface and keep them safe.

CHAPTER TWENTY-SIX

Ali

Ali hurried through the rain towards the cottage. Beyond the cliff, the sea was a black abyss. Whitecaps were the only thing that pierced the darkness, appearing then disappearing like tiny puffs of smoke. She yanked open the door, the scent of damp curling around her. Standing in the nursery, her gut twisted at the water trails through the grey paint, the rotting floorboards and the saggy roof overhead. The whole thing seemed better suited to a horror film than an idyllic repose for a baby. For a second, she felt the rot start to swallow her too.

No. Ali forced away the feeling, walking into the bedroom, then climbing under the duvet. She was being ridiculous. Come morning, she'd call Michael to return home. He'd be there to keep both Jem and Meg safe; to wrestle Meg from the strange place she'd disappeared into. Soon, things would go back to how they'd been before that night Meg had met Caro: long walks in the sun, picnics on the beach, and hours and hours of chatter about all things baby, with Meg's cheery enthusiasm chasing away any lingering darkness.

After a restless night, Ali awoke early, wondering how she could get in touch with Michael. She threw off the duvet and went into the kitchen for a cup of tea, thinking that with his own business, he must have a website with a number listed. By the sounds of things, drumming up commissions was important, and surely, he'd want his clients to be able to reach him at all hours. Ali turned on her mobile, steadfastly ignoring all the pings as message alerts flashed up on her screen. Jon, Sapna, work… she didn't care. All that mattered was finding Michael.

She was opening up the browser on her phone when she heard the crunch of tyres on gravel. Could it, by some miracle, be him? It was too early for Meg to be going anywhere, but then… Ali bit her lip, remembering how adamant her friend had been to drive last night. Her heart dropped as she spotted Meg speeding down the lane with Jem in the back seat.

Was she going to see Caro now? Please may she drive carefully, Ali prayed, remembering what Meg had said about an accident. Please may she remember Jem was with her. The very thought of the baby getting hurt in a car crash, or a repeat of what had happened a few days ago, was unbearable.

She had to reach Michael.

She typed his name into Google, holding her breath as she hit 'search'. Bingo! 'Michael Walker, Solid Oak' came up. She clicked on the link and punched the air as a number filtered onto the screen. One phone call and then she'd be able to relax a bit.

The number started ringing, and Ali tapped her foot. *Pick up, pick up, pick up.* It kept ringing, though, and oddly she could hear another phone ringing in time to the one on the line. She cocked her head. Was she imagining things? She held the mobile away from her ear. No, she could definitely hear it ringing… coming from… where? She stepped outside of the cottage, the ringing getting louder, her gaze following the sound.

It was coming from the open window of Meg's bedroom.

Michael's mobile was somewhere in there.

Ali hung up, trying to take this in. Michael had gone to his parents' house to try to drum up business, right? That was what

Meg had said. So why would he leave behind his mobile – the mobile with the number that was listed on his work website? That was like leaving behind a limb, particularly when you were a small-business owner.

Maybe he had another phone, or… Well, whatever the reason, it didn't really matter. Ali only cared about contacting him and getting him back here. Meg had said he was at his parents', somewhere in Spain. Somehow, Ali had to find their number and reach him there.

She stared up at the open window. Michael must have his parents' number in his phone contacts. And if not, surely the number would be written down somewhere? An emergency contact list in the kitchen drawer; a diary in the bedside table, *something*. Jon always insisted they keep a list of numbers on the fridge door, but then he was a bit of a technophobe, never completely comfortable relying on his phone. Did Meg and Michael have the same list? She hadn't seen one, but she'd never really looked.

Ali peeked at the driveway in front of the house. Meg was still out with Jem. If she was going to Hastings, it'd take at least an hour to get there and back again. And if Ali wanted to find Michael's parents' number, now was as good a time as any.

But how would she get inside the house? Meg was fanatical about locking the door, and Ali didn't have a spare key. Meg had never given her one, despite having that spare set – there was really no need since they were always together.

Ali looked back up at the open window, her mind spinning. It wasn't too high, but it wasn't low either. Gran had a ladder by the side of the cottage, and it would definitely reach, but… Ali bit her lip. She wasn't afraid of heights, and in the past, she'd have been up there in a heartbeat. These were hardly normal times, though. She had a baby to keep safe, a baby to protect. What if she slipped and fell?

She drew in a breath, thinking of the world inside that house: of the mother she'd learnt from; of the child who'd taught her how to care for the baby inside of her. They needed her now too – as much as she had needed them.

As much as she needed them still.

She'd be all right. She'd take every step carefully and hold on tightly. The risk of falling was so small it wasn't even worth thinking about.

She slipped on her shoes and went back out into the misty morning, then around the side of the cottage to where Gran's ladder was, rusty and covered with spider webs. Ali dragged it across the wet grass, then propped it up against Meg's house. Making sure it was steady, she climbed onto the first rung, telling herself not to look down. Taking it step by step, she made her way to the top, then eased herself through the open window and into the bedroom.

She stood still, scanning the room, her eyes meeting another black camera lens. *Another camera?* Meg's words about how Michael didn't want to miss a minute with Jem floated into her mind, and she tilted her head. Ali could understand that – a camera in the nursery, yes, and maybe the kitchen – but the master bedroom? In all the time Ali had been here, she'd rarely seen Jem inside this room.

Well, she wasn't here to think about that. She had to find the phone. Ali crossed to what was clearly Michael's side of the bed – Meg's side was drawn back, the bedside table littered with earrings and lip balms – and pulled open the drawer of the bedside table. It was empty except for a box of tissues. She crossed the room and yanked out Meg's drawer, sifting through the contents. There was nothing apart from an old paperback and a packet of tissues. On a whim, she went to the heavy chest of drawers, shuffled a few papers on top and spotted what looked like a charger cord. She followed it, shoving aside more books and papers... bingo! A phone, with – she squinted at the notifications on the home screen – what looked like a lot of missed calls.

She struggled to her feet, wondering once again why Michael's phone was here. With all the missed phone calls, it was obvious this phone *wasn't* a spare. Ali shook her head. She needed to find his parents' number, and that was all. Holding her breath, she tapped the screen. The mobile was an old model, thankfully, and it didn't demand a password. Fingers shaking, she navigated to Contacts, relief flooding through her when she spotted 'Mum and Dad'.

Thank *God*. With no time to waste, she hit the contact. One quick phone call and Michael would be back. Maybe he'd be here as soon as today, if he could catch a flight.

She tapped her foot as the phone rang, pleading under her breath for one of Michael's parents to answer.

'Michael!' The woman's voice on the other end was full of surprise, and Ali drew back. Why did they sound so shocked to hear from him? 'How are you?'

'Um, it's not Michael,' Ali said slowly, wondering why they were asking how he was when they saw him every day. 'But could I speak to him, please?'

'Michael's not here.' His mother's voice was curt, and Ali's eyebrows flew up. Well, that would explain why they'd asked how he was doing. Maybe he'd gone to another town to drum up business. Or maybe… hope darted through her. Maybe he was on his way back home already! 'Who is this? Why are you calling from my son's phone? Is everything all right?'

'Oh yes, everything is fine,' Ali responded. Meg would never want Ali to reveal what was happening to her mother-in-law, she was sure. 'I'm a friend of the family. Do you know when he might be back?'

'Might be back?' The woman's voice rose. 'We haven't talked to him for ages, let alone seen him. He won't even let us visit our granddaughter, did you know that? We wanted to fly over when she was born, but he told us not to come. Anyway.' She cleared her throat, and Ali silently applauded Michael for having the backbone to protect his child from anything that could potentially hurt her.

By the sounds of things, they'd done a number on him. She could certainly relate. 'Why would you think he's with us?'

'I guess I got the wrong end of the stick.' Ali forced a laugh. 'Sorry to disturb you. Thanks anyway.' She clicked off and put the phone back on the chest, her mind churning. Meg had said Michael was at his parents', right? She'd talked to him there every day, hadn't she? Ali bit her lip. Maybe she *had* got the wrong end of the stick, or perhaps Michael had decided not to see them, after all.

What was she going to do now?

She left the room, her heart lurching as she peeped into Jem's room. It hadn't even been a day and already she missed that little girl so much. She went down the stairs and into the lounge, noticing that Meg had started working on another painting, this one in the same vivid reds and blacks. The shapes were undefined, but something about their frenetic energy made Ali shiver and move away.

Right, time to get back to her cottage. Ali went out the door and grabbed the ladder from the side of the house. She put it back behind the cottage, hurried inside, then flopped onto the bed, glancing up at Jem's window. She wasn't going to give up. Not for Jem, not for Meg… and not for her or her baby.

Somehow, she'd find Michael.

CHAPTER TWENTY-SEVEN

Ali

Ali was lying in bed trying to think of what to do next when someone banged on the door so hard that the whole cottage shook.

'Ali! Ali? Open up!' Meg sounded anything but happy, and Ali hesitantly eased the door open. Was she still angry about last night? Ali had hoped some sleep would calm her down a bit.

'Hi,' she said, taking in Meg's paint-splattered T-shirt. She must have been in such a rush to get to Caro's that she hadn't bothered changing. 'Did Caro like the painting?'

Meg didn't even respond. 'I had a call from Michael's parents. They said someone called from his phone – a woman – asking to speak to him.' Her voice was steady, but her body seemed to be vibrating. 'That was you, wasn't it? It had to have been. You were going to tell him about me... and about what happened with Jem. Weren't you?' She stepped closer to Ali, and Ali moved back, remembering how Meg had pushed her.

'How did you even find his phone? Did you take it last night before you left?' Meg shook her head. 'I can't believe you went into my bedroom, went through my things. *Our* things. Why would you do that? Why the *hell* would you do that? I never should have invited you in. God, you and your grandmother...' Something flashed across her face so quickly that Ali couldn't identify it.

'Me and my grandmother?' Ali asked slowly. What was Meg talking about? Hadn't Meg said they'd rarely even spoken?

'Forget it.' Meg waved a hand. 'Look, give me Michael's phone back, okay? You shouldn't have taken it in the first place.'

'I don't have it. I didn't take it, I swear. It's still at your house,' Ali said calmly, trying to smooth things over. She didn't think mentioning how she'd used a ladder to crawl through the window was wise, and she prayed Meg was too agitated to think more about how she might have got it.

Meg drew in a breath, as if she was trying to contain herself. 'I know you're worried, and I know you want to help, but there's really no need, okay? I'm fine.' She paused. 'But if it makes you feel better, I've called Michael myself and asked him to come home. He should be back soon. Okay? You don't need to worry any more.' She smiled, but it didn't reach her eyes. 'All right?'

Ali nodded mutely, watching as Meg disappeared into her house once again. She should be relieved: Michael would return, Meg would be okay, and Jem would be safe and secure. But questions niggled, creating a tight coil of tension inside. What had Meg meant about Gran? Why was Michael's phone on the chest, with all of those missed calls? Where *had* he been for so long?

Ali closed her eyes and rested her hands on her stomach. There had to be logical answers, she was sure. Soon, Michael would be home, and she'd find out. The most important thing was that Michael *was* coming back.

He'd be there for his family, just like he'd always said.

CHAPTER TWENTY-EIGHT

Ali

Ali spent the next few days trying to repair some of the damage at the back of the cottage, eagerly awaiting Michael's return. So far, though, there'd been no sign of him. She bit her lip, staring out at the gravelled drive for the millionth time. Meg *had* called, right? If she was so desperate to keep painting, she probably wasn't in a hurry to ring someone who'd tell her to stop… or, at least, to slow down. But without Ali taking care of Jem, would it even be possible to continue painting with such absorption? The baby still needed to be fed and put to bed, and her crying definitely wouldn't be easy to ignore.

She must have called him, Ali thought, turning from the window. Hopefully, she was getting the rest she needed, and she'd soon be back to her true self. Although Ali had tried to keep herself busy, the past few days had seemed so empty without the comfort and warmth she got from caring for Jem. Ali had loved being part of the family; loved the ebb and flow of the day with a young child.

And it wasn't only Jem she missed. She missed Meg… the person she'd been before painting took hold of her. She missed their talks every night, and her energy and enthusiasm. She missed their *friendship* – missed the woman who always made Ali remember that holding her baby in her arms was a moment well worth waiting for. Every day that went by without Meg, the shield Ali had erected against the past – against Jon and everything that had happened – wobbled more and more.

Ali wandered into the bedroom and sat down on the bed her grandmother had used for so many years, wishing once more that she was here. She may not have said much, but when she did, she had a way of making even the most complicated situation seem simple. Ali had always admired how she viewed the world in absolute terms: things were either good or bad, with punishment meted out accordingly. She'd seemed so strong and unyielding, exactly how Ali wanted to be when she grew up.

Ali closed her eyes, remembering how Gran had punished her once when she'd eaten the last chocolate biscuit after Gran told her no. Ali had tried to explain that she'd been starving, but Gran was having none of it. She'd looked Ali straight in the eye and said Ali knew what she'd done was wrong, and that it was better to admit her mistake than try to justify it.

Ali had swallowed and said she was sorry, hoping that, like with her mother, those words would be enough. But Gran had said that now was a good time to learn that although saying sorry was important, it wouldn't erase what had happened. There were *always* consequences to any mistake, whether the person had meant it or not. Her eyes had filmed over when she'd said those words, and Ali had wondered what she was thinking of – surely not the silly biscuit! Gran had pronounced that Ali would spend the next day weeding the back garden, and that was that.

Meg's words about her grandmother scrolled through Ali's head once again, and her brow furrowed. Had Gran seen something that worried her… something that might have terrible consequences? Had she tried to help? Surely not: Ali couldn't imagine her gran getting involved enough to even notice anything amiss. Anyway,

Meg's strange behaviour had only really started with her painting. Ali had no doubt that before that, she'd been the perfect neighbour, just like she'd been the perfect mother. So, what was it, then?

Ali wandered out to the back garden, squinting as she spotted something moving on the beach. In the evening light, she could see Meg crossing the sand and diving into the water. Her mind flipped back to the dinner with Meg and Michael, when Michael said that Meg used to swim every day and how Gran would sit out back watching. Funny, in all the time Ali had spent with Meg, she hadn't seen her in the water once.

She was a beautiful swimmer: her strokes were smooth and strong, and something about her confidence and power made Ali feel at peace, like everything was under control again. Michael *must* be back if Meg was down here swimming; she'd never leave Jem alone. It was a good sign that she'd pulled herself free from painting too. Relief surged through her, and she picked her way carefully down the path, breathing in the fresh air as Meg cut through the sea back towards the shore.

Meg emerged from the water, and Ali raised a hand.

'Hi,' she said tentatively as Meg wrapped a towel around her body. The mark on her arm had faded now to a light rose, barely visible in the falling light.

Meg nodded but didn't respond, but Ali wasn't going to give up. After the past few days, perhaps it'd take a bit of time for things to settle between them.

'How's Michael doing?' Ali asked. 'He's back, right? Jem must have been so happy to see him!'

Meg nodded again.

'And… and how are things with you?' Ali didn't want to probe, but she had to know.

'You mean am I back to being just a mother now that my knight in shining armour has returned to put some sense into me?'

Ali drew back, stung by Meg's sarcastic tone. And what did she mean, 'just' a mother? She'd told Ali over and over that it was the most important thing she'd ever done.

'I'm great. I'm perfect,' Meg continued, before Ali could respond. She slipped on her shoes and walked across the sand. 'Why don't you have a dip,' she said, turning around again. 'You look a little pale, a little stressed. A bit of relaxation would do you good. And the baby too.' She stopped, her eyes shining in the dim light. 'You know, maybe it's time for you to go home. Your real home: back to London, back to where you belong. There's nothing for you here, is there?'

Ali blinked. What? Nothing for her here? What about them living together until Ali's baby came? What about being by her side?

Meg was obviously still upset by what had happened, and maybe… Ali tilted her head. Maybe she had a right to be upset? Ali had to concede that from her friend's perspective, snooping around in the bedroom, using her husband's phone and disturbing her in-laws did seem extreme – particularly if Meg hadn't recognised there was a problem in the first place. Ali sighed, wondering for a second if perhaps she had gone too far. She was already in protective mode with her own baby. Had she gone overboard to protect Jem too? How would she feel if Meg contacted Jon behind her back?

She didn't even need to answer that.

But something *had* been off with Meg, whether she realised it or not, Ali reminded herself. Ever since Meg had met Caro, she'd been like a different person, caring only about her work and neglecting both herself and her daughter. And then… Ali shuddered, remembering when Meg had wanted to drive to Caro's, knocking into Ali and trying to grab the keys. That look in her eyes had been terrifying. Was it only artistic obsession, or was there something more behind Meg's behaviour that night? Ali dismissed the thought. Meg had been drunk. She'd been tired and anxious, and she'd lost control for a minute. That was all.

'Look, I'm sorry if you think I overstepped the mark,' Ali said finally. 'I… I wanted to help, that's all. I was worried about you – how you weren't eating or sleeping. Jem missed you. I did too.' She swallowed. 'I *do*.'

But Meg didn't answer. She just continued to gaze at Ali, her eyes boring through her. Then she turned and disappeared up the path.

Ali looked back at the water, watching the waves froth and bubble as they broke on the sand. She'd been naïve to hope that as soon as Michael returned, things would go back to normal. Meg must be drained – she'd pushed herself to the brink.

Jon's words filtered into her mind once again… that sometimes, people needed time. She let out a breath, thinking how that certainly wasn't true for her husband or her ex-best friend. But Meg wasn't like Jon or Sapna, people who wouldn't come around, no matter how long you gave them. Given time to regain her equilibrium, Ali was sure her friend would recognise that Ali had only been trying to help keep her family protected and safe, the same way Meg had done for her.

Hopefully, she wouldn't need *too* long, though, because time was the one thing Ali was starting to run short on.

CHAPTER TWENTY-NINE

Violet

July 2018

I may be determined to help Meg, but without her husband's support, I'm not sure what else I can do besides keep reaching out. I've knocked on the door to try to talk to her, but no one ever answers. She's going for a swim most nights again now, which I hope is a good sign – exercise is sure to help, and it will give her that break she's been craving. I sit out back, watching from above as she wades into the water… making sure she returns to shore. She must know I'm watching, but she doesn't even turn in my direction. She's clearly upset that I told her husband about the accident.

I still can't believe his angry words. Even though I know he was shocked, they continue to ring in my ears… how I should keep out of it, how none of my family can be bothered to visit. That's another thing he's right about, actually. Andy hasn't come here in months. In fact, I can't even remember the last time he called – maybe at Christmas, when he repeated his annual invitation for me to move into the granny annex at his house? The hurried way he offers it always make me think of how, when he was a boy, he'd ask if I wanted a sip of his cola, then run off with it before I could even answer. He's inviting me out of obligation rather than love, although I shouldn't be surprised.

Love. The word seeps into my mind, and suddenly, a memory floods into me... the last time I told Andy I loved him before leaving for good. I'd finally let Robert know I wasn't coming home; I *couldn't*. Ben had been gone for four months, and every day was a desert stretching out in front of me, a vast sea of time I dragged myself through. It would have been easier to leap off the cliff – there was a strange kind of peace when I pictured falling through the blue sky towards infinite blackness – but that was too easy, and I couldn't take the easy way out. Jumping betrayed the gravity of what I had done... or, rather, what I had failed to do. I needed to be punished, although I knew that nothing could ever help me atone for my mistake.

Every minute that passed, I lurched between grief at losing Ben and grief at losing my family. When I saw the car pull into the drive, I wasn't sure I could face my husband one more time; see the face I loved so much. I opened the back door and ran into the garden, crouching down beside the decking and hoping he'd think I wasn't home. It was cowardly, yes, but it was preservation: not of self, but of the path I had chosen... the life I now had to live.

'Violet?' I could hear Robert's voice through the thin cottage wall, and I pressed up against the deck, making myself as small as possible. 'Vi? You here?'

I stayed still, staring at the scrubby grass. I could barely breathe. I longed to run from here and into his arms, but I couldn't. I couldn't let myself lean on anyone.

'Mummy?' I looked up as Andy came towards me, squatting down next to where I was hiding. My heart squeezed, and everything inside me quietened as I gazed at my son. Even though it had only been months since I'd left, he seemed so different – so much bigger, his unruly hair cropped shorter than I'd ever had it, wearing clothes I didn't recognise. And yet I knew every inch of him: the half-smile when he was nervous, the birthmark on the back of his knee, the timbre of his voice. He was mine, even though I wasn't there. He would always be mine.

'When are you coming home?' he asked, pressing even closer. That was how I knew how much he'd missed me: while Ben had always stuck to my side, Andy had been so independent, wiggling away from my hugs even as a toddler. I pulled him against me and kissed his head, breathing in the scent of him.

'Please come home,' he whispered, as my already splintered heart shattered into more pieces. 'Please. I miss you.'

'I miss you too,' I said, tears streaming down my face. 'I miss you so much.'

'Then come,' he said, winding his arms around my neck. '*Please.*'

'Oh, Andy. I—' I took in a breath. 'I love you. I love you, but I can't come home.'

'No!' Andy shouted, his voice echoing off the wall behind us and bouncing out to sea. 'You don't love me!' He pulled away and streaked off as the sound repeated around me, and I lowered my head to my knees as the grief ripped me apart. I didn't try to stop it. I let it come, uncurling only when I heard footsteps approaching.

'He needs you,' Robert said softly, staring down at me. 'You're his mother, and he needs you. We both do.' But I couldn't move. I sat there, listening to the car drive away. I sat until the darkness fell. And when I finally got up, I'd been still for so long I could hardly walk. Every muscle ached, but I welcomed it, hoping the pain in my body would block out some of the pain in my heart.

I catch my breath now as the realisation hits. I didn't fail only Ben. I failed Andy too. He *did* need me. No matter what I'd done, I was still his mother, the one he turned to when he cried. And I couldn't be there for him… the same way I couldn't be there for Ben. I thought that removing myself from his life was punishing only me – I couldn't keep him safe, anyway – but I can see now it was punishing him, as well.

His words that day scroll through my mind. *You don't love me. You don't love me.* Does he still believe that? I know he's an adult now and he seems happy, but do you ever get over your mother leaving? I know better than anyone how appearances can be deceiving. Anyone looking at me would probably believe I'm happy with this life too.

I think of the baby in Meg's arms, and of that bond between parent and child. For so long, I couldn't be a mother, even though I still had a son. But I never stopped loving him. No matter how much pain I buried myself under, that love was always there. I just couldn't let myself show it.

Can I now? Will he even want to hear from me? I'm fighting for a family I barely know. Can I pick up the phone and call my own son?

Before I can stop myself, I cross the room to the landline. Guilt sinks into me as I realise I don't even know his number, and I flip through the address book, then pick up the receiver. I punch in the digits and wait, my pulse racing. What am I going to say? It seems ridiculous that I'm this nervous about speaking to my son, but despite my love, he's practically a stranger. His voicemail comes on, and my heart sinks. I replace the receiver, telling myself that maybe it's a good thing he didn't answer. Maybe there is too much distance to cross.

Sighing, I gaze out the window. It's still raining but across the water, rays burst through the clouds and light a patch of sea in the distance, making the heavy grey water appear opalescent. I shove on my shoes and step onto the grass, the scent of damp earth and salty water filling my nose.

I draw in a breath as I catch sight of Meg and her baby in their back garden, staring out to sea. The wind is whipping in and rain splatters down, but she's not moving. It's like she and the baby are statues... as if life has drained from both of them and they've turned to stone. For a second, I wonder if my eyes are playing tricks on me again. I've been thinking about them so much that maybe what I'm seeing isn't really there.

A shiver sweeps over me, and I tell myself not to be ridiculous. I'm about to go over and gently tell her she needs to get out of the rain when I hear her husband calling and see her turn. He strides across the grass towards her. I can't see his face, but by his hurried motion, his concern is obvious. He must see that something is wrong. He *must* realise that she needs help.

But what I see next horrifies me because he doesn't lovingly guide her to the house. She takes a step away from him, but he catches up and grabs her arm – hard, it seems, by the way she's wincing. She tries to jerk away, but with the baby in her arms, she can't get free. I can hear her cries as he drags her back across the garden and into the house once again. I catch a glimpse of his face, and the cold anger makes me shiver.

I stand rooted to the spot, trying to absorb what I've just seen. I'd thought he was helping; that he was supporting Meg. But now… Thoughts fly through my head: how Meg came over that day, telling me she had to get out for a minute. How I'd overheard her begging him for space, how he didn't want her to take medication or even see a doctor, how they never left their house. And then the accident and her words that she had to get away… I'd thought at the time she'd meant the baby. But could she have been talking about her husband?

Had she been trying to escape from him?

As a former GP, I know what can happen behind closed doors. I know how some men can try to control women and every aspect of their lives – and I know pregnancy and having a baby can make things infinitely worse.

Is that what's happening here?

I swallow as I remember the first night I noticed Meg was pregnant, that strange scene in the sea. Maybe he wasn't grabbing Meg to help. Maybe he wasn't saving her. Maybe… Fear sweeps over me, accompanied by guilt and panic as I realise that if what I suspect now is true, I must have made things even worse by telling him about the accident.

I go back inside, closing the door firmly behind me. When Meg is out for her swim tomorrow evening, I'll head to the beach. It's well away from her husband and a safe place to talk about the future. I'll tell her that I'll help any way I can: get her to a doctor, take her to a hostel, *anything*. I quiver at the thought of going down to the sand – I haven't been there since Ben died; it's the one place I couldn't face – but in a way, I feel like I'm doing this for her as much as I am for our shattered family.

I couldn't rescue my son, and I couldn't be there for Andy when he needed me. But I'm going to be there for Meg if it's the last thing I do.

CHAPTER THIRTY

Ali

The next couple of days dragged by, time seeming longer than ever. The house next door was quiet. Even Jem's window was firmly closed, denying Ali a peek into the world where she'd learnt so much; of the little girl she'd cared for. After being apart for so long, the family must be hunkered down, finding their stride once again. Every inch of her longed to be back inside that wonderful place, but she knew she had to give them time.

Still, with every minute that passed, Ali felt her barrier growing weaker, allowing more and more of the darkness to seep in… allowing the questions to multiply. What if Meg didn't talk to her again? Was Ali really going to stay here alone until the baby came – and afterwards? Could she do all this – face all this – on her own?

There's nothing for you here. Meg's words echoed in her head, and Ali breathed in. She'd tried so hard to focus on everything good in her pregnancy, but without Meg's friendship, maybe she was right. But if there was nothing for her here, then where? Definitely not back in London. Ali screwed her eyes shut at the memory of her and Jon, curled up on the sofa in their cosy flat as Jon hummed a silly tune to her belly… then the pain and agony on his face when he sat in that exact spot, saying over and over that he was sorry, but he couldn't do this. Ali had been so certain *she* could, but now…

Looking for something to pull her from her thoughts, Ali resorted to yanking up weeds that had sprouted in the front garden. After the recent heavy rains, everything was green and flourishing. She knelt on the wet grass, tugging and digging, her mind flashing back to the first day she'd met Michael and Meg. She'd been out in the garden like this, desperate for something to do, and they'd passed by with Jem like something in a vision… drawing her away from her anger and pain, propelling her into a place of positivity and light.

Meg *would* come around, Ali told herself.

She was pulling a stubborn weed from the ground when she heard a loud beeping. She lifted her head, noticing a large lorry backing down the narrow lane. She watched as a man got out and went to Meg's front door. He banged the knocker and waited, shaking his head when no one answered. Then he went back down the steps and over to Ali.

'Morning. I'm looking for a Michael Walker,' he said. 'Is this the right place? I've got a stock pick-up here, for Oak Furnitureville.' Ali's eyebrows rose. That was a huge furniture chain all across the UK, running massive advertising campaigns on almost every available outlet. You'd have to be living under a rock not to have heard of them. Had this been the large order Michael was working on? Meg had said he was about to finish, and then he'd taken off to Spain.

'Yes, you've got the right place.' Ali paused. 'Maybe check the studio? It's down the little path there.' The car was gone from the drive, but perhaps Meg had finally taken it to get the window fixed.

'All right, thanks. I'll go have a look. Don't want to back down that lane again if I can avoid it.' He set off down the pathway towards the studio. Ali hung back, watching as he knocked on the door and waited. He paused, then banged again – so loudly that the sound echoed off the house.

He lumbered back towards her, puffing. 'No one there. I knocked, but there's a huge padlock on the door anyway. I tried ringing, but it's gone straight through to voicemail.' He shook his head. 'The boss isn't going to be happy about this. If you happen to see your neighbour, please tell him that I was here. He'll need to call to reschedule pick-up. Sooner rather than later.'

Ali nodded, watching as the man got into the lorry and drove away. Where was Michael? Meg had been talking about this order for weeks now, saying how proud she was of Michael and that this could be his big break. How could he miss such an important pick-up?

He *was* back, right? Ali still hadn't seen him, but Meg had been out swimming that night, and she hadn't given Ali any sign that he hadn't returned. She'd said she'd called him, so surely... surely Meg wasn't still alone with Jem? Fear shot through Ali at the thought of it.

Ali was still weeding when a car pulled up and Meg got out. She glanced at Ali as she swung Jem out of the back, but she didn't say a word as she went towards the house.

'Wait!' Ali called, and Meg turned around. Ali was relieved to see that her hair was neatly combed and the dark circles under her eyes had vanished. While she still didn't look like the woman Ali had met that first day, at least she seemed rested and calm. 'There was a lorry here to pick up the order that Michael was working on? Oak Furnitureville? They said they're going to call to reschedule.'

'Okay, thanks.' Meg didn't even bother meeting her eyes.

Ali swallowed. 'Michael is back, right?' She had to know.

'Christ.' Meg's face twisted, and she shook her head. 'You're not going to leave us alone, are you? You're going to poke and poke, and pry and pry, and—' She stopped and put a hand to her chest, taking in a deep breath. 'Michael's not back, no.'

'Okay,' Ali said slowly, that fear rearing up again. She paused, wondering what to say next. 'But you called him, right? He knows you need him?'

Meg shook her head, letting out a little laugh. 'I don't need him. I haven't called him. And I'm not going to.'

Ali stared, trying to take in the words. Meg hadn't called Michael, after all – he'd never been home?

What the hell?

'Michael's gone.' Meg met Ali's gaze. 'The night of the big storm. He left.'

'I know,' Ali said softly, worried once more for her friend's state of mind. 'I know. He went to Spain, on a work trip.'

Meg was shaking her head. 'No, no. No, he didn't go to Spain. He went... away. From us. From me and Jem.'

What? Once again, Ali strained to catch the words, to hold them in her brain long enough to process them. But as much as she tried, she couldn't. It was impossible. Michael wouldn't leave his family.

'But... but you're so happy,' Ali sputtered, the words emerging even as she realised how stupid it was to try to tell someone how they felt; how they should feel. 'And Michael's such a great husband, so hands-on, so loving. He's committed to you both. You guys are the perfect family.' She wasn't exactly sure why she was telling Meg all this, but... All she knew was that she wanted the old Meg back: the woman who looked at her husband like he was everything; the one who loved the life she led.

The one who had taught Ali how to be a mother.

'None of that was real,' Meg said. 'None of it, and I...' She paused. 'It couldn't go on any longer.'

Silence fell between them as Ali tried desperately to understand. All that time she'd believed Michael was away for work, that he'd be coming home soon, that Meg was talking to him every day... that had all been lies.

The family had been broken. Michael had left.

It was almost unfathomable, and if Meg wasn't standing here right now saying the words, Ali never would have believed it.

'Why didn't you tell me?' she asked finally.

Meg sighed. 'When we met on the path that morning, you looked at us like… I don't know, with something like admiration, maybe. As if everything was bright and shiny. As if I *was* the perfect wife; the perfect mother.' She let out a breath. 'I wanted that. I wanted someone to think of me like that because I'm not. Far from.' She winced and looked away, as if she was remembering something painful. 'Things have happened… I don't even know. All I know is that I couldn't pretend with Michael any longer, and I can't pretend with you.' She met Ali's eyes. 'Jem and I need to get away from here. We're packing up and we'll go stay with Caro for a bit.'

Ali nodded, thinking that at least Meg would be with someone who could make sure she and Jem stayed safe.

'And Michael?' she asked in a soft voice. Ali could understand wanting to flee. And she could understand, better than anyone, the desperation to believe that everything *was* bright and shiny. But to think that the perfect family that she'd envied and admired hadn't been real…

Meg's face hardened. 'I can't think of him. I don't want to.' She shook her head. 'Good luck with your baby. You'll be fine, I know. You're ready. If I can do it, anyone can. God knows I never even wanted to in the first place.' And then she went inside and shut the door behind her.

Ali stood, frozen, staring at the closed door. Michael hadn't been a committed father and husband. Despite all his words to the contrary, he'd left weeks ago, and he'd never been back. Meg had lied – lied about where he'd been, lied that he was home again… and lied about their marriage.

And the mother she'd admired... *I'm not the perfect mother; far from. I couldn't pretend with Michael any longer, and I can't pretend with you.* The words floated through Ali's head and dismay curled into her heart. She remembered what Caro had said back at the pub: how Meg had never wanted kids. And she thought of how once Meg started painting, nothing else seemed to matter – not even Jem, to the point of forgetting her in a hot car. Her sarcastic words on the beach, how now that Michael was back, she'd return to being 'just a mother'.

Was it possible that *that* had been the real Meg and not the other way around? That all her happiness and excitement about Ali's pregnancy – all her words about how wonderful motherhood was – and everything that had propped up Ali... that none of it had been real either? That the woman who'd shown Ali how to be a mother hadn't even wanted to be one herself? *Still* didn't want to, if her recent actions were any indication?

Ali turned towards the cottage, anger flooding through her. She'd believed she and Meg were friends; that they'd bonded over a common vision of family, of motherhood... a world where your baby deserved everything you could give it. She'd pulled Meg's words – Meg's life – around her, like a comfort blanket keeping her from all the pain of the broken world she'd fled.

But that shared vision had never existed. The comfort blanket was a ragged cloth stitched together with lies.

And Ali was alone now, with nothing to protect her.

CHAPTER THIRTY-ONE

Ali

Ali walked slowly towards the cottage. Memories pressed down with every step, piling on top of her. She opened the door and went inside, her legs pulling her towards the damaged nursery until she couldn't stand any longer. She sank onto the cracked floor, horrific images pushing on her chest until she had to inhale. They rushed into her, filling her every pore, and she had no choice but to remember.

Anencephaly. Ali still couldn't pronounce the word without tripping over the letters, but she didn't have to say it. She knew exactly what it meant: her baby's brain hadn't developed properly. Her daughter wouldn't talk or walk. Wouldn't make it to her first birthday. And might not even make it to the birth.

When the consultant had delivered his diagnosis, it felt like someone had reached in and pummelled her heart. She could barely breathe; barely take in anything except her baby on the screen.

Except the horror on her husband's face.

'You can fix that, though, right?' Jon had said to the doctor, his voice shaking. 'I mean, it's still early. There must be something you can do.'

But the doctor had shaken his head. 'I'm afraid not. I'm very sorry.'

'But…' Jon had sputtered, struggling for words. Ali didn't think she'd ever seen him at a loss. He always knew what to say. 'But she's alive, right?' He pointed to the screen, where their baby – their *daughter*, the sonographer had told them earlier, before the smile faded and she'd quickly disappeared – was bobbing around. 'How can she be alive if her brain hasn't developed properly?'

'She's alive for now,' the doctor had said gently. 'But I'm afraid this condition isn't compatible with life. Some of these babies are stillborn, but there is a chance your baby will make it full-term. But she won't live for more than an hour or, if you're very lucky, a couple of days at most.'

He paused and waited for them to say something, but neither Ali nor Jon could speak. Ali could only stare at the screen: at the one thing that made sense in all of this. Jon was still holding Ali's hand, but his fingers had gone limp, as if he no longer had the power to do anything.

'We can do further testing, such as an amniocentesis, to see if there are any other chromosomal abnormalities, if you'd like us to. But I can definitely give your baby a diagnosis of anencephaly right now, based on this ultrasound. I'll have a midwife come over and talk you through some options.'

'Some options?' Jon had tilted his head. 'I thought you said there was nothing you can do?'

The doctor nodded. 'I meant whether you'd like to terminate or proceed with the pregnancy. If you choose to continue, there are some maternal risks that you need to be aware of. Like I said, the midwife will talk you through all of that.'

Ali had flinched at the words, her eyes still glued to the screen. Terminate? No. No *way*. This was their daughter, right in front of them now. They'd heard her heartbeat; seen her move. She was alive, and Ali already loved her with every cell of her body. She'd made a vow to stand by her no matter what, and she'd meant it. Besides, if there was a chance that Ali could hold the baby in her arms for even a second, that was worth carrying on. That was worth everything, and she was sure Jon felt the same. She didn't have to ask – he'd never turn away from their daughter. He'd be there for as long as she needed him, the same way he'd promised with Ali.

She'd gripped his hand as the midwife's words swirled around them, never letting go even as they took the Tube back home. They were silent but together, and Ali was certain that whatever happened, they could face it. They could both be strong for their child.

Inside their flat, Jon had folded Ali in his arms. She'd leant against him, tears filling her eyes as she breathed in his love.

'I guess, given the risks, we should schedule the termination soon?' Jon said, stroking her hair. 'I can call if you want to. I'll be with you every step of the way.'

Ali had jerked back from his embrace. *Termination?* She shook her head, unable to believe what he was saying. She knew the doctor's words were a brutal shock. This was a terrible thing to happen; an awful tragedy that she couldn't even begin to grasp. She knew it was hard. Hell, it was happening to her, too. It was happening *inside* of her. But he couldn't mean those words.

He did, though. Over the never-ending night and day that had followed, he'd told her again and again that he couldn't bear to spend the next few months watching her bump get bigger, only to know that the baby growing inside would never get old. That it was better now for everyone if they accepted the inevitable.

That he didn't want this baby.

And when she couldn't take any more – couldn't listen to this stranger's horrific words about their child any longer – she'd escaped. She'd fled to the cottage to hunker down and wait for her husband to come, uncertainty and pain clinging onto her.

But Meg had reminded her that, no matter what, every second was precious. This baby was something to celebrate, not something to mourn. Whether she lived for long or not, this was the baby that would make Ali a mother, and she deserved to have a mother who was *ready*. And it was Meg, with her excitement at Ali's pregnancy and her eagerness to share her mothering skills, who'd given Ali exactly that. She'd lifted her up and pulled her away from the darkness – away from anything that would taint the pregnancy Ali was desperate to cherish, and away from the bleakness of the days ahead. And with the nursery, learning all she could and Meg's talk of the future together, Ali had almost let herself believe that her baby *would* have a full life.

God, how she desperately wanted to believe that.

But her daughter wouldn't live. Ali would never feed her baby or put her to sleep. She wouldn't have picnics in the back garden. She wouldn't splash in the waves, or clap her hands with a gurgling grin. She wouldn't grow up.

Grief and anguish poured into Ali now, mixing with the memories to create a riptide she didn't even try to escape. She clutched her stomach, her chest heaving and her whole body contracting as the current swept her under.

Meg may have been pretending that everything was fine, but Ali had been too.

CHAPTER THIRTY-TWO

Ali

Ali spent the next few days in bed, sorrow and pain weighing her down. All she wanted was to lie here under the covers, keeping her baby safely tucked inside. All she needed was to be alone, with no one to hurt her or let her down. She was dozing one afternoon, floating somewhere between waking and sleep, when she heard a car pull up outside. Who could that be? Both Meg and Michael were gone from the house at the moment, and there hadn't been any traffic on their little lane for days… but then, she hadn't exactly been keeping watch.

'Ali?'

She froze at the sound of her husband's voice. What was he doing here?

'Ali, are you in there?' Jon paused, then sighed. 'I've been so worried. I wanted to come and see you sooner, but Sapna said I should give you more time… more space. She said you weren't alone.'

Ali stayed silent, images of the last few weeks with Meg running through her head. She hadn't been alone, but she might as well have been. Anger and hurt filtered through her once again that everything she'd believed – everything she'd wanted to believe – had all been an act.

'Ali, please come home. Please.' Jon's voice faded away, and Ali heard the seagulls crying in the distance as if they were joining his plea. 'I can't take back what I said; how I felt when I heard...' He fell silent. 'When the doctor told us about our baby. I was worried about you, yes. But I was worried – I was scared – for myself, and for us. I was scared of loving something so much and then losing it. Of loving something even knowing you're going to lose it, and what that might do to us. Because I *do* love this baby. Of course I do. How could I not? I just... I wanted to protect us.'

He cleared his throat. 'But then I realised something. Love isn't on a timer. You can't simply turn it on and off. It isn't finite, not like life. Even if you'd decided not to carry on with the pregnancy, I'd still have loved our baby – loved her forever. She'd still be my daughter, and the pain would still be there. When something – someone – is a part of you, you can't stop it hurting by ending things. I was wrong to even think that.' He stopped talking and Ali could picture him rubbing his face, like he did when he was nervous. 'I'm not going to lie: I am still scared. I'm terrified, actually. And I know it won't be easy. But I love her, and I love you. I always will. I want to be there for her – for you. I want us to be together, as a family.'

A *family*. The word floated towards her, and Ali breathed it in, memories flashing through her mind. How they'd talked excitedly about having a baby. Discovering she was pregnant and designing the nursery. Lying in bed with Jon's hand on her stomach, dreaming of their future together.

His vow that he'd love their child, no matter what.

And now he was finally here, ready to be with them. He *had* come through in the end. A shard of light pierced the darkness inside her, and she threw off the covers and stood. There was still time, she told herself, shoving her feet into slippers. They could still be a family. Yes, he'd wavered when she'd needed him most, but what they were going through was horrific. He'd only been trying to protect himself… to protect *them*. She knew that impulse better than anyone.

She threw on a jumper over her thin T-shirt, her heart beating fast as she stepped into the lounge. Jon was right: love wasn't on a timer. His words back in London might have disappointed, hurt and angered her. She'd tried to block him out to stop the pain, but the love had still been there, dormant and waiting. She felt it now, as strongly as the day they'd married. Her pace quickened as she neared the door, every inch of her straining to invite him back into her life – into their daughter's life.

Then her father's face flashed into her mind, and she paused. She remembered how he'd hurt her over and over, making new promises, then not following through. All those weekends she'd sat on the stairs, waiting for him to come, believing that this time, he'd actually be the father he'd pledged. The hours she'd wasted trying to understand his rejections, and the heartache that had followed her until even now, shaping her life and relationships. She'd given him countless chances and he'd failed her every time, the fresh pain cutting through her like a knife.

Would Jon be the same? *Was* he like her father? Maybe he was here, but he *had* let her down – he'd watched her and his baby walk out the door, something she never could have imagined. And it wasn't only that: his fear had kept him away for weeks, allowing him to miss so much of this time together. She understood why he'd been so afraid, but could she rely on him now to really be there for their daughter… and for her? He might think he could, but what if his fear became too much? After all, hadn't he just said he was still terrified?

'Ali? Are you there?' Jon's sigh filtered through the door. 'I don't even know if you can hear me. And maybe there's nothing I can say to convince you, but… listen to the song I sent you, okay?' He cleared his throat. 'I emailed you a link. Just… have a listen.'

Ali was silent, her mind still whirling. He'd written a new song? She couldn't remember when he'd last done that. In the past few years, his teaching job had overwhelmed him. He'd started saying that by the time the day was over, he was lucky his brain could still function, never mind indulging in creativity.

'I'm going to leave now,' he said, when the silence stretched. 'Maybe you need more space. I understand that. I'll come back in a bit – I'll come as many times as I need to. And know that you can call me any time,' he continued. 'Please. Please think about what I said. I love you.' His voice broke, and Ali bowed her head, still frozen as tears dripped down her cheeks. She wanted that family – she wanted it so desperately. But she couldn't bring herself to move from this protected place towards the unknown… towards him. She *couldn't*.

Jon's vow to return as many times as it took rang in her mind, and she sighed.

Could she ever push aside the memory of her father? Could she believe in her husband again?

'What would you do, Gran?' she whispered, rubbing her belly. Would no-nonsense Gran give Jon a second chance? Ali had no idea. Her grandmother didn't suffer fools gladly, but she'd never seemed to hold onto her anger… not like Ali's mother had. If Gran had, she'd kept it all hidden inside.

Ali went into the bedroom and lay down on the bed. Then she crawled back under the duvet and closed her eyes, alone with her baby once more.

CHAPTER THIRTY-THREE

Violet

July 2018

A knock on the door shakes the cottage the next morning, and I turn from where I'm wiping down the counter after breakfast. Who could that be? I cross my fingers that somehow it's Meg and I can talk to her here, in this safe place.

'Mum?' A deep voice cuts through the walls, and my eyebrows rise in surprise. Goodness me, that's Andy. What's he doing here? Does he know I called yesterday? He must, because he hasn't come in months. Something had to have prompted him to visit. Hope and pleasure shoot through me that he's here, accompanied by that nervous feeling from yesterday. Can I show him now that I love him? Can I explain to him why I left?

Will he understand?

I tighten my robe around me, taking a quick look in the mirror before pulling open the door. My white hair stands up like static around my head, creases score my face like someone's folded it over and over again, and the skin on my neck has come loose from its moorings. This is why I try not to look at myself too closely: the image of me in my mind never matches the reality. Somewhere along the way, I got old. I run the comb through my hair, then hobble towards the door. It takes a while in the morning for my joints to warm up.

'Hello.' My voice is rusty, and I cough, giving myself time to take him in because he doesn't match the image in my mind either. When I think of him, I picture the boy on the beach that day, sitting beside me and leaning against my legs, dark hair tufted from salty water and long skinny body shaking. I should have reached out to comfort him, but I didn't. Guilt curdles through me once more – this time not for Ben, but for Andy.

'Hi, Mum.' He leans in to kiss my cheek, and I catch a whiff of his manly scent, so different from the little-boy-smell of sun and sea he used to emit. 'Can I come in?'

'Of course.' I stand aside and usher him forward, thinking how sad it is that he needs to ask. But then, this was never his home – not like it is for me. This was a holiday place, full of light and fun, until it suddenly wasn't. He went back to London to the family home with his father, making the odd journey out here every couple of months… until the visits trickled off to only once a year or so.

He stands, looking around the room, his large frame making everything feel even smaller. 'How are you feeling?' he asks, staring closely at me. 'You all right?'

'Of course! I'm not losing my marbles yet.' The words emerge curter than I'd like, and I want to hit myself. I do love him. I want him to believe that. I'm just so used to… to keeping everything pushed down, and the way he's gazing at me is unnerving.

'Cup of tea?' I ask, to fill to silence that's descended.

He pulls out a chair to sit, then gets up again and stares out at the sea. It's as if he doesn't know what to do with himself; where to place himself here.

'You called yesterday.' He turns to face me, and I nod as I put the kettle on. 'You… you never do that. Is everything okay?'

I swallow. Everything's not okay, and it never will be. But maybe… maybe I can do something to help him. Something to let him see that, despite what he may have believed, I never stopped loving him.

I swing round to face him. I want to speak, but somehow whenever I try to form the words, they die away before they reach my lips. I can't push them past the barrier inside me, and silence fills the room again.

'I know it's been years now since…' Andy looks away. 'Since Ben died. And I know I've never said I was sorry: sorry for not watching him like I should have, to make sure he didn't go into the water that day. I couldn't, because, well… I guess because it was too much for a boy to admit to himself and to the person he loved most that he was to blame.'

I listen to his words, my mouth falling open and my heart pressing against my ribs so much that I can barely get in air. Andy blames himself? Has he lived with this for so long – thinking it's his fault his brother died? I never thought that: not for even one second. I never even suspected he'd think that. I suppose now I should have, but I was so caught up in my own blame and guilt. He'd never once uttered anything to give us a clue, although I wasn't exactly listening.

I grip his arm, so big and strong now, and stare into his eyes. I *have* to speak. I can't let him live with this any longer because I know what it does to people. I know what it's done to me. I have to be strong for him. I take a deep breath and force the words out, pushing them past the wall I've built around myself; the wall that's now crumbling in an attempt to save my son… the son that remains.

'It's not your fault. It never was. How could it be?' I pause, willing what I'm saying to sink in. 'I was the adult. I should have been watching. I knew Ben was getting cheeky, and I should have gone down to the beach with you.' I turn now and look out to sea. 'I should have been able to pull him out.'

We're both silent for a minute, and I meet my son's eyes again. Even though they're grey now and not the blue of his childhood – even though they're surrounded by wrinkles – I can see the boy he once was. 'I'm sorry I let you down,' I say, fresh pain flowing through me that I've failed not only one, but both my boys. 'I'm sorry I let your brother down.' There's so much space between us that I'm not sure anything I say can fill it, but I need to try. 'After he died, I felt like I didn't deserve to be happy. And I couldn't leave him out there alone. Being here beside him was the least I could do.' I hold Andy's gaze, and thankfully he doesn't turn away.

'It had nothing to do with you.' I shake my head. 'No, I mean it had *everything* to do with you, and how much I love you. I couldn't keep your brother safe. And I worried that I couldn't protect you, and I couldn't bear that. You were safer with your father. I never blamed you. I never felt anything than absolute love.' And for the first time in years, I put my arms around my son and hug him. I'm afraid he'll move away, but instead I feel him tense, then soften in my arms, tightening his grip on me. Relief floods in that maybe, just maybe, he believes what I've said.

When we finally pull apart, his face looks... different, somehow. Lighter, less heavy, and I feel part of the pain inside me weaken too. I might have failed him before, but hopefully I haven't now.

'Right.' I squeeze his arm, then turn to bustle about the kitchen. 'Let me pour you some tea and then you can catch me up on all the news.'

We sip our tea as he fills me in on his travels with his wife, how Ali's doing with her husband (fine, although I'm not sure if he'd know otherwise), and what the rest of the summer holds in store. Although our words are nothing special or significant, something has changed between us. I know I can never make up for the damage I've done, but it feels like there's an understanding – a kind of connection now – that wasn't there before.

Andy puts his teacup down, his eyebrows lifting in surprise as he glances at something in the corner.

'Is that Hasty?' he asks, and I follow his gaze, surprised he still remembers the teddy's name. Then again, it's ingrained in my memory too.

'It is.' I smile as an image of Ben stroking the soft fur comes into my mind, and I remember that I still need to give the bear to the baby next door.

Andy glances at his watch. 'Right, I'd better get home. It's been so nice seeing you, Mum. I'll come visit again soon, okay?'

Mum. The word rings in my ears, and I touch his arm, feeling for the first time since Ben died that I *am* a mum. I've managed to do something good for my son. I've managed to show him that I do love him.

'And remember, that offer to come live with us is still open.' I meet his eyes, expecting him to move away before I can respond, but instead he pauses… like he's actually waiting for an answer this time. Could he really mean it? My heart fills up, and I struggle once more to find words. 'It's there if you need it,' he says finally.

I hug him goodbye, then watch through the window as his car pulls away. I try to picture me going with him… driving away from this self-imposed prison and towards a new life. But I can't. I may have opened the door to my cell – I may have reached towards the light – but I don't think I can ever leave.

CHAPTER THIRTY-FOUR

Ali

No matter how much Ali attempted to block them out, Jon's words echoed in her head over the next couple of days. Whenever she shut her eyes to try to escape into sleep, she saw his face. Twisting and turning, she couldn't think of anything but the way his voice cracked when he'd pleaded with her to come home; how he said that of course he loved their baby – how could he not? Several times she'd reached out for her mobile to play the song he'd written before shoving the phone away as if it would burn her fingers. If she heard his voice, she wasn't sure she could hold out, and there were still so many questions battering her brain. *Could* she give him another chance? What if his first instinct had been right and he really couldn't deal with their situation?

With sleep no longer a refuge, Ali got up early one morning and decided to go for a walk. She forced her heavy legs into the village, her stomach rumbling and her mouth dry. The air was cool and Fairview was quiet, and Ali wandered through the village streets, then ducked into a shop. Might as well get some food while she was here; the cottage shelves were almost bare. She bought what she needed and made her way down the narrow pavement, the handle of the heavy carrier bag biting into her palm. She paused for a moment, fighting for breath. The world swam around her, and she started to sway.

'Whoa!' Strong hands under her arms kept her from falling, and she blinked to try to clear her vision. 'Come, sit down here.' She was lowered onto the pavement, and she slumped over gratefully. Finally, when she felt all right again, she lifted her head to see a vicar looking down at her.

'Thank you,' she said, her voice wobbling.

'Do you want me to call someone?' he asked, and she shook her head. 'Come with me. I'll get you a cold drink or a nice cup of tea. You can have a little rest to make sure you're all right.' She didn't want to – all she wanted was to get home – but she didn't have the energy to argue. She let him guide her through a black metal gate and across a tiny graveyard into the cool, dark interior of a church.

'Have a seat here,' the vicar said. 'What would you like?'

'Just some water, please,' Ali said, and the vicar nodded and disappeared through a door at the side of the sanctuary.

She sank back into a pew, breathing in the silence. When had she last been in a church? She wasn't religious – neither of her parents were and Jon hadn't been – but there was something about the hushed quiet she found appealing. Back in London, whenever she had a few minutes to spare on her way to or from somewhere, she used to stop in and sit, soaking up the silence as her body relaxed. And okay, sometimes she had sent up a prayer that she'd have the family she'd longed for... that her life would have the happy-ever-after she'd dreamed of.

Pain curled through her, and her stomach clenched again.

'Here you are.' She opened her eyes to see the vicar standing over her, holding out a glass of water. She took it and gulped it down, savouring the cool liquid sliding down her throat.

'Are you here visiting?' he asked.

Ali paused for a moment, unsure how to answer. The future she'd fallen into with Meg would never happen – not that it ever would have. Was she really going to stay here now, in a ruined cottage, all alone by the sea? She'd do her best for her baby, but *was* she strong enough to do it all on her own? Jon's face floated into her mind. Did she want to?

'I'm staying in Seashine Cottage on Farm Lane,' she said, hoping the vague answer would satisfy him.

'Great. Good to have you here. I hope you're enjoying it.' The vicar smiled, and Ali drained the glass and got to her feet. 'I'd better go. Thank you.'

'Are you sure you're okay?' he asked. 'I can call a taxi for you, or—'

'I'm fine.' She was far from, but what else could she say? At least she could breathe once again, even if she did feel like she'd run a marathon.

'Don't forget these,' he said, handing her the bag of groceries. 'By the looks of things, you're eating for two now.'

Ali forced a smile. 'Thank you.' She left the church and wandered through the cemetery, touching the tops of the weathered stones and savouring the rough texture beneath her hand. Her grandmother hadn't wanted a grave. She hadn't even wanted a funeral; just asked for her ashes to be scattered in the ocean. Ali's father had gone to the cottage one day and done it himself without even telling her. Ali had been furious when she'd found out. Her father had looked surprised, saying he didn't think Ali would mind since she'd been so busy with work and life. He hadn't meant anything by it – he couldn't, coming from him – but guilt had seeped into her, anyway. She *had* been too busy... too busy to visit; too busy to call. For once, her father had been right.

Ali was about to open the churchyard gate when a gravestone reared up, the letters looming towards her. *Benjamin Carey, 1966–1973. Beloved son of Violet and Robert. Beloved brother of Andy. Always our little boy.* She stared at the words, reading them over and over as she tried to take them in.

Ben.

Gran had lost a son… a child who was only seven, and who'd barely had a chance to live.

Her father had lost a brother.

How had she not known this? Why had no one ever told her?

Ali walked slowly back to the cottage, her mind spinning as the pieces fell into place. The bag of clothes. The teddy bear that Gran had said belonged to another little boy – how Gran hadn't wanted her to touch it. Why she'd stared out into the ocean, as if she was missing something; as if she was seeking something. The sadness and pain Ali had sensed sometimes, and the way Gran would curl up into silence.

And maybe… maybe this was why Gran had come to the cottage, to seek solace and refuge, exactly like Ali. To learn to live again, in a future she'd never imagined but had to survive in. A place where being alone wasn't a negative, but a good thing – because then you could barricade yourself inside your shell, gaining protection from the outside world. You could allow yourself to fall into your grief, the only compatible companion.

Ali drew in a breath, feeling a connection with her gran now more than ever. She would understand better than anyone the pain that Ali was feeling. She would understand Ali's instinct to protect her child; to hang onto every little piece of her, like Gran had with that teddy. And Ali knew beyond a doubt that Gran would have encouraged her to make the most of these days too… that unlike Meg, she would have meant it with every fibre of her being, the way only someone who understood loss could mean it.

Ali stared at the glittering sea stretching out to the horizon and blinked away the tears in her eyes. She didn't want to hurt Jon. She loved him. And she knew he loved her and the baby, but that wasn't enough to regain her trust. She wished so much that it was, but it just *wasn't*. Gran was right: every mistake had consequences. She'd believed in him and his promises, but he'd done the unfathomable. He'd watched her leave, letting his fear triumph over love.

That had touched something deep within her, reminding her of the pain of broken bonds she'd experienced first-hand… a pain she could never forget, and a pain she never wanted her child to experience. She'd do *anything* to keep her from it.

Time was short – Ben's grave was a harsh reminder of that – and this baby deserved to experience only love in whatever days remained. Nothing should risk threatening these precious remaining moments. That was the very reason Ali had come here in the first place.

She went into the cottage and closed the door behind her, her heart heavy but the questions finally silenced. Like her grandmother, Ali was going to get through this the safest way possible: on her own.

CHAPTER THIRTY-FIVE

Violet

July 2018

I'm staring out to sea the next day, waiting for Meg to go for her daily swim. Andy's face flies in and out of my mind, along with images of somewhere comfortable and warm… of a life where I wouldn't be alone, of a world with people who care. I know it's too late for me to begin again. I know that after all this time, I can't leave Ben – can't leave my grief behind and start afresh. But with every minute that passes, my desire to be with Andy grows stronger. I want to be there, to be by his side. I want to be his mother, in a way I haven't been able to all these years. And yet… yet I still feel rooted here, unable to move.

Meg emerges from next door, and I push the thoughts from my head. She picks her way down the cliff path, and I hurry after her, watching as she wades into the waves, then smoothly dives in. She swims out to sea with steady strokes, and I walk onto the sand, stepping gingerly as if I'm afraid of triggering a landmine.

Finally, I'm here. Finally, I'm at the place where it happened. The beach where my son died.

I close my eyes and wait for the explosion of memories and pain, but only silence swirls inside. I open my eyes in surprise, gazing at the water in front of me. For so long, I avoided this place, certain

I could never recover from setting foot here. But maybe… maybe it's because I've already punished myself as much as possible. I've relived those terrible events over and over. I've lived pain every minute. I didn't push it away. I invited it in – into me. No matter where I am and what I do, it will be there.

A seagull cries, and I look up to see it gliding out to sea. I will always remember that I couldn't save Ben. I will always remember that it's my fault he died. I don't need a cottage or a beach to remind me of that. Leaving here doesn't mean leaving behind my guilt and my grief. I can be with Andy and carry those with me too. I can be his mother – at last. I can do that for *him*, if not for me.

But before I go, I need to help Meg. Because without her, I wouldn't be able to take this step. Seeing her and the baby… that stirred something inside. That made me open up, in a way I hadn't since Ben died.

I stand there watching the waves as Meg swims towards the shore. Finally, she's in shallow water and she stands, then starts walking closer. I lift a hand, wondering how to begin. Will she talk to me if she's angry? Will she let me help her?

Will she be able to trust me now after I didn't keep her confidence?

'How's the water?' I ask, wishing I was better at small talk.

She stares at me, but she doesn't answer, and I take a deep breath. What did I expect? I broke a promise by telling her husband about the accident. Of course she's angry and upset. And from what I suspect is happening inside that home, I can see that she has every reason to be.

But I'm not giving up.

'Good to have some time to yourself,' I say. 'How are you feeling? After the accident and everything? Is your baby all right?'

Her eyes swing towards me at the mention of the accident. 'I'm fine,' she says, although I can tell by the robotic tone that she's anything but. 'Jem is fine. We're all great.'

Never have I heard a less convincing response. 'Meg, if something's not right, there are places you and Jem can stay – where you can be safe. I can take you, if you want.' I watch her face closely. 'And you can get the help you need. Have a chat with a counsellor, get started on some medication… I meant what I said earlier. You will be fine.' I stare at her hard, praying that this time I've been able to reach her. If I'm right and that accident was a failed attempt to get away from her husband, then she needs to believe I will help her leave. And even if she's not ready for that – even if somehow, I'm wrong – she needs someone to take her to a doctor. Neither she nor her baby can stay here like this.

She pauses for a minute, and hope leaps inside me. Then she glances up at her house on the clifftop, lights blazing in the windows.

'I don't know,' she whispers. 'Maybe.' She doesn't say more, but my heart lifts as she hurries back up the pathway, head down, as if she's afraid there's someone watching. I glance up to see her husband silhouetted in the window, swallowing my unease at the way he's staring. Even from here I can feel his eyes burning through me, and I know my suspicions were right. Meg is scared of him. She *was* trying to get away.

I turn to look at the sea, determination and purpose flooding through me. I'm still here. I haven't fallen apart. I'm going to be with my son again, and I'm going to help Meg. It's too late for me to escape my life of guilt and grief, but it isn't too late for them.

CHAPTER THIRTY-SIX

Ali

Back in the cottage, Ali stared around the tiny space, determination running through her despite her fatigue. She was going to redo the nursery, this time without Meg's help. This time, it would be all her and no one else. First things first, she'd need to repaint the walls… maybe a light blue, the colour of the ocean when the sun shone on it; the colour of the sky when it had been rinsed of heavy clouds after a storm. One wall might still be too damp, but getting started would make her feel better. It would prove that she could do this journey on her own.

She *was* strong enough.

Ali spent the next few days painting. Despite having to sit down every five minutes or so to rest – it felt like the baby was squatting right on Ali's ribs – she was making steady progress and feeling stronger inside with every hour that passed. Her daughter may not have a long life ahead. She would never come to this room; never see how the sun made the blue appear like silvery slivers of the sea. This nursery would be to honour the memory of her child and nothing else. Each time that knowledge hit, grief cut into Ali like a barbed wire. But she didn't need to hide away from the misery. She didn't need to block out the pain – not any longer. She wanted to remember. And whenever Ali looked at this room, she'd think of her daughter… the same way Gran had clutched her son close to her heart whenever she cuddled that bear.

Ali was making her morning cup of tea when she noticed two police officers walking down the steps of Meg's house and approaching the cottage. She caught her breath. What was going on? She padded over to the door and yanked it open, questions flooding her mind. Well, she wouldn't have long to wait to find out.

'Hello,' Ali said to the woman officer, not even caring that her feet were bare and her hair was a mess. The baby kicked furiously, and she put a hand on her stomach to soothe her. 'Is everything okay?' She could barely catch her breath.

'Sorry to disturb you. We've had a few reports recently of a man behaving suspiciously in the area.'

'Behaving suspiciously?' Ali raised her eyebrows.

'Lurking around holiday homes, that kind of thing. There was a break-in down the coast about a month ago and several residents have reported seeing someone on their property, so we're telling everyone to be diligent and make sure to lock up properly.'

'Okay.' It was difficult to imagine anything threatening happening in this calm, quiet place, and yet a tiny knot of fear formed inside.

'You haven't seen anyone around here, have you?' the male officer asked. 'Nothing out of the ordinary?'

Ali shook her head. 'No, nothing. Sorry.'

'All right, thank you. If you do see something, please give us a call.' The woman handed her a card. 'Are you out here on your own?'

Ali nodded. 'Yes, I am.' She tried to make her voice loud and strong, but instead it sounded shaky.

'Take care of yourself and stay safe, all right?' The officers smiled and got back into their car, then reversed down the lane. Ali stood in the doorway watching them go, their words echoing in the tiny space. *A man lurking. Behaving suspiciously. Stay safe.*

She shook her head, trying to dislodge the fear, but something was stopping her. She caught her breath as fuzzy images inside her brain slowly came into focus.

Meg's terrified face the day Ali had taken Jem to the studio, asking if she'd left the door unlocked. The dark shape Ali had seen late at night in the field by the house. How, when Meg forgot Jem in the hot car, her first instinct had been to ask if Ali had locked the door, or if she'd seen or heard anything.

Had someone been lurking near the house? Had Meg seen him? If so, why hadn't she said anything? Why hadn't she called the police?

Ali froze as a thought hit: could that man be Michael? Could that be why Meg hadn't rung the police… because she knew it was him? He *had* been gone now for about a month, around the time of the break-in the police had mentioned. But why would he skulk around, breaking into cottages? Why not just get his things and leave?

And if it was him, then why was Meg so afraid?

Ali shook her head. Meg and Michael weren't important any longer. All that mattered was her baby. She picked up her tea and took a sip, savouring the warmth, but even that couldn't melt the icy shard of fear inside. The thought of someone – whoever it was – peering into her cottage in the night made her shiver. She pulled the door tightly closed and locked it, wishing it wasn't so flimsy.

Her safe place didn't feel quite as safe any more.

CHAPTER THIRTY-SEVEN

Ali

Ali opened her eyes the next morning, feeling just as tired as when she'd gone to bed. She'd jerked awake at every noise, only really drifting off once the sky started brightening. In the dark of the night, the urge to call Jon had been almost unbearable. She'd only managed to stop herself by repeating over and over that she had to be strong for her daughter. Whatever lurked outside, they were safer here, on their own. Anyway, like Gran had said, there was nothing of value inside the cottage. No burglar in his right mind would be tempted to plunder this place.

'Okay, guess we'd better get up, right?' She put a hand on her stomach, waiting for the usual answering kick. There was nothing, though, and worry shot through her. Usually at this time, the baby was performing somersaults and stretches inside Ali's belly, as if she was waking up too.

Ali sat up, her heart thudding. What did people always say? Give the baby a bit of chocolate or something, and that will get her moving?

Trying her best not to panic, Ali slid from the bed and walked over to the kitchen cupboard, her bare feet curling on the cold gritty tiles. She rummaged inside and grabbed the bag of Galaxies she'd bought one day on a whim – the only chocolate the tiny off-licence had. It was a throwback to her summers here with Gran, when Gran would dole them out once a day after tea-time if Ali had been good.

She scooped up a handful and unwrapped them quickly, then shoved them in her mouth, hardly taking the time to chew before swallowing them down. *Come on*, she pleaded, running a hand over her stomach. *Come on, little girl.* Ali clutched her belly, pressing gently down, but there was no response. No kick, no squirming, no tiny bubble of hiccups…

Hands shaking, Ali pulled on jogging bottoms and a T-shirt, reached for her keys, then hurried out of the cottage and got into her car. All the way to Hastings, she prayed her daughter was fine, coaxing the baby to move with all her might; to show Ali she was still there. But there was nothing.

Please be okay. Please be okay.

Ali tried to stay calm as she followed the signs to the hospital. Sometimes, babies were a little lethargic, she told herself, but she knew that with her baby, it could be more than lethargy. Ali parked the car and hurried into the A&E, hardly able to breathe as she explained why she was here. What felt like a century later, a midwife came and helped her up to the maternity unit.

The midwife probed her belly with the foetal heart monitor, then smiled as the galloping sound of the baby's heartbeat filled the room. Ali felt every muscle relax as relief poured through her.

Her daughter was alive.

'The heartrate is fine,' the midwife said, meeting Ali's eyes. 'I'm sure you'll feel her move soon. She's probably having a little lie-in. You're booked into a hospital in London, you said? When are you due?'

'Oh, I'm only coming up to twenty-six weeks,' Ali said, remembering that she'd yet to change hospitals. 'We have a way to go.'

The midwife raised her eyebrows. 'Only twenty-six weeks? Would you mind if I measured you?'

Ali shook her head and lay back down. She'd submit to anything now that her baby was okay.

'You're measuring very large,' the midwife said, brandishing the tape measure. 'How are you feeling?'

'I'm okay. I do find it difficult to catch my breath sometimes, but I think it's because the baby is pressing on my ribs.'

The midwife tilted her head. 'Do you have a feeling of heaviness?'

Ali nodded. 'Well, yes. But isn't that normal?'

'It can be. But combined with breathlessness and how big you're measuring…' The midwife sat down across from Ali. 'Have you heard of polyhydramnios? It's a condition where you have too much amniotic fluid. It can make you feel quite heavy and sometimes breathless.'

Ali nodded slowly. In the recesses of her mind, she vaguely recalled the midwife saying something like that to her as one of the risks of continuing her pregnancy.

'It can cause preterm birth,' the midwife continued, 'so I'd like to ask one of the consultants to have a look. We might need to do a few more investigations.'

Ali swallowed, fear shooting through her. Preterm birth? She was fighting for time as it was.

The midwife met Ali's eyes. 'Do you have any medical conditions we need to be aware of? How has your pregnancy been so far?'

'My baby…' Ali slid a hand down to her bump. 'My baby has anencephaly.' It was the first time she'd said those words aloud, and she hated how the midwife's face changed from professional concern to sympathy and sadness. Ali's daughter may have anencephaly, but she didn't want that condition to define her – to define how others felt about her. Her child was more than the pain the word evoked, and Ali didn't need to live in a fantasy world to feel excited at meeting her or happy to hold her in her arms. She didn't need to drown in grief either. She could let herself feel the complicated mix of emotions. She could bear it because above everything else was love… a love so strong that it gave her strength to face the days ahead.

'Anencephaly can often cause polyhydramnios,' the midwife said softly. 'Relax here for a minute, and I'll go find a consultant for you.'

'Okay.' Ali closed her eyes, listening to the hustle and bustle of the ward around her.

Two hours and one ultrasound later, and Ali was back in her car on the way home. The doctor had given her medication that should help reduce the amniotic fluid, telling her to come back for a check-up every week. She pulled into the drive of the cottage and got out of the car slowly, still feeling heavy and weighted, exhausted inside and out. She'd known she wouldn't have much time with her daughter, but now… She shook her head, her heart aching. If the baby came early, that time could be even shorter.

Ali stood on the doorstep, thinking of Jon and the words he'd said right here: how he loved them both, and how he wanted to be with them. How he wanted time to be a father too. Before she could stop herself, she reached for her mobile and turned it on, then navigated to her email. She clicked on the one from Jon, then opened the link.

The first notes of guitar sounded, chords that were tender and warm. Jon started singing and tears filled Ali's eyes as she listened to the words. It was a tribute to their daughter… to the life they could have had and to the love they had now. She went inside and collapsed on the sofa, the song swirling around her and the baby, tears streaking down her cheeks. No matter what had happened between them and what had been said, this was the music of a father who loved his child with everything he had. She felt his emotion so intensely it was almost a palpable presence in the room. This love was real, bumping up against hers – matching its strength.

A love that *could* overcome fear and pain… just like her own.

She breathed in, her head snapping up in surprise as the sharp scent of smoke filled her nostrils. Where was that coming from? She put the phone down and got up, her eyebrows rising when she spotted Meg's car in the driveway next door and a light on upstairs. Ali could hear Jem crying inside, just like that night when she'd first arrived. Ali bit her lip. Meg must have returned to get some things – or maybe she was back from Caro's for good?

Ali's thoughts were interrupted when she noticed a plume of smoke seeping slowly from Meg's open window. 'Meg!' she screamed, panic tearing at her voice. '*Meg!*' But no one responded – no one came to the window – and fear erupted inside. Where the hell was she? The baby's cries grew louder, and Ali froze as an image of Jem in the stifling car swept into her mind. Had Meg been painting and got distracted? Had she drifted off to sleep and…

Ali shook her head. She didn't have time to indulge in theories. All that mattered was getting Jem out.

She grabbed her mobile and called 999, relaying the location of the fire. With the fire brigade in Hastings, though, she knew it would be at least thirty minutes before they arrived. She rushed across the grass and up the steps, trying to move as quickly as she could yet feeling as if she was underwater.

She tried the front door, relief flooding through her that it was open. Inside, the smell of smoke was even stronger, tendrils curling through the air.

'Meg?' she called, gasping for breath as her heart pounded even faster now. Fear shot through her again at the thought of navigating the thick smoke upstairs, but she couldn't leave Jem there. Her own baby kicked as if urging her on. Ali took one big gulp of air and stepped forward, Jem's weak cry radiating through the air like a distress signal.

CHAPTER THIRTY-EIGHT

Violet

July 2018

I've spent the last few hours clearing out the bedroom, getting things ready for leaving here. I can hardly believe that, after all this time, I'm actually going… but I know I'm not, really. Wherever I am, Ben and the pain of what happened will come with me. Now, though, it's time to do this for Andy. He's driving down tomorrow to pick me up and take me… home. I smile, warmth flooding into me as I think of his surprised and happy reaction when I told him I'd accept his offer to stay. His response has made me even more certain I'm doing the right thing.

I gaze into the cracked mirror and put a hand to my cheek, not even recognising the rough, wrinkled texture of my skin. I'm definitely not the same woman who came here that summer weekend – in more ways than one. Grief and age have scarred me. Grief and age have scarred my son, too, but maybe… maybe my love will help heal him.

Finally, I've sorted through most of the bedroom. I'll leave the rest of the back room for Andy to help me with at some point. I'm sweaty and dusty and feeling a little lightheaded; I've been working non-stop for hours. I know I should sit down, but there's one more thing I need to do – one last thing, before Andy comes to get me.

I need to make sure Meg will be all right, and that she and Jem will be safe. I need to convince her to leave. I've been into the village and bought her and Jem everything they'll need – nappies, bottles, a few sets of clothes – and packed it all into a carrier bag. My rusty car is ready to go, and I've cleaned out the back to make room for the car seat. I'm all set to drive them to the shelter in Hastings and towards a new life.

I grab Hasty from the corner of the room and give him a cuddle. This will be the last time I see the baby, and I need to finally hand this bear over. I'm letting go of something so dear to me – to my son – but I know that wherever I am, I'll never forget him.

'I think we're ready,' I say to the bear, not caring how silly I sound.

I slide on my shoes and head outdoors. It's a beautiful day: the sun blazes from a clear blue sky, the air is warm yet fresh, and the sea glistens like a carpet of jewels. It's like nature is showing me exactly what I'll be missing when I go. I pause for a minute, tilting my head. *Will* I miss this place? I've spent most of my life here, but I don't think I will. It's time to pass it on to someone who can make new memories here – untainted ones; a fresh start. It's time for someone to make this place into what it should be: a summer home full of light, freedom and fun. I hope Ali will be able to do exactly that.

I hear the sound of the husband working away in his studio, making whatever it is he makes. I rap on the door of the house, praying he stays away… praying Meg answers.

She doesn't come, so I knock again. 'Hello?' I'm going to stay here until she appears.

Thankfully, I don't have to wait long. I hear footsteps approaching, and then the door swings open. 'Hi.' She pushes her hair away from her eyes and blinks, as if she's trying to focus on me. Then she quickly looks behind me, fear on her face. I can see she's as worried as I am about her husband spotting us.

'Meg.' My voice is low, and I know I need to speak quickly. I may not have much time. I tighten my grip on Hasty, crossing my fingers that she'll come with me. 'I have a bag in the car for you and the baby, packed full of everything you'll need. There's a refuge in Hastings where you can stay, and they have room… I checked. I'll drive you.' I stare into her eyes. 'I know you want to get away – for you and the baby. I can take you now, before I leave tomorrow.'

'Leave? You're going?' She looks panicked that I won't be here any more, and my gut clenches. I need to get her to that refuge.

'I'm moving in with my son in London,' I say. 'It's time.' I take her arm. 'And it's time for you to go too. Now's your chance to do it safely.'

She stares at me, and I hold my breath.

'I can't,' she says finally, shaking her head. 'I want to, but I can't. You don't… you don't understand.'

'I understand being trapped,' I say, desperate now to convince her. 'I understand not being able to move.' I think of Andy and his invitation to come and stay – how we connected, and how I finally managed to leave… for him. 'But sometimes, if someone gives you a way out, you need to take it. You deserve it. Your *daughter* deserves it.' *Just like Andy does.*

'If I leave, he's going to say I'm not a fit parent.' She looks down at the ground and I hear the terror in her voice. 'And he's right. I'm not.'

I touch her arm. 'You *are*. I can see that – see how much you love your baby. And having depression doesn't make you a bad parent. It doesn't mean you love your baby any less.' I hope my words are getting through. 'And if he does say that you're not capable, I'll speak up for you… for you and your child. I promise you that.'

'Promise her what?' Meg's eyes widen, and I swing round to see the husband coming up the steps. A tiny thread of fear waves through me, but I push it aside. Most bullies back down when faced with someone who's strong and unwavering. That's exactly what I intend to be now.

'Meg and the baby are coming with me,' I say, my tone firm. I may be old and a little frail, but I can still whip out my authoritarian doctor-voice when I need to.

But the husband doesn't back down. Instead, he steps closer.

'Oh?' His lips stretch over his teeth in a semblance of a smile, but I know it's anything but a happy one.

'Come on, Meg. Let's go.' I beckon her forward and try to go past him, but he takes my arm and squeezes it so hard that I draw in a breath of surprise and pain.

'She's not going anywhere.' Each word is punctuated by a shake, and I try to speak – to say that she *is* – but my chest tightens, like the grip on my arm has extended to my heart. My vision blurs, and the ground sways beneath my feet. He lets go, and I stumble down the stairs, trying to grab onto something to stop myself lurching forward.

The edges of my vision begin to tinge black. I sink onto the grass as my legs crumble beneath me, but I manage to keep my grip on the teddy, as if I'm holding Ben close. For a second, it feels like Ben himself is wrapped around me, like he's emerged from the waves.

It's not your fault. Ben's voice echoes in my head as I struggle to stay conscious. *You don't need to be so sad. It's not your fault.* I blink, knowing the voice isn't real yet hearing it so clearly that it must be. And I feel the guilt start to slip away... the guilt that kept me imprisoned in grief and pain for so long. Ben wants me to be free – free of everything now, free to live again, in a way he never can.

I smile, and the last thing I see before the darkness closes in is the sparkling water – the 'seashine', like Ben calls it – stretching out towards forever.

CHAPTER THIRTY-NINE

Ali

Ali yanked her T-shirt up over her nose and mouth to block out the thick smoke, her eyes stinging as she made her way up the stairs. She forced herself to keep moving forward – moving towards the dark and heat as the crackle of the fire rattled in her ears. It was like someone had plunged into the depths of her brain and drawn out all her horrors, except this was real. She felt her way down the hallway towards Jem's room, barely able to see now. The crying had stopped, and she prayed the little girl was okay. Where the *hell* was Meg?

Finally, Ali reached Jem's door. It was closed, and she put a hand on the handle and twisted it, the hot metal searing her palm. She tried to open it, but it didn't give way. Was it locked or had the heat damaged it? She took the T-shirt from her mouth, wrapped her hand around the loose fabric, and tried again.

The door would not budge.

She started hammering on it. But nothing made it open, and she looked around frantically for a chair or some other object she could ram it with. The heat of the fire was growing, and the smoke was even thicker and blacker, and she knew she didn't have much time. Finally, she heaved a solid oak chair from the corridor against the wood, and the door gave way.

'Michael!' She blinked, not sure if she could believe what she was seeing, but beyond relieved that he was here. Why *was* he still here... why hadn't he tried to escape the fire? God, he looked awful, with his clothes practically hanging off of him. Wiry whiskers covered his chin, his hair was shaggy and unkempt, and his eyes were unfocused.

'Come on, let's go.' Whatever had happened, they didn't have time to talk about it now.

But Michael was just staring at her, clutching Jem tightly in his arms. He shook his head without saying a word. Ali gazed back, confusion swirling inside. What the hell?

'If you're worried about Meg, she's not here. *Come on.* We have to go now.' If they waited any longer, they wouldn't be able to get past the fire.

'I'm not worried about Meg.' Michael's face twisted, and Ali was stunned at the rage she saw there. 'No, I'm not worried about her any more. She won't hurt me again. And she won't hurt our daughter either.'

Ali nodded, trying not to breathe in the smoke. The room was starting to wave in front of her and she was struggling to stay awake; to stay on her feet. She held out her hand. 'Let's go.'

But Michael didn't move. 'Meg thinks she can take our daughter and get on with her life without me – after everything I've done for her; after all of this time.' He shook his head, tightening his hold on Jem. 'I was the one who took care of her. *I* was the one who kept her well. She has all of this – this house, this baby, this life because of *me.*'

Ali nodded. Okay, he was angry. She could understand that. He'd been so committed to his family, and all that was over. But now was hardly the time to discuss it. They had to leave. 'I'm sure she appreciated all of that. But sometimes, things don't work out.' She knew that better than anyone.

But Michael was still talking, glued to his spot. 'I'm the one who kept her on track, no one else. I kept her away from anything that could hurt her: friends, her painting… kept her safe here in these four walls. She wanted to go back on her medicine after Jem was born. She told me she needed something more than me to cope. But she didn't need any drugs. I was enough. I should be enough.'

Michael's voice washed over Ali, and she shook her head. *What?* Nothing made sense; she couldn't even start to try to puzzle all of this out. There wasn't time, anyway. They had to get out of here. 'Come on.' She coughed on the words.

But Michael took a step back. 'No. This is it. It's *over.* Your grandmother learnt her lesson. Meg will now too.' He held Jem even closer as the heat intensified. 'The fire will make sure of that.'

Ali stared, unable to process what she was hearing. *Michael* had started the fire? He was willing to kill his child – and himself – to stop Meg from having a life without him?

And her grandmother… She coughed again in the smoky air, trying to grab onto the thoughts flying through her head. Had he hurt her grandmother? It was too much to grasp, but Ali knew she had to. She had to do something if she wanted to survive this.

'Where is Meg now?' Please God, may he not have hurt her too. Please, may she be okay.

But Michael didn't answer. Ali stood rooted to the ground, knowing she couldn't stay here much longer but also knowing she couldn't leave… not if she was going to save Jem. Michael was in the corner now, his eyes glazed over again as if he didn't even realise she was still here. She meant nothing to him, she knew. Meg and Jem meant nothing to him either. They couldn't, if he was prepared to let his daughter die in the fire.

All he cared about was himself and keeping his family together – in a way that he could control; in a way that met his own warped vision. Ali had admired his determination when they'd first met, mistaking it for the loyalty and strength she'd thought Jon was missing. But she could see now that it wasn't strength… far from. It was something dark; something twisted.

The heat in the room became even more intense, the smoke now curling around her like a thick fog. In the corner on the shelf, she could make out Hasty sitting jauntily in his captain's outfit. Seeing that bit of her grandmother in this place gave her strength, and Ali knew she had to do something before it was too late. She took a step forward into the grey haze, grabbed a tiny chair from the corner of Jem's room and lunged towards Michael.

Caught off balance, he lurched and swore, instinctively putting out a hand to stop himself from falling. As Jem started to slide from his grip, Ali caught her. She was limp, but her eyes fluttered open for a second, and Ali knew she was still alive. She held onto the child with all her strength, her heart pounding as Michael stepped forward.

Then the window shattered with a sharp crack, and a firefighter appeared. He motioned towards Michael to follow him out the window, but Michael shook his head. He looked into the corridor, now devoured by flames, then walked straight into them, his silhouette lighting up as the fire consumed him. Ali watched in horror, tightening her grip on Jem as the firefighter climbed into the room and took her arm.

Then everything went black as her muscles gave way and she slid to the floor.

CHAPTER FORTY

Ali

Ali opened her eyes slowly. She stared at the ceiling for a minute, trying to figure out where she was. For a second, she thought she was back home with Jon. She turned to cuddle into his warm body before something tugged at her arm and she felt cold metal rails at her side. She sat up quickly, gazing around the room as the knowledge seeped in. She was in hospital. There'd been a fire. Somehow, she'd got out. She was alive. Her stomach squeezed, and relief flooded through her as she felt her baby kick. Her daughter was alive too.

And Jem? If the fireman had got her out, then he must have rescued Jem. Ali prayed the baby was all right – and Meg. What had Michael done to her?

Michael… Ali closed her eyes tightly against the memory of him in the flames; against the shock of his words, words which she still hadn't been able to fully process. She lay back down, fatigue tugging her towards sleep once more. She was so, so tired, and it was still too much to even think about now.

A knock on the door made her eyes fly open, and she sat up, yawning. Her stomach squeezed again, and she let out a little groan.

'Ali?' Meg's voice filled the room. 'Can I come in?' Exhaustion pulled at her face, her clothes were smudged with dirt and her hair fell messily from a high ponytail, but she seemed unharmed. Ali let out her breath. *Thank God.*

'How's Jem?' Ali's heart pounded as Meg walked towards her and settled on the chair.

'She's being treated for smoke inhalation, but the firefighters managed to get her out before too much damage was done. She'll be fine.' Meg met Ali's gaze, her red-rimmed eyes filling with tears. 'I can't say thank you enough. If you hadn't been there… if you hadn't gone inside…'

Ali swallowed. Going up to Jem in the midst of the fire hadn't been a conscious decision – she hadn't weighed the risks or what might have happened. It had been instinctive, born out of a fierce sense of protection… born out of love for the little girl who'd taught her how to be a mother, who had allowed her to be a mother in a way she never would to the baby she was carrying now.

A tear streaked down Meg's cheek, and she swiped it away. 'Please tell me everything is okay. That *your* baby is all right after all of this.' She shook her head. 'I couldn't bear it if she wasn't.'

Ali put a hand on her stomach. 'My baby is all right. She's doing as well as she can, given the circumstances.'

Meg tilted her head. 'What do you mean?'

Ali met Meg's puzzled gaze, thinking how they'd both been pretending for so long. Finally, she was ready to tell Meg the truth. 'She has a condition where her brain hasn't formed properly. We found out at our twenty-week scan, right before I came here. If she can hold out long enough to be born, then she might live a few minutes or even a few hours, but no longer than that. It's just not possible.'

Meg's mouth fell open, and she sat down on the bed beside Ali. 'I'm so sorry. And here I was, bringing you clothes for the baby and making you do up a nursery… oh my God. You should have told me. You should have told me to stop.'

Ali sighed. 'I didn't want to think of her like that. I *couldn't.* I wanted to be excited and happy, like I would with any other baby. To learn how to be a mother, to create a wonderful place in the future for her… for her to live, even if that world was never real. And the more time I spent with you and Jem, the more real it seemed.' Ali met her eyes. 'But it wasn't, was it? None of it was.'

'No.' Meg shook her head, her eyes full of sadness. 'I desperately wanted it to be, but it was far from. And I know exactly what you mean when you say that you didn't want your daughter to be defined by her condition.' She sighed. 'I… I have bipolar disorder. I feel like I've been trying to escape that, too, ever since I was diagnosed. Michael was the one person who knew me before I had it. He always told me that, together, we could be stronger than it. I wanted to believe him.'

She gazed into the distance as if she was watching her past unravel. 'He convinced me I'd be fine if I went off my meds, so we could start trying for a baby. I wasn't keen, to be honest. I'd had some bad episodes in the past – that's why I left art school – but I was stable, and things were good. We'd got the house exactly how we wanted it, Michael's business was taking off, and I was hoping that soon I could take some night courses and get back to painting again. Having a baby can be a dangerous thing for someone with my condition.'

She swallowed. 'But Michael… well, he'd always wanted a family, and I wanted to think that everything would be fine. He said he'd keep me safe and that I could go back on my meds when the baby was born.' She paused and Ali stayed silent, wondering when and how her grandmother came into all of this. Had something happened to make her question if Meg was okay?

'The pregnancy… it was hard.' Meg shook her head. 'The hormones and all the changes… they threw me off, like I feared. Michael started getting obsessive about watching over me and keeping me safe. Swimming was the only thing that made me feel free.' She tilted her head. 'Remember when he said he couldn't follow me there because he's not a great swimmer?'

Ali nodded, memories of that dinner together flooding into her head. She'd thought they were so in love, but…

'One night, I don't know. I guess I felt so trapped, like I wanted to get away. I went into the water and I… I stood there for ages. I wanted to swim and swim, and never come back.' Tears formed in her eyes. 'Michael must have seen from the window that something was wrong, and before I could do anything, he came down to the beach. I went further into the water so he couldn't reach me. But even though he couldn't swim, he managed to get close. He tried to grab me; tried to pull me to shore. I fought him, hard, and I got away. I didn't want him to touch me.' She swiped a tear. 'I don't really know what happened after that. I don't know how he managed to make it back – the current was powerful that night, especially for someone who couldn't swim. But somehow, he did. Maybe it would have been better he hadn't.' She shook her head. 'I can't believe he's gone.'

Ali reached out to touch her hand. What could she say to stop the pain and distress Meg must be feeling right now?

'We never talked about that night, but it scared me. I wanted him to watch over me after that. I didn't really want to get away, and I didn't want to hurt the baby. When he set up the cameras, I was happy. He was protecting me from myself until our baby came.' She paused. 'But then Jem arrived, and he still wouldn't let me go back on my meds. He wanted me to breastfeed, and I didn't argue at first. I wanted to do everything I could for Jem, and I wanted to think it would be fine.'

She smiled sadly. 'But of course just wanting something isn't enough, and I started sinking. The worse I got, the more controlling Michael became. He went from someone who always had my back to someone who wanted to control everything I did. It was like being a father had unlocked a desire to have the perfect family, no matter what it took. Things started to get pretty bad.'

Ali nodded, still trying to get her head around the fact that the Michael she'd thought she'd known hadn't been real at all.

'Your grandmother…' Sadness swept over Meg's face. 'She saw something was wrong. She knew I needed help. I don't know how, but she seemed to know what Michael was really like. She said she'd help me leave, and I told her maybe. I knew I wouldn't, but I wanted that hope. Hope that one day, I could.' Meg sighed. 'She came over the next day when Michael was in the studio. She said she was going to move in with her son in London, but first she wanted to help me escape. She wanted to take me and Jem to a women's refuge.'

Ali's eyes widened. Her grandmother had planned to leave the cottage? To live with Ali's father?

'She had everything we'd need in the car, and she had that teddy… the one you gave Jem later.' Ali's heart squeezed. Gran had been planning to give Jem the same teddy Ali had passed on? That explained Meg's strange reaction when she'd seen it.

'Michael saw her; heard her trying to get me to go into her car.' Meg's face twisted. 'He grabbed her arm and shook her, and then… then she must have had her heart attack because she kind of stumbled down the steps and collapsed on the grass. I wanted to try to help her, to do what I could, but Michael…' She shook her head. 'He wouldn't let me. He only let me call 999 when she was already gone. Then he put the teddy back in her cottage and brought all the things from her car inside.' She looked at Ali, her face full of pain. 'I'm so sorry.'

Ali nodded, thinking of her grandmother lying on the grass – not alone, but with a man who was refusing to help her. A man who had as good as killed her. Anger surged inside, and she wished Michael had survived the fire so he could pay for what he'd done.

'After that, I knew what Michael was really capable of. I was scared – for me and for Jem. I stopped swimming; stopped trying to escape. I started pretending to be this perfect wife, in a way kind of hoping it might take: that my actions would mirror my insides. Michael believed it, I think – or at least, he wanted to. He was so happy with what he thought was me, with his family. When we met you, that's what you saw.' She stopped, drawing in a breath. 'What I told you before was true. Even though it wasn't real, I liked how you looked at us – as if we had something you wanted. As if it *was* real. And I guess like you, part of me wanted to believe it was. It was easier than facing the reality.'

'But then Michael left?' Ali tilted her head, trying to understand. If he was as protective and controlling – as dangerous – as Meg had said, why would he do that?

Meg gazed out the window. 'I still can't believe what happened that night.'

'What night?' Ali asked softly, almost afraid to disturb Meg's reverie. 'What happened?'

'It was the night of the big storm, the one that damaged your cottage. We'd been talking so much about babies with you, and Michael believed I meant it when I said I wanted more kids. He wanted to start trying for another one,' she said. 'I knew there was no way I could – there was no way I wanted to, not with Michael, now that I'd seen this side of him, and not after what had happened with your grandmother. I was barely managing to hold it together with Jem, counting the days when I could stop breastfeeding and go back on my meds.' She swallowed. 'And maybe figure out something to get away. You'd shown me it was possible... you and your grandmother. I wasn't sure I could survive having another baby, and I made the mistake of telling Michael that.'

Meg met Ali's eyes, then looked away. 'He laughed. He told me I'd do whatever he said or he'd take Jem from me – he'd go straight to the GP and tell them I wasn't well; that I was endangering our child. He'd make sure that I wouldn't have access to her for a long, long time. He had cameras everywhere, even in places I didn't know about – even one in your cottage, he said, so he could see what we were up to. And I knew with all the video he had, he probably could prove I wasn't fit.'

Ali drew back in surprise. Michael had put a camera in her cottage? But when? A memory of how he'd lingered when he'd brought the mattress filtered into her mind, and she shuddered.

'I lost it,' Meg continued. 'I was so angry. Started shouting and screaming, pushing him… but he shoved me away, like I was nothing. I fell against the corner of kitchen counter, and that's how I got the mark on my arm. It was bleeding so much, and I was in pain, but he just told me not to wake up Jem and then went upstairs to bed. I was furious. I can't even explain how I felt. It was like I couldn't see. I…' She shifted on the bed. 'I grabbed a knife and I followed him up to the bedroom. I wasn't going to hurt him. I only wanted… I guess I wanted to have some power. Power over my body, my *life*. I was so angry. But when he turned around and saw me, he laughed again, like I was nothing.'

She stopped talking, and Ali willed her on. 'And I couldn't take it any more. I wanted him to disappear so I could have a life. I told him to get out or I'd hurt him. I held the knife up to him, and I think he could see then that I was serious. It was the first time I'd ever seen him scared, and it felt so good. He'd always been the strong one, always had the power, but not then. I forced him out the door and slammed it closed.'

Ali blinked, remembering the bang she'd heard that night. 'But where did he go?' she asked, trying to puzzle it all out. If he really was so controlling, why would he stay away for so long? *Had* he been the one the police had warned her about?

'He broke into an empty cottage down the coast from here. He told me he'd planned to stay a day or two – enough time for me to see that I couldn't do it on my own. But when he tried to come back, he saw that you were here. He wasn't sure how much I'd told you… about your grandmother, about everything. I think he was worried you might call the police if you saw him.' She paused again. 'He said he'd been waiting for you to leave, and then he'd return. I think the more time that went on, the angrier he got. He couldn't control me, and without his phone and the studio, he couldn't work either. He'd lost everything.'

Meg met Ali's eyes. 'You were a godsend. I was terrified he'd come back – I couldn't think about what might happen if he did. I didn't *want* to think about what might happen. And so I threw myself into being who you thought I was. I loved who I was through your eyes. Someone calm, someone practical, who was an expert in all things baby. Someone with an amazing husband who was supportive and loving. Someone who had a great future, rather than the absolute mess I'd made of things.'

She smiled. 'And for the first time in years, I could do what I liked. I could spend what I liked. I was *free*.' Her shoulders heaved. 'But I wasn't really, was I? He was still out there. And I was being controlled by my condition – a condition I'll never be free of. I could feel my mania creeping up, but I couldn't stop it. I suppose in a way, I didn't want to stop it. It gave me the power I'd been craving; made me feel like nothing could touch me. And to be painting again after all of those years…' She shook her head. 'But I never wanted to hurt Jem or put her in danger. If you hadn't been there, then I don't know what might have happened. I never wanted to hurt you either. I'm sorry if I scared you.'

A tear dripped down her cheek. 'Caro got me help. She'd seen what had happened in art school and she knew what was wrong. She got me back on my medicine, and I was starting to be stable again and see clearly. I thought I might have a chance at building a life, after all.'

She wrapped her arms around herself, as if she could ward off what had happened next. 'Caro was going on holiday and she invited me along with her. It seemed like the perfect time to get away. I went back home to get some more things, and Michael walked out from behind the house.'

She took a deep breath. 'I was terrified. I tried to get back in the car, but he grabbed the keys from my hand and told me to give him Jem. I said no – that if he tried to take Jem away, I'd say he wasn't a fit father, either, and I'd tell everyone how he'd treated me and stopped me from getting help… and what he'd done to your grandmother.' She swallowed. 'That was a mistake. I've never seen him so angry. He yanked Jem from me and locked me in the studio. I could smell the smoke from the house, but I never thought…' Her face twisted. 'I never thought he'd hurt her.'

She reached out and grasped Ali's hand. 'I need you to know that even if I was pretending with Michael, I wasn't with Jem. I have made mistakes – terrible ones – but I meant every word I said about her. And showing you how to be a mother made me realise that I am a good one, despite everything. And now that I have the medication I need, I can be the mother I want to be. The mother I *know* I can be.'

Ali held her gaze, a current of understanding and empathy passing between them. They'd both been through so much, living in their own private hells. They'd both clung to a version of reality, of the future, that hadn't existed to help them through. But now that had been swept away. Now, they'd faced the pain of their pasts and they were still here… stronger than ever.

Ready to face whatever might come.

CHAPTER FORTY-ONE

Ali

Ali lay in the silent room, so many thoughts running through her head. Michael, Meg, Gran… Gran, who had reached out from her solitude to try and help Meg. Gran, who had finally been going to leave her beloved cottage – the place where she'd sheltered, alone with her memories and grief. What had changed? Ali wondered. Had Ali's father reached out and for once her gran had let him in? Or had she got in touch with him? After all of these years, what had made her grandmother want to leave her isolation and connect with others – connect with her family?

Ali heard the door open and close, and she opened her eyes as a nurse came towards her.

'How are you feeling?' the nurse asked with a kind expression. She put a hand on Ali's arm, and Ali felt tears come to her eyes at the gesture.

'I'm all right. But—' She grimaced as a pain hit again, and she slid a hand down to her stomach. 'Sorry, just a bit of a pain. Think I need to eat.'

The nurse's eyebrows lifted. 'What kind of a pain? Is it a tightening?'

Ali nodded, fear shooting through her. This wasn't labour pains, was it? It couldn't be… not yet. *No*.

'Would you mind if I examined you?' The nurse didn't wait for Ali to answer before stepping closer and putting a hand on Ali's stomach. 'I'm going to do a quick internal examination, if you don't mind. Won't take a minute.'

Ali held her breath as the nurse closed the door, pulled the curtain and pushed aside the covers. 'Yes, you're about two centimetres dilated, actually.' She snapped off her gloves, then smiled at Ali. 'I think this baby is on the way! I'll bring you through to the labour ward once they're ready for you. In the meantime, try to relax, okay?'

Ali nodded and closed her eyes, resting her hands on her stomach. Her daughter was coming. Only a few hours remained until she'd finally hold her little girl in her arms... until she would slip away. Ali felt the warmth beneath her skin, the soft mound that had become harder the more her body had swelled. She prayed that she'd never forget how it felt to have this child inside – how it felt to be her mother.

A tune emerged from her throat, raspy with the effects of the smoke, as she stroked her belly. She hummed a melody, slow and tender, wondering where it had come from. She stopped abruptly as the realisation swept over her: it was the song Jon had written. She'd only listened to it once, but it had stuck in her mind – in her soul.

She started humming again, her soft voice now filling the room. Everything inside her calmed as the strength of Jon's love went right to her heart, filling up empty spaces and pushing aside any lingering hurt and doubt. Jon wasn't like her father. He hadn't abandoned her. Reeling from his own pain, he may have watched her walk out, but he hadn't let her go. He hadn't hidden away despite the loss he'd been feeling too. Given time, he had come around... ready to fulfil his promises and to be the father her daughter deserved. This love *was* enough, and she believed that he meant those vows – she believed now that he could follow through. She could feel the power of his conviction with every note of this song.

Ali thought of their baby, and how she'd finally learnt to accept the mix of grief and happiness… how Jon had realised he loved their child despite the coming pain. That was true strength, she realised, rubbing her stomach. Not standing still, unwilling to move while everything burnt around you like Michael, but letting in every emotion, no matter the painful reality. Moving forward and trusting despite the past.

Allowing yourself to live… and love.

Gran's face filled her mind, and Ali thought of how her grandmother had reached out after so many years of solitude – first to help Meg, and then to move in with her son. Ali still didn't understand what had prompted her to leave the cottage, but she knew the decision to leave her independence and rely on others must have been huge. Sadness flowed through her that Gran never had the chance to follow through on a new life, with people around her who cared.

It was too late for Gran, but it wasn't too late for Ali. She turned to her side, reached to the landline and punched in Jon's number, thinking of all the times in the past she'd rung him: to arrange those first dates, accompanied by the swirling excitement inside. And then later, for mundane items like milk or bread, the phone call downgraded to text messages. But this phone call… this was in another time, another place.

She was calling to tell him she was going to have their baby. She swallowed, and a tear dripped down her cheek. They'd have a child who wouldn't need them for long, but they'd love her forever. They'd be her parents forever.

'I'm sorry I can't keep you safe inside me any more,' Ali whispered to her daughter as her belly contracted again. 'But you don't need to be afraid. Your mum and dad are here for you… both of us, together. Finally.'

CHAPTER FORTY-TWO

Ali

Light was creeping across the sky when their daughter entered the world. Ali waited, straining to hear a cry or a grunt, *something* to show that their child was still with them. But the room was hushed despite the doctor and midwife there – despite the bevy of machines – and a tear dripped down Ali's cheek.

'Is she alive?' Ali could barely get out the words. She prayed that their daughter had made it, even though she knew many babies like hers didn't survive labour. Every second that passed felt like torture, and finally the doctor nodded.

'She is,' he said. 'She's very small, but she's breathing. Just.' He smiled over at them as the midwife wrapped their baby in a special blanket to keep her warm. 'She must have really wanted to meet you both.'

'Not as much as we wanted to meet her.' Jon's eyes were sad, but he smiled as the midwife placed the tiny bundle in Ali's arms. 'Hello, little girl. Welcome… welcome to our family.'

'Hello,' Ali whispered, staring down at their daughter. She was so tiny, so delicate, resting lightly on Ali's chest. Her black lashes grazed her pale cheeks; her lips curled delicately together like a swirl. Her nose was a little squish on her face, and Ali couldn't tear her gaze away. She knew that despite the pain, she'd never – not in a million years – regret this moment. With her baby's condition – and without any extra oxygen to help her lungs; Ali and Jon had opted to spend the short time with their daughter by keeping her as close as possible – Ali knew she wouldn't be here long. She wanted to memorise every detail; every feature. She'd hold this time close for the rest of her life… these first moments as a family.

The labour had been long and hard, peppered with surreal moments of comedy – like any other labour, Ali guessed. A half-smile pulled at her lips as she remembered the midwife's disgust when Jon got lost on his way back from getting a coffee; how Ali had thrown up on his shoes when he'd bent to pat her back. How he'd snored so loudly in the chair next to her bed that Ali lobbed something at him to wake him up, and how Ali had discovered swear words in her vocabulary she didn't even know she had. Her labour had been full of all those clichés, and yet it was anything but normal.

'Can I hold her?' Jon's voice interrupted her thoughts, and she glanced over at him, her heart swelling. Her husband looked terrified yet determined, and she couldn't have loved or admired him more right now. He was here, beside her. He was doing everything he could to be a part of their family, overcoming his fears. He'd been surprised when she'd called but had come without any hesitation, arriving at her side a couple of hours after she'd rung. She'd taken his hand, instantly knowing she'd made the right decision. She could do this alone, but she didn't want to. She wanted her husband, the man she'd trusted with her love. She wanted her daughter to have a father, and for Jon to be one.

Carefully, Ali moved the baby to Jon's arms. He gazed down at their child, his face full of emotions, from sadness to grief to pride. It felt like ages, and Ali was itching to have their daughter back in her arms when Jon finally looked up again.

'What should we name her?' he asked, his voice loud in the room, and Ali realised that they'd never had a serious discussion about what to call their baby. They'd tossed around crazy names, laughing and joking, but that was it.

She didn't even need to think. A name just popped into her mind. She turned it over, considering it, and then nodded. It felt right.

'What about Hope?' she asked, because even though their child would not survive, she *had* made it this far. She'd given Ali hope and showed her that love could buoy you up in even the darkest moments. This baby was a gift, now and for the future.

Jon met her eyes, and she could see that he understood. 'It's perfect,' he said, sliding an arm around Ali's shoulders. And as they both gazed down at Hope, she felt safer than she ever had before.

CHAPTER FORTY-THREE

Ali

Ten days later

Ali stood on the cliff, looking away from the sea towards the blackened walls of her grandmother's cottage. The house next door had been destroyed, and the cottage had suffered extensive smoke damage. It still stood proudly, though, as if determined to remain no matter what burnt around it. And while Ali might try to restore it in the years to come, right now all she wanted was to be home again.

She stepped towards the cottage, memories flooding into her head: the light and sand underfoot when she'd come here for her summers with Gran. Arriving late one night a short while ago, full of pain and anger, just wanting to be with her baby. Constructing a whole new life, desperate to block out the reality ahead.

And now here she was. The worst had happened. Her baby had died after only ten minutes in her arms, and yet she felt a kind of peace and acceptance swirling amidst the grief she knew would always be there. She wouldn't try to run from it because that would mean running from her baby. But she wouldn't let it cage her in, not like Gran had for most of her life… until the end; until it was too late.

Ali shook her head, remembering the call she'd made to her father after Hope had been born. She'd told him how Gran had died and had asked him about Gran coming to stay. Her father had told her everything then: about how he'd always felt to blame for his brother's death, how Gran had thought it was her fault, and how all of that guilt had torn their family apart. About how it had affected him in his relationships… and how it had stopped him from reaching out.

Ali had felt something shift inside her at her father's words, a weight she hadn't even realised she was carrying. Her father's detachment had nothing to do with her. It didn't mean that he didn't love her; that he'd stopped loving her enough to be her father. It was his own childhood trauma and grief that had stopped him. The final remnants of anger and pain she'd been holding for so long – the anger and pain that propelled her to protect her daughter so fiercely; to protect *herself* so fiercely – had slipped away.

She walked slowly into the cottage, gazing around the back room she and Meg had converted into a nursery, her mind filling with images of Meg's bright and energetic face, with Jem cooing by her side. Meg had used this place as an escape too… a place where she could be trusted and respected, in a way her husband hadn't trusted or respected her. Ali still couldn't process everything that had happened, but she knew that Meg would be okay. She was getting the help she needed for the kind of life she wanted.

'Ali?' Jon's voice drifted into the cottage from where he was waiting by the car. 'Ready to go? Do you have everything you need?'

Ali glanced down at the holdall beside her. It was what she'd come here with and what she was taking away – taking home. Because London was her home, not here. Her life was with Jon, back in the flat they'd made their own, in the life they'd crafted together. Jon had asked if she'd wanted to scatter Hope's ashes here, but Ali had shaken her head. This was the place she'd come to hide. She didn't want that any longer.

She stared out to the sea, watching the whitecaps disappear and reappear, one after the other, and she thought of Meg and

Michael. How Jem had almost disappeared into the void, and how Ali's father and grandmother had watched a loved one die in front of them. Life was precious; life was fleeting. It could change in an instant, leading you down a different path than you ever expected. You could choose light – Hope – or you could choose darkness, dwelling alone in grief, uncertainty or pain.

Ali had never been more certain which direction she wanted to take.

'Coming!' she yelled to Jon. Then she gazed around the cottage one last time and turned to go.

A LETTER FROM LEAH

Dear reader,

I want to say a huge thank you for choosing to read *A Mother's Lie*. If you want to keep up to date with all my latest releases, just sign up at the following link. Your email address will never be shared, and you can unsubscribe at any time.

www.bookouture.com/leah-mercer

I hope you loved *A Mother's Lie*. If so, I would be very grateful if you could write a review. I'd love to hear what you think, and it makes such a difference helping new readers to discover one of my books for the first time.

I really enjoy hearing from my readers – you can get in touch on my Facebook page, through Twitter, Goodreads or my website.

Thanks,
Leah

 AuthorLeahMercer

 @leahmercerbooks

 www.leahmercer.com

ACKNOWLEDGEMENTS

A huge thanks to everyone who has helped make this book the best it can be: Madeleine Milburn and Georgia McVeigh for their encouragement, support and feedback; Laura Deacon for her invaluable editorial input; and the whole team at Bookouture. And, as always, thank you to my husband and son for putting up with me staring off into space for hours on end and dragging them into endless discussions about fictional characters!